BLOOD
EAGLE

**Robert
Barr
Smith**

BLOOD
EAGLE

Robert
Barr
Smith

Medallion Press, Inc.

Published 2007 by Medallion Press, Inc.

The MEDALLION PRESS LOGO
is a registered tradmark of Medallion Press, Inc.

Printed in the United States of America
Typeset in Adobe Garamond Pro

Library of Congress Cataloging-in-Publication Data

Smith, Robert B. (Robert Barr), 1933-
  Blood eagle / by Robert Barr Smith.
     p. cm.
  ISBN 978-1-933836-10-2
  1. Intelligence officers--Fiction. 2. Munich (Germany)--Fiction. 3.
Bavaria (Germany)--Fiction. 4. Raubal, Geli, 1908-1931--Fiction. 5. Hitler,
Adolf, 1889-1945--Fiction. I. Title.
PS3569.M537927B55 2007
813'.6--dc22

                            2007004855

10 9 8 7 6 5 4 3 2 1
First Edition

DEDICATION

To my son, the best officer and the best man I know.

EAST BERLIN
AUTUMN 1951

BRUNO WINTERHALTER SWORE SOFTLY TO HIMSELF AS HE squirmed his stocky body deeper into the dripping concrete crawlway, lit only by the underpowered electric torch he pushed ahead with his right hand. Marta did not like him to swear, but she was not here, and he did not like this place.

He was alone, deep beneath the *Potsdammer Platz*, following a maze of old electric cable, his tools in the worn leather holster he had hitched around into the middle of his back. There was a little stale, greasy water in the bottom of the concrete conduit, and his belly and thighs were already soaked from it. He shivered and wrinkled his nose at the musty, oppressive stench of the place. It was an ogre's lair, he thought, a tomb, a dank place where neither sunshine nor fresh air had ever come. He sighed, and pulled himself forward another three meters.

He knew he had to be close to the wall of the bunker. *Scheissen!* he murmured. *Shit, I wonder what evil things are still left in that damned place. Corpses, maybe, munitions, God knows what else.* The Russians had never let anyone go in there, not since the city fell in '45. There were still guards on the bunker; not the Siberian beasts anymore. Nowadays it was KGB troops.

Bruno shivered, and reluctantly pulled himself on down the ranks of rubber-covered cables. The break had to be down here someplace. He could not come out until he found it, and decided whether it could be repaired, or a new cable was required.

He grinned sourly in the stinking gloom. The city administration would not like to have to put in a brand-new cable. Everything in the people's paradise had to be made to last. He shook his head. As always, something was wrong with the horn of plenty. All the good things somehow came out in the direction of the party leaders, and the lousy Russians. *I should have gone to the West with my brother in '45,* he thought, *and now they will not let me go.*

He pulled himself around a curve in the conduit, and found the bundle of cables that branched off to his right, and the little steel door through which they led. He knew instantly what the cables had to be. They were heavy-duty, designed to carry a great deal of power. With that capability, in this place, they could have only one purpose. This was the power entry to the *Fuehrer* bunker.

My God, he thought. *Dear God, that's where the Fuehrer died, and all the others.* He lay transfixed, staring at the small grey door in the light of the tired flashlight. And then he saw it in the gloom, the steel box, painted grey, lying just inside the crawlway next to the door, as if someone had reached through the access door from inside the bunker and laid the box there. It would have been easy to retrieve from inside if you knew it was there,

2

but it would be entirely hidden from anyone peering through the access door.

Bruno laid his wrinkled forehead on his hands and thought hard. Maybe it was nothing, but maybe not. Maybe it was something from the old days, even gold or precious stones. Those things he could sell, no questions asked. Or even documents. And those he perhaps could sell to someone with connections in the West. Or they might be worth a reward from the party, or the Russians.

Ja, he thought soberly, and maybe a quiet one-way trip to Siberia, too, or an unmarked grave someplace. In East Germany, certain kinds of knowledge could be a dangerous illness, even a terminal one. He raised his head and stared at the steel box again. But it could not hurt to look; the chances were slim that he would pass this way again. He reached for the box.

Bruno found it unlocked, but he had to use a screwdriver from his tool holster to wedge open the lid, thick with rust. He turned his torch inside the box at last, and saw only two packages, carefully wrapped in oilcloth. He was a bit disappointed to find nothing obviously valuable, but curious enough to open one of the packages. He found only a slim document, typewritten, faded and soggy with the years and humidity.

He carefully unfolded the crinkled pages under the flickering glare of his torch and read, his lips moving with the effort. What he read made him suck in his breath and glance reflexively over his shoulder down the length of the dark and empty crawlway behind him. He quickly rewrapped the document in its oilcloth and carefully stuffed both packages deep inside his shirt, under

3

his tattered coat. He shoved the steel box far out of sight on a tier of cables running just beneath the top of the tunnel.

Bruno lay still a moment longer, the torch beam flickering slightly with the trembling of his hands. *My God*, he thought, *my God! I will go on and find the damned short, and fix it, and then I will finish work and go home as if nothing has happened. And there I will think this out. My God! I am sure I cannot give this to the Russians and go on living. It could mean Marta's death, too. Go slow, Winterhalter! Don't do anything stupid.* And he wriggled on deeper into the crawlway.

It took Bruno Winterhalter two long months of musing to come to a decision. Even then he did not tell his wife of thirty-five years, afraid to expose her to what he knew. Only in the spring, on a Sunday when the green began to return to the grey, drab land, he and his wife went to the Treptower Park near the river Spree for their weekend stroll, almost the only luxury his slim pay would permit in the grim days of postwar East Berlin.

The elderly couple sat quietly together afterward by the front window of *Gasthof Blum*. The café was only a faded relic now, filled with the hovering shades of happier days before the war. It was shabby now, like its aging customers, its brave green and yellow paint faded and peeling. It was almost empty, although the afternoon was fair, and the old linden trees outside were green again with spring. Only two other tables were occupied, both by older couples like the Winterhalters. Like them, Bruno and Marta still came to the dying old *gasthaus*, remembering better, brighter days long passed away.

They still dressed in their best as they always had, though the suit and the dress were now old and threadbare, like the *gasthaus*. But the memories that went with them were evergreen, of youth and love and high hopes, and of two handsome boys, then young and smiling and excited over their weekend treat of ice cream and pastries.

But now one of the boys was buried somewhere in the rich black earth west of Kiev; the other was simply gone, vanished with the fragments of his fighter over the English Channel. And now the greying, tired couple held hands across the table, he nursing a stein of beer, she sipping a glass of wine, taking at least a little happiness from each other and the memories that crowded about them in the dingy little *gasthaus*.

Bruno had at last decided. He glanced furtively about the room—the only other customers were the elderly couples at two tables more than twenty feet away. The innkeeper, aging like his visitors, leaned wearily against the counter at the back of the room. He occasionally glanced hopefully at the tables, wistfully wondering whether someone wanted another order, but then his rheumy old eyes glazed, and he stood in silence, lost in memories of his own.

"Marta," said Bruno softly. "There is something I must talk to you about, something very important."

He glanced around the room again. "It can be very good for us, or very bad. I need to know what you think about it."

He looked fondly into the faded blue eyes of the worn woman he had never ceased to love

"*Ja, Schatz,* what can it be? I have known there was something on your mind; I have not seen you so lost in thought in many years. I am all ears."

The tender smile faded as she watched his face. "It is very serious, too. I have thought you are worried; I have thought so for weeks now. Tell me."

Bruno gave her hand a gentle squeeze. "How well you know me, my dear. Yes, I have been worried. At first, I did not want to tell you. I thought it would be . . . safer for you if you knew nothing. But now, well, I need your good advice as I always have. So, then, here it is. I have found something. I found it on one of my jobs, one during which I came very close to the old *Fuehrer* bunker."

He shook his head quickly when he saw the alarm leap into her eyes. "No, I was not inside. I could not get in, and I did not want to. But what I found *came* from that terrible place, through a utility port, a door through the bunker wall into the passage where I worked."

He glanced about him again and lowered his voice still further. His wife leaned toward him to hear his words.

"Marta, I found two documents signed by Hitler himself! Yes! And they are not just any documents, although God knows anything connected with those times is dangerous to have today."

He was almost whispering now. "One paper is a will, leaving sums of money and annuities to various people to whom . . . to whom he was close. I do not think it is important, except perhaps to historians. It is the other paper that frightens me. It is enormously valuable, I think, and I know it is terribly dangerous. It is something that both East and West would give much to know. The Russians would kill for it, I am sure. Those bastards have killed for much less, and sometimes for nothing at all, except that it pleases them."

Bruno sipped at his beer, and glanced again around the silent *gasthaus*. "But, Marta, this paper is also worth much money, I think, if one could find a way to sell it without the Russians or the party finding out. It would be a way, perhaps, for us to live a little better. Certainly, it would be a way for you to be a little more comfortable when I am gone."

He saw the fear and misery spring instantly into her face, and was sorry. "No, no, my love, it must be spoken of. That time must come to us all, and I want to know that my girl will not want for warmth and food as so many do. This paper may be the sort of insurance policy I have dreamed of.

"I will show you where the papers are hidden, and you may read them both and see if I have judged them accurately. We will not try to do anything with them yet, not unless we see a safe chance, or there is great need. When you read them, you will see why such great care is necessary."

At last he smiled into the eyes of the woman he had loved for so many years. "And today, my dear, I think we may have another glass for old times' sake, and maybe for a better future."

BRUSSELS
OCTOBER 1965

THE LITTLE SQUARE OFF *PLACE ROGIER* WAS A QUIET ISLAND of shops and hotels, a pleasant relic of old Europe, a placid, gentle yesterday that would never come again. It lay close to the bustling *Boulevard Adolphe Max* and the heart of the city, but its manicured grass and trees and pansy bed might have been in any small Belgian town. Cooper crossed the cobblestoned square with long, easy strides, sucking in deep breaths of the cool, early morning air, savoring the day.

Early autumn is a good time in Brussels. It is cool, often breezy, with lots of faded sunlight and only the occasional light drizzle to wash the city clean and fresh. And this day was vintage Brussels October, pale and pleasant, with scruffy cirrus clouds hurrying along high up, scudding away to the east. A breeze kicked up leaves and cigarette packets from the gutters and sent them whirling and clicking along the quiet side streets off the square. The distant rumble of traffic on the *Boulevard Max* was subdued here, not loud enough to disturb the placid peace of *Place Rogier*, dreaming quietly of other days.

Cooper had been out for a walk and early coffee, leaving Heidi and the kids to rise at their leisure and come down to breakfast in the restaurant of their hotel. The hotel was tiny but comfortable, and the dining room was excellent. Their kitchen did a wonderful job with the specialties of the city, tiny shrimp stuffed in monstrous tomatoes, and the marvelous small mussels, swimming in their own broth.

Cooper grinned. Here it was morning, with breakfast yet to come, and he was already thinking about lunch. Well, that was what leave did to him. "My darling," Heidi had said, only the night before: "My darling, the minute we begin to travel, you are all stomach and cock. I do not complain, love, but what is it about a vacation that turns you into a starved satyr?"

Cooper grinned again. Why not, after all? Surely he'd eaten enough C rations in 'Nam and other places to indulge himself in good food from time to time. And as for Heidi: "Beloved," he had said, "as for you, I am married to the world's most beautiful woman—I simply cannot help myself." He had reached for her slim body, and she had met him more than halfway.

And anyhow, he thought a bit sadly, this was farewell to Europe, probably for a long time. They should have taken a few days more leave. Tomorrow there would be the swift ride back to Frankfurt on the Trans Europ Express, pounding across the lovely countryside of Belgium and Germany, back to catch the flight to the States.

He sucked in another deep breath, and then another, almost light-headed with the flavor of it, so sweet and sharp with autumn that he could not get enough. He relished the taste and the scent of it, full of the melancholy of the dying year, of change, of something ending, never to return. Tomorrow it was good-bye to the green fields and red tile roofs of Germany, to the stone of ancient walls and the cobblestones of narrow streets that were old when America was born.

He could see the square ahead of him now, and he quickened his long strides. He looked forward to the Ranger School, to Fort Benning again, and the red dirt and scrub pines of Georgia, to the new job. *A damn good job, Cooper, a plum of a job for a junior major, a chance to lead, and teach, to put on a parachute again.*

He shook his head. But still. To leave Germany, the land he loved, the land where he had met Heidi, where the kids had been born, where they had spent so many wonderful days. *"Mein zweite Heimat,"* as he often said to their German friends. "My second homeland."

And suddenly he was eager to see his family. He smiled and started across the square. A young secretary, sipping early coffee at a café, watched him as he passed, admiring the square jaw, the athlete's build, and the long, purposeful stride. She wondered who he was, and why he smiled. A policeman, maybe, she thought, or a soldier. Yes, with the short haircut, surely a soldier. And the smile . . . she decided, somewhat wistfully, that he was on his way to see a lover. And in a sense, she was quite right.

Now he could see the hotel plainly, a narrow, grey, four-story brick building at the back of the square, shoulder to shoulder with its elderly companions, sturdy and respectable and sedate. *There,* he thought, *the restaurant is on the ground floor, there, with the big window. I'll bet they're already downstairs; the kids will be starved, as always. Heidi will have them neat as a pin, and she'll get them to speak French to the old waiter, and to greet any elderly people in the dining room. And they'll charm everyone, as usual.*

He smiled again, looking forward to seeing them. Tough little four-year-old Tom, pretty blond Liesl, at three the image of her lovely mother. And Heidi. Those level deep blue eyes could still bring a lump to his throat and a spreading heat to his groin. After five years, still lovers. He grinned broadly, now halfway across the square.

The explosion knocked him down. One moment there was the plate-glass front window of the hotel dining room, with its small chaste neon sign. The next there was a brilliant flash of white light where the window had been. As the white flash changed to roiling red and black, the shock wave hit him, and he went down, flung helplessly into a light pole and a wire trash container, sprawling in the street.

Half-dazed, he lay still for a moment. Old instincts kept him lying flat on his belly as shards of jagged glass and chunks of brick clattered down all around him, and his nose was filled with the acrid stench of explosive and smoke, and something else . . . the vile, unforgettable stink of burning flesh. Someone screamed away to his right, over and over again, an awful wailing, without words.

As the rain of debris died away, he pulled himself to his feet and lurched toward the hotel. There was something wrong with his left leg, but he limped on into the smoking ruin that had been the dining room. There was no front left to the building, only a black ragged hole in the neat line of grey-brick facades, a gaping cavity filled with black smoke and gouts of red-orange flame.

The old waiter the kids had charmed so often lay just inside what had been the front door. His white jacket, always so immaculate, was black and crimson now; his head was red pulp; his out-flung right hand still clutched his tray. Farther inside, the dining room was a wilderness of smashed furniture and glass fragments, burning wall paneling, and smoldering carpet.

Ahead of Cooper hung the gleaming mahogany staircase, down which they had come for their meals. Now it ended in jagged splinters eight feet from the floor, sagging and twisted. Most of the roof paneling was down, but the lovely old crystal chandelier still hung, swinging gently in the smoke, its pendants tinkling over the crackling of the flames.

An elderly woman sat on the floor to his left, legs splayed out before her, covered with plaster dust and fragments, but apparently unhurt, talking incoherently to herself. A wrinkled hand protruded from a pile of fallen masonry against the back wall. There was no sign of movement in the wreckage.

Cooper looked desperately around the ruined room, hoping against hope that maybe his family was still upstairs . . . and then he saw he saw the doll, lying undamaged on the edge of an enormous fall of brick, the little Dutch doll with the smiling china face and tiny lace cap, bought only two days before in Amsterdam.

He threw himself at the pile of brick, hurling aside the debris with both hands, crying out the names of his wife and children, tearing loose a fingernail without feeling it go. He only dimly realized that other people were helping him; a tiny paperboy, a bearded taxi driver, a police officer.

They found Heidi last. Her clear blue eyes were open, but there was no light left in them. He held her hand and called her name as the other rescuers gently moved away the last debris that covered her body. But she could not hear him; she would not ever hear him again. And at last he sat there in the dust and glass and ruin, held her head in his lap, and cried. Three bodies with the life and joy gone out of them, and nothing more.

Finally, with infinite gentleness, an ambulance crew moved all that was left of his life and his love, and helped Cooper away to a hospital. He endured the patching of his own wounds with mute patience, and in time, in the arms of an enormous sedative, he slept at last.

CHARLOTTESVILLE, VIRGINIA

NOVEMBER 1965

GENERAL ANDREW JACKSON LAWTON, UNITED STATES Army, retired, lived in Piedmont Virginia, in lovely Charlottesville, tucked away below the Blue Ridge Mountains. Just now the city was dressed in its party finery, all gold and crimson and orange for the turning of the year. The students at Thomas Jefferson's old university walked laughing through windrows of fallen leaves, sere and brittle, and the early mornings were clear and chill, with a hint of frost.

Cooper admired the general's modest home as he walked up the flagstone path. It was an immaculate white colonial with the inevitable green shutters, guarded by oak and flaming maple and a rich lawn. Cooper could not hear any sound when he pushed the bell by the heavy oak door, but it opened within seconds.

He looked for a moment into steady, hard brown eyes in a creased, tough, unsmiling black face, which cracked into an enormous smile. "My God," said the stocky man in the doorway. "My God, Major Cooper. All the Way, sir!"

Cooper returned the grin. "Airborne, Sergeant Godfrey!"

Cooper stepped into the cool hallway, pale-blue stucco, polished molding, a line of bright military prints along the wall to his right. The door swung shut behind him, and he turned to the black man. The two shook hands, and held the grip a moment as friends do who have been long apart.

"I didn't know you were still with the Old Man," said Cooper.

"Yes, sir," said Godfrey, "since we both retired. I guess it's for keeps now. Come on back; the general will be tickled to see you again."

They walked together through a comfortable study, its walls lined with hundreds of books and pictures, a Chinese SKS rifle, and a tattered Viet Cong battle flag. They passed through a bright and pleasant greenhouse addition, warm with the late afternoon sun, hung with dozens of houseplants and ranks of potted flowers, all neatly lined up as if on parade.

Godfrey noticed the direction of Cooper's glance, and laughed deep in his chest. "As you see, Major, the Old Man can't abide anything that's slovenly or out of formation. Even foliage. I'm in charge of day-to-day care and training."

Cooper smiled. "As I remember from Jump School, Sergeant Godfrey, you could make trees and rocks fall in and double-time. You sure as hell had a way with second lieutenants of infantry. I must have done five thousand push-ups in those three weeks."

Godfrey grinned, remembering. "Second lieutenants of infantry are the world's most precious commodity, sir, but they need to be polished some before they're ready to run and bite alone. That's what NCOs are for."

They walked through open French doors out onto a flagstone

patio overlooking a sloping lawn, a bank of crimson salvia all around it, and a thick wall of pines at the foot of the lawn. General Lawton looked up from his book, squinted against the light, and smiled.

He had not changed, except that the close-cropped hair was a little greyer. The rest was the same: the slight, hard, compact body, the square shoulders, the piercing light blue eyes that could freeze an errant soldier at twenty paces. *The man*, thought Cooper, *who taught me how to be an officer, the father I never had.*

"Tom," said the general softly, "how very good to see you." He rose and stepped forward with the same old grace, the grace of movement of his parachute infantry days. They shook hands, and the general put his left hand over their clasped right hands as they did so.

"Come and sit, Tom, and Jasper will bring us a beer."

They sat together at the edge of the terrace, looking down across the green of the lawn toward the encircling pines. A breeze ruffled Cooper's hair, and they sat for a moment in silence. Sergeant Godfrey quietly set two bottles of Beck's on the terrace rail, the green bottles open and beaded with cool drops. Both men took a long pull, and then another, still in silence.

And then the general spoke. "Tom, it's been almost five years since I last saw you in *Heidelberg*. I can't tell you how pleased I am you came to see me. But I'm going to presume on long friendship and be blunt. Something's wrong, and I know it. We've known each other a very long time, and I can see trouble in your face. I'd like to listen if you want to talk. Is it the new job at Fort Benning? Surely not you and Heidi . . ."

Cooper took a deep breath, and raised his eyes to meet the general's. "It concerns Heidi, yes, sir. I don't know how to say it gently; for a while I had trouble saying it at all. General, she's dead, and so are the kids. They were killed by terrorists. In Brussels, a little more than three weeks ago. It was a bomb."

Cooper could feel the tears beginning to rise, but he fought to keep his voice level and quiet.

"They were at breakfast at our hotel, sir, at the very end of our leave. I was out walking. The Belgian police are sure the bomb was meant for some Germans who were in Brussels for some kind of remember-the-holocaust convention. They weren't hurt. Instead, the bomb got my family, the hotel owner, a gentle old waiter, and three other customers . . . and a poor damned dog that came by every morning for a handout."

Cooper wiped his eyes with one hand, sucked in a deep breath, and mistily watched the bees busily enjoying the brilliant crimson blossoms below the terrace wall.

The general leaned forward, and gently rested his hand on Cooper's arm. "Oh Tom," he said quietly. "I'm so sorry. I loved Heidi myself. If Sarah and I had ever had a daughter, I would have wanted her to turn out like Heidi. And those beautiful kids . . . Christ! I wish I could do or say something."

Cooper met the general's eyes. "I know you do, sir. And maybe, just maybe, you can. I came here to see you because you're my old boss, and my friend. And I wanted you to know what happened. But I have another reason, too. I need a very great favor."

He took a deep breath. "Sir, I want to get some back. I want to get into the real war against the kind of sons of bitches who killed my family, and the people who pay them."

Cooper barely recognized his own voice, tight and twisted with hate and mourning. "Sir, we don't talk about it in public, but I know damn well we have people who go after neo-Nazis and Libyans and the IRA and all the other bastards of the world. I want you to put me in touch with someone in the terrorist-killing business, CIA or whoever. You know I'm good in a fight. I've got a reasonably good brain. I speak fluent German, and I can get by in French and Italian."

He paused, and his voice was thick with anger. "And, sir, I hate now, and I'll go on hating for a long time. That may be a pretty fair qualification, too."

The terrace was silent in the warm afternoon. There was only the humming of the bees in the crimson blossoms, and far away the laughter of children and the excited barking of a dog. Cooper drank the last of the icy Beck's, and listened to the happy faraway voices and the barking.

"The kids wanted a dog," he said softly. "We were going to get them a big, tolerant, loving dog, a Lab, maybe, or a Golden . . ." He felt the tears begin again and shook his head gently, as if to force them back.

At first the general did not reply; he sat silent, watching the industrious bees. Then he drew from his shirt pocket a battered, ancient pipe with a Sherlock Holmes curve to it, and began to suck pensively on it. Master Sergeant Godfrey walked quietly from the house, carrying two more bottles of Beck's, uncapped and beaded with moisture, and set one next to each man.

And finally the general spoke, his voice quiet and musing.

"You know, Tom, I love Bavarian beer dearly, but this . . . ah!" And he held the dark green bottle up as if proposing a toast. "North Germany makes the finest beer on earth, except maybe for the real Czech pilsner."

He turned suddenly to Cooper, the piercing blue eyes shining as they had in the old days before action, or a jump. "All right, son, maybe I can help. No promises, but I'll try. I shall have to make some calls." He paused.

"You're qualified, Tom, better qualified than you know. You're what the French colonial army used to call a *Barodeur*, a scrapper. You're one of those rare men who really enjoy fighting. You were born to soldier. Your brain is not just pretty fair, it's excellent, and you have the finest motive in the world for clandestine work."

He fell silent for a moment, watching Cooper over his pipe. "I know you've thought about this a great deal. But I also know what a fine, dedicated soldier you are, and how much you love soldiering. You must understand that if you get to do what you've asked me about, it will probably mean the end of the profession of arms for you. Leaving what you love is bad enough, but there are some other devils you'll have to be prepared to face."

The general took a long pull at the bottle of Beck's. "You'll step into an ugly, sordid, twilight world without any kind of security. You'll live for months without warmth, or morality, or recognition. You'll have to do some things that will nauseate you, for a country that may or may not be grateful. Even if it is, it can never publicly say so. It may even have to deny you, or abandon you.

"And if, somehow, one of your jobs becomes public knowledge, there will be any number of radical politicians and harebrained journalists ready to condemn you as a murderer. They'll call you a mercenary savage. They'll say you indiscriminately murder innocents in the name of America. You won't be able to defend yourself, and neither will anyone else. Your country may even have to disavow you entirely."

The general looked long and steadily at Cooper. "Son, I know you're not afraid to die, and you're full of hate, but have you thought about these other things?"

"Yes, sir," said Cooper. "God knows I've thought about very little else over the last few weeks. Remember, I was on some jobs out on the Cambodian border that got very lonely and very hairy. And remember the one CBS got wind of, and the government officially denied ever happened?"

The general smiled, a tight little grimace with no warmth in it. "Oh, I remember, Tom. I remember as if it were yesterday. I remember how we crossed that invisible border and bloodied the dinks in their sanctuary. I also remember how the left-wing critics howled. And I remember we were not allowed to go in force again. I remember how the White House and the State Department quaked for fear some twit in the United Nations would shed tears about violating Cambodian neutrality."

He sighed. "All right, Tom. Your qualifications are impeccable. So is your motivation." He paused, those steady blue eyes on Cooper.

"And remember, your motivation has *got* to be powerful. Because if you go through with this, you are going to be a murderer.

You will be murdering your country's worst enemies, to be sure. You will kill people who would kill you and me in a heartbeat. Your targets will be a rich variety of bastards."

General Lawton leaned forward, and his voice fell almost to a whisper. "Nevertheless, son, make no mistake about it, you will have to kill in cold blood. It will not be soldier's work, in the heat of battle. It will be murder most foul, any dirty way you can pull it off. Are you really content with that?"

Cooper nodded. "That's what I want, sir."

The general took another pull at the Beck's. "Then so be it. For now, there is nothing I can do until tomorrow. And as it happens, I have a couple of fine mallards in the refrigerator, only a day out of Chesapeake Bay. They require eating by people who appreciate such things. And we can have a little good Mosel with them, and another Beck's beforehand, and talk of other days. The guest bedroom is free. Can you stay?"

Cooper smiled broadly for the first time since that terrible day in Brussels. "I'd love to, sir."

The general returned the smile. "Jasper," he called to the stocky black sergeant, "bring a Beck's for yourself and pull up a chair. Let's talk awhile about old times. We'll worry about dinner a little later."

Godfrey returned with another tall green bottle, and the three men settled down on the flagstone patio. The bees were still busy in the brilliant crimson flowers, but the air was growing a little cool. The sun was dropping low, a brilliant orange globe over the lavender and dark green of the Blue Ridge Mountains far out to the west.

THE ATLANTIC, EAST OF NEW YORK CITY

DECEMBER 1965

YUSSUF ALI WAS ECSTATIC. HE PUSHED THE BACK OF HIS seat to the rear as far as it would go and stretched, his eyes tight shut. He heard none of the happy chatter of the tourists around him, for Yussuf Ali was lost in a vision of his own. *Thank you, lord Mohammed!* he murmured under his breath. *Thank you! I will be your warrior against the infidel!*

The Boeing 747 was well aloft over the Atlantic, with nothing below the great wings but cold, deep water. The seat belt sign had gone off, and he thought briefly about starting back for the restroom, but decided against it. There was plenty of time for that. He would take just a little while to savor the moment.

"Sir?"

Yussuf started, his eyes flickering open like a startled deer's. Immediately he relaxed. It was only the flight attendant, a tall willowy black woman in a neatly tailored blue uniform. She was smiling at him.

"Sir, we are serving soft drinks or coffee. Would you care for something? Or you can have beer, or a mixed drink."

Yussuf's lip curled. "I am Muslim, woman. Alcohol is forbidden. I am surprised that you would even ask."

The flight attendant's smile vanished. "I'm sorry, sir. I did not know of your religious beliefs. There is no way I could have known. Would you like something else?"

Yussuf turned away without an answer.

Damned niggers, he thought. *None of them are real believers, and the American blacks are the worst.* He smiled. Perhaps it was time for the restroom after all. He unclipped his seat belt, slid out into the aisle, and turned toward the tail of the airplane.

On his way down the aisle, he passed a slim blond woman with a little boy sitting next to her, playing with a toy jet fighter. The little boy looked up and started to smile, but the smile faded when he saw the ice in Yussuf's eyes. *Brat,* thought Yussuf. *Western brat. You and the blond bitch will be nothing but atoms in just a few minutes.*

Once inside the tiny restroom, Yussuf unbuttoned his shirt, unbuckled his belt, and dropped his trousers. Around his waist he wore a thick nylon belt, a long tube two or three inches thick, tightly stitched by hand. He undid the cloth ties that held its ends together, pulled it loose, and laid it on the diminutive sink in front of him.

He smiled. The belt was full of *plastique,* a wonderful plastic explosive made in Czechoslovakia in the old iron curtain days. Yussuf remembered his lectures from the training camp in Iraq. This explosive was very powerful and easy to mold. It contained no ingredient the educated noses of the bomb dogs could detect. Nowadays the Czechs were being good little boys, he thought. Now they make their *plastique* with something in it the dogs could pick up. But this stuff, the stuff in Yussuf's belt . . . this you could take anyplace, straight through the gates of nearly any airport.

His smile broadened. *And now,* he thought, *now for the final touch.* He reached into his breast pocket, pulled out his sleek ballpoint pen, and unscrewed the top. He tipped the barrel upside down over his open left hand, and into his palm slid a slim brass tube, a blasting cap in place of the ink cartridge. Yussuf opened the belt and slid the little cap smoothly into the *plastique.* He stooped awkwardly in the tiny room to place the belt on the floor.

And then Yussuf Ali, his face lit by a beatific smile and his pants down around his ankles, threw back his head and screamed at the top of his voice, *"Allahu Akbar!"* . . . jubilant, triumphant, *"Allahu Akbar!"* . . . and stamped on the blasting cap with his heel.

SOUTH YEMEN
DECEMBER 1965

SERGEANT-MAJOR GEOFFREY BARNES REGARDED THE BUN-
kers and the barbed wire below him with professional distaste.
How I wish, he thought, *how I wish I had some proper soldiers to
work this misbegotten place, instead of these bloody lazy Yemenis.
Local levies, my flaming behind. More like bloody local layabouts.*
The defensive perimeter around his dreary little hill was almost
finished, but it had taken forever. The local sheikh's soldiers
moved so slowly, so listlessly, the work never seemed to advance.

Barnes shaded his eyes, staring out across the endless dirty
yellow-brown of the Yemen, hostile, appallingly hot, almost
trackless. Looking through the shimmering lens of the broil-
ing heat was like looking through water, distorting everything.
"Bloody arsehole of the planet," he murmured, and moved back
into the skimpy shelter of a tarpaulin strung, lean-to fashion, between the cabs of two Land Rovers and a pair of poles jammed
into crevices in the rock. *That's what I get*, he thought, *spending
me life in the bloody SAS.*

Lance-Corporal Simmons was still hunched over his radio in

the dubious shade of the tarp, listening intently through the static for the distant voice that was their only link to help and support. Simmons was the youngest man in the detachment, a Royal Marine radio man attached when Barnes' own man went down with dysentery. *Good lad,* thought Barnes. *Give him a good report when he goes back. Make sergeant in three or four years.*

Simmons hunched forward farther now, straining to hear and understand a tinny voice far away. He turned his head quickly to Barnes.

"It's our higher, sar'nt-major," he said, then turned his attention back to the voice from far away. At last he stood up and turned to Barnes, his young face troubled.

"Sar'nt-major. The message is for Captain Berwick." He paused, and Barnes thought the young man was going to cry.

"Spit it out, lad."

"The captain's wife, Mr. Barnes. She's dead. And his little boy. Remember, he showed the pictures the other night? In a bloody airplane, Mr. Barnes. Crashed in the ocean in America. I mean near it. A fookin' bomb, it was!"

He took a step toward Barnes, and held out one hand imploringly. "Please, sar'nt-major, don't make me tell the captain. He's such a damn fine bloke."

Barnes nodded. "I won't, lad. That's for me to do. And that's damned fine *officer*. Just remember. Now get on to the captain. His patrol ought to be on the way back in anyhow. Tell him to come back, but you don't have to tell him why."

Sergeant-Major Barnes watched the long trail of dirty-brown dust snaking its way back toward his miserable hill. *Bugger me,* he thought. *What a hell of a thing to happen to a good man. Jesus, how I wish I didn't have to tell him.* He stood stolidly in the heat, trying to decide what to say, until the pair of Land Rovers pulled through the gap in the barbed wire and parked a little below him. His eyes were on the slim figure trotting uphill toward him, sunglasses under Arab *kaffiyeh,* khaki shorts and short-sleeved shirt, web harness with ammunition pouches, scope-mounted rifle in his right hand.

Barnes saluted. "Captain Berwick, sir."

The slim man returned the salute, his eyes narrowing at the formal address. In the SAS, only first names were on active service. "Let's get under cover, Sim. I need some water and some shade." As they moved under the sparse shelter of the tarpaulin, the slim man pulled off the *kaffiyeh* and ran his hand through his crew-cut black hair. Barnes handed Berwick a canteen and watched him drink off at least half of it.

"Ah!" Berwick sighed, and turned to Barnes. The captain's eyes were a very dark blue, almost cobalt, and his aquiline nose was a little crooked, as if it had been broken long ago and poorly set. "So, Sim, why so formal? You had something you needed to pass on to me. I'll tell you about our pointless damned patrol later. What's the news?"

Barnes clenched his fists at his sides. "It's bloody awful bad news, sir. I don't know how to say it except straight out. It's Mrs. Berwick, sir, and your son. They're dead, sir. In a plane crash. The message said it was a bloody bomb. God, I'm sorry."

The captain looked at Barnes for just a moment as if he were a stranger. Then, very softly, "No chance of a mistake?"

27

"No, sir. Higher said it was confirmed. They're sending a helo for you, and Captain Martin's coming in to relieve you."

Berwick stood silent just a moment more. "Thank you, Sim. I wish . . . I think I need to be alone a little while. Call me if you need me."

Barnes watched his officer walk haltingly away, to finally sink down on a rock overlooking the indolent native crew, slowly laboring to finish a bunker. As he watched, a plume of cigarette smoke rose above Berwick's head. Barnes shook his head. *Poor bastard. One of the best men I ever served with. A Military Cross and a DSO and a bright future. And now this. Got to get his* kaffiyeh *on his head, or he'll get flamin' heatstroke sittin' out there.*

He could already hear the helicopter on its way in.

THE ALPS BELOW BERCHTESGADEN, WEST GERMANY
11:00 P.M., FEBRUARY 1966

THE FINE SNOW SWIRLED SOFTLY, SIFTING DOWN GENTLY through the gloom of the deep forest. Dense thickets of pines loomed black and brooding on both sides of the snow-covered slope, making a natural aisle downhill into a little valley. Nothing moved in the silence. The slope was smooth and unbroken between the darkness of the pines, its shadowed whiteness broken only by the black outlines of five or six young pines.

At the base of the slope was a little river, gleaming obsidian black in the night, bubbling gently over smooth rock and pebble. Beyond the river was the winding road up toward the town of *Berchtesgaden*, higher up the mountain. Two-lane blacktop, gleaming and slick with moisture, the road followed the river, then turned abruptly away from the stream and the dark slope above it to run through a tiny village, a single lighted street with dark houses stretching away behind it on both sides. Six streetlights illuminated the short main street, six lonely pools of light turning the grey snow to bone-white.

A few shop signs hung over the streets, still in the cold, windless night. There were five or six dimly lighted shopwindows, a dozen parked cars mantled in snow, empty sidewalks. On a back street, a dog barked twice and then was still. Far away a railroad engine shrieked, the *Bundesbahn* on its way over the summit to Salzburg, far downhill into Austria. The village dozed in the winter chill, neat half-timbered stucco houses with patches of red-tiled roofs showing around the chimneys, where the snow had slid away. Now only the river broke the deep silence, chuckling softly to itself in the darkness.

Cooper lay motionless just inside the heavy woods at the top of the slope. He lay on his stomach, cushioned by a thick layer of sodden pine needles, intently watching the sleeping village through binoculars. He was tired and cold, but the glasses never wavered. He was dressed in cross-country ski clothing, light blue and white, practically invisible against the snow. Over his head, like a hood, lay a white bedsheet, powdered now with new snow.

He rested his elbows on another sheet before him. Nestled within it was the eight-millimeter Mannlicher: a heavy Zeiss telescopic sight was screwed to the receiver, and a tubular flash-hider clamped to the muzzle. A bipod supported the barrel.

Cooper slowly lowered the big Steiner glasses, and wiped his tired eyes with his right hand, careful not to move quickly. He shifted his weight very gently, rolling up a little on his left side to ease the dull ache in his right thigh. He wished he could rub the ragged scar where the VC bullet had torn through the thigh, but he did not want to change his position far enough to do so.

He settled back down on his belly, still moving very slowly, and again rested the glasses on the village. He focused on the *gasthaus* behind the first pool of light. A large, brightly painted sign hung over the street in front, on it a leaping stag and in large letters the name of the inn, *"Zum Hirsch."* Yellow light flowed through diamond-paned windows, to form a warm pool on the sidewalk snow.

He began to wonder whether the three hours of waiting would be wasted, whether the cautious twilight trip in on cross-country skis, and the bitter cold watching hours had gone for nothing. And then he heard the car, its high-revved engine suddenly loud in the primeval silence, grinding up the long grade from the village of *Bad Reichenhall* and the *autobahn*. The falling snow, heavier now, picked up flickering reflections of light, white and yellow, as the car came into view and slowed for the turn into the village.

He gently lifted the bedsheet from the Mannlicher, and tucked the butt into his shoulder. He pulled the protective caps from both ends of the scope, and settled his cheek against the stock of the rifle. The village street and the car leaped into brilliant focus.

It was a brown Opel, four doors. That fit the description. He swung the scope just a little onto the license plate. "M," *M* for Munich. That fit, too. He took a deep breath, tucked the Mannlicher deeper into the cup of his shoulder, and gently eased off the safety. The crosshairs of the scope settled on the *gasthaus* doorway, worn, warm pine and big, old wrought-iron hinges set in the thick door with enormous studs.

The Opel pulled into the village street and eased to a stop

under the first pool of light, tires crunching on the crusted snow in the gutter. Three men climbed out, laughing together, bulky in thick overcoats, their breath forming little puffs of white vapor in the cold. Cooper swung the scope across their faces.

Not the big one, he thought. *He must be six-four and 300. He's just a goon. Two-bit hired help, probably low-level KGB, maybe even a local party enforcer. Not the skinny driver, either. There,* he thought, *the one getting out now, the other one, the blond Adonis in the long black leather coat.*

Cooper steadied the scope on the tall man's head. Now he was sure it was the Bulgarian. Alexandr Akovich the killer, angular chin arrogantly tipped up, ramrod back, long blond hair combed straight down over his collar. *Just like the telephoto photographs MI6 showed me,* Cooper thought, *except no baggy suit this time; the bastard's a real fashion plate tonight.* Oh, yes, it was surely Akovich, the face in the photograph he had printed in his memory. Cooper took another deep breath, let half of it out, and pressed gently back on the Mannlicher's trigger, taking up the slack.

But the bulk of the Bulgarian's huge bodyguard filled the scope, completely blocking out Cooper's view of his target. The three men were in the archway of the *gasthaus* entry, and Cooper felt a small stir of anger.

"Not now," he whispered aloud in the chilly silence. "Not after freezing my ass off out here for three hours! Get out of the way, you sorry bastard." He swung the scope gently, following the three men as the big bodyguard reached for the wrought-iron door handle. Still no shot. But now the big man ducked an obsequious bow to Akovich, and stood aside to usher his boss into the

32

doorway. Yellow light flowed through the opening door onto the snow, and a tinkle of zither music floated up the snowy slope.

Akovich stopped just an instant, turning in the doorway to make some joke to the other two, perfect white teeth showing as he laughed. The brief pause was long enough.

The crosshairs rested just a heartbeat on the arrogant, hawkish face, and Cooper squeezed the trigger. The Mannlicher bucked against his shoulder, and the flat bang of the report skipped up the Alpine valley like glass smashing in a quiet room, the echoes tearing at the winter silence.

Akovich was still standing, but now his right cheek was a red hole; his mouth hung open, and his pale blue eyes had gone flat and vacant. Cooper worked the bolt of the Mannlicher and locked the crosshairs on the Bulgarian's forehead, following the tall man as he slipped down the door frame, smearing the smooth pine with a crimson mess. His coat bunched up around his shoulders and neck as he slid heavily to the snowy sidewalk, spittle dripping from his slack mouth onto the red snow beside him.

Akovich's head lolled forward as he sat down heavily, his back against the archway, and the Mannlicher boomed again. The second bullet smashed through the top of his skull and out the back into the door frame, and blood sprayed across the mellow wood of the door, spattering the bone-white snow. Akovich toppled slowly sideways over onto the sidewalk, flopping convulsively, like a beached fish.

The peaceful zither music had stopped, and Cooper could hear cries of alarm and panic from inside the *gasthaus*. The gigantic man was gone, ducked inside the doorway, but the skinny driver was still outside, crouched, a pistol in both hands, staring fixedly uphill in Cooper's direction.

But you didn't see either flash, did you? Well, you're a bonus. And the Mannlicher roared again.

Cooper did not waste a second glance on the driver, sprawled facedown in the dirty brown snow of the gutter. He moved swiftly to his feet in a shower of snow, dropping the bedsheet that had covered him. He slogged quickly through the snow, slinging the Mannlicher and the binoculars over his shoulder as he rose. Deep in the trees, he stepped quickly into cross-country skis, snapped shut the bindings, seized his poles, and without a look behind him, skied swiftly into the gloom of the forest.

The trail was smooth and easy, popular with *lang-lauf* skiers during the daylight hours all winter. It wound tightly through the trees, slipping downhill gently at first, then more and more steeply, until it took great skill to stay erect and make the turns on the long, edgeless cross-country skis.

Cooper pushed hard on his heelpieces and hunched a little lower on the skis, but he did not slow down; he dared not. All his concentration, all his mind and body, he poured absolutely into the track of his skis. There was no sound but his steady, deep breathing and the hissing and crunching of the skis over the crusted snow.

He broke through the crust only seldom, for the going was fast and good. What a pleasure it would have been to ski this track just for fun: no mission, no danger, no worry about what was behind you, no dead men sprawled in the bloody snow back in that village street. He shook his head and pushed hard into a tight, skidding turn. Maybe another day. . .

And then, suddenly, he saw the light ahead through the dark pillars of the pines; his heart jumped, and he began to snowplow a little to reduce his speed; and then he realized it was the hotel and its parking lot, and it was coming up much sooner than he had expected. Then there were more lights and the sound of music in the night. In a long, sweeping, Telemark turn, one knee almost on the snow, he reached the edge of the woods above the hotel and halted just inside the tree line.

He stood stock-still inside the black shadow of the trees, ignoring the driving urge to hurry, to run. His eyes swept slowly, carefully, across the neat, half-timbered hotel. But there was nothing, only muted music and laughter, warm yellow light through drawn blinds and drapes. He sucked in a deep breath and then another, working to slow his heart rate. Now the parking lot: twenty cars, maybe a few more, some mounded in snow, some later arrivals still free of it. There was no movement against the white of the snow, no car lights, no rising exhaust fumes. Nothing. Nothing but the softly falling snow.

He skied slowly to the corner of the lot and stopped again, his eyes ceaselessly sweeping the cars. Still nothing. He snapped his bindings loose with the point of a pole, stepped out of his skis, and swiftly moved to a dark green Mercedes sedan tucked away under the thick pines at the rear of the lot. He opened the trunk, laid the Mannlicher and the glasses inside, then snapped skis and poles into the cartop rack, unlocked the front door, and slid into the dark car.

No dome light went on; he had unscrewed the bulb when he

left the car. His eyes swept the hotel and the parking lot again. There was still no movement, no sound but the distant music from the hotel. The big car started smoothly; he eased into gear and drove slowly from the lot, crusted snow crunching under his tires, wipers pushing accumulated snow from the windshield.

As he drove past the hotel and approached the lot exit, a green-and-white *Polizei* Volkswagen bus roared up the *Berchtesgaden* road, blue light flashing, two-tone horn tearing the night, headed uphill toward the little village. He flicked on his lights and turned the other way, downhill, on to the road to *Bad Reichenhall,* to the *autobahn,* to Munich. To safety.

He drove as fast as the narrow road would permit, the big Mercedes tracking steadily through the corners. His eyes flickered often to the rearview mirror, but the road behind stayed dark. It was snowing more heavily now, big wet flakes swirling and dancing in the glare of the headlights. There was no other traffic, either uphill or down.

He remained alert as he drove sedately through the silent, empty streets and grey buildings of *Bad Reichenhall,* past chaste signs telling motorists that the town was a spa and a place of rest, *bitte,* and kindly be quiet. And then there was the *autobahn,* almost empty, smooth and straight and true to the west, and Munich.

He settled back in the leather seat and lit a cigarette, shaking his head at the slight tremor in the hand that held the lighter. He shuddered suddenly, a single tremor of shivering, and he reached down to turn the car's heater up to high. God, how cold it had been on that silent hillside! Then he grinned wryly in the darkness of the car. *'t the problem, was it? It was the fear, too, or mostly . . . just like 'Nam. No sweat in action; too busy, no time for it, but afterward . . .*

He pulled deeply on the cigarette and settled into the seat, already thinking carefully ahead, rehearsing his prearranged plan. He would drop the Mercedes in the lot at the Munich *Hauptbahnhof*—the main railway station. It would be collected by someone else. He did not know who; he did not want to know. It did not matter.

Then he would take the tram for a dozen blocks, walk a few blocks more, and, finally, pick up his BMW. After that it would be an easy run up the *autobahn* to Frankfurt. Somewhere on the road, maybe Ingolstadt at the Danube crossing, he would stop at a service area for something to eat. Then home, a couple of beers, maybe, and sleep. He wanted a woman badly, but that would have to wait.

The *autobahn* hummed smoothly beneath the Mercedes at 140 kilometers per hour; about 85, he thought, fast enough. He settled into the drive, still keyed up and tense, waiting for the fatigue he knew would creep in as the adrenaline passed away. The black heart of the winter night surrounded him like a shroud, a dark blanket pressing in around the Mercedes as he swept past the occasional car and a few scattered lights out in the gloom of the countryside, dimly seen and suddenly gone in the darkness.

The snow swirled into the headlights, more gentle now, and perceptibly growing lighter as he passed the Rosenheim *autobahn* junction. The snow faded away to a spiteful spatter of rain as he crossed the broad, smooth River Inn, flowing placidly up from

Innsbruck and the south. Only then, with Munich coming up fast, did he begin to relax. And only then did he permit himself to savor his revenge, and think of Heidi . . . and of Brussels.

The lights of Munich were much brighter, the snow slackening, when he pulled his thoughts back to the here and the now. *God, I'm tired. This job should be the last for a little while. Time for a rest. Maybe I can get some skiing in, or maybe fly to London for a few days.*

He sighed. *I need to be someplace clean and safe for just a little while.*

LUCERNE, SWITZERLAND

APRIL 1966

LUCERNE, SWITZERLAND

APRIL 1966

LUCERNE DOZED PLACIDLY IN THE SPRING SUN, WASHED clean by the morning's gentle rain. Berwick stood on the medieval wooden bridge across the Reuss River. He leaned on the handrail and watched the broad Reuss on its way out of Lake Lucerne, only a few hundred meters upstream, starting its long trip north to greet the Limmat and the Aare, and finally the mighty Rhine.

He breathed deeply of the sweet cool air from the lake, and watched the gulls circling and crying over the water. The city basked in the dying sunlight of spring, red-tiled roofs and grey church steeples against the pale blue sky. Berwick savored the lovely town, as he always had. He had come here first with his wife, in happier days. He smiled at the memory. They had been youngsters then, he a new lieutenant in the Fusiliers, down from Minden in Germany with his new bride.

The smile faded. *She's gone, Berwick*, he thought. *She's gone for good until you see her and our little boy again in the Lord's good time. Lock her memory in your heart and keep your mind on your business, man. Concentrate on the job. That's all that matters in the world just now. It's time to pay them back a little.*

This time he had come by train as Samuels, a book buyer from Ontario. He was comfortably settled in a quiet hotel in the *Brienzergasse,* his room littered with maps and tourist pamphlets, his Minolta hung over a chair back, Frommer's *Switzerland* on the bedside table. A typical foreign visitor, just another tourist, like a thousand others. Nobody important, nobody to notice.

He had wandered for three days, obviously gawking at the sights of Lucerne, snapping pictures, renting a bicycle each day to ride, apparently aimlessly, through the fresh, neat countryside around the town. On the first and third days he had passed Lonergan's chateau, a lovely old picture-postcard building fronting the lake, down its southwestern shore, below the tiny hamlet of *Schoenbuhl.*

On both days Berwick settled on a quiet knoll capped by a plantation of young pines, overlooking the chateau some seven or eight hundred meters away. And there he spent several hours each day, eating the hotel's enormous sack lunch, sipping a passable Mosel from the bottle, and watching the chateau through the telephoto lens on the Minolta.

It was all exactly as it was shown in the photos and plans he had been given in Frankfurt. His information was exact, down to the high perimeter fence and the two Dobermans loose on the grounds. He could see the surveillance devices at the corners of the wide stone walls. They looked like electric eyes, black boxes simply bolted to the wall tops, nothing fancy. Break the beam, trigger the alarm. Manageable.

On the second day he saw Lonergan in the formal, park-like yard, and focused the telephoto on his quarry. Tall, skinny, maybe forty-five, with a hook nose and thinning hair, artificially bleached a sort of faded blond. He wore skintight Gucci jeans and a green silk shirt with very wide sleeves, open to the waist to show his bony, hairless chest. *So there's the American turncoat,* mused Berwick. *The fairy who sold his country's secrets for Russian money. The man who sold CIA agent names around the world. Nothing dirtier.* Berwick smiled. *This one is a favor for the Yanks. It will be a pleasure.*

Lonergan was followed closely by a squat middle-aged man carrying a heavy revolver in a shoulder holster. *Big pistol,* Berwick thought. *But the bodyguard is flabby and badly out of shape. He hasn't missed any meals, and he looks very bored.* The portly man waddled along some ten or twelve feet behind Lonergan, and the two did not speak throughout the half hour Lonergan walked.

Not friends, thought Berwick. *The ape is only a hired gun. Not bedfellows, either, chances are. Professional goon. Probably bored with no action. I'll bet he's working as a well-paid errand boy. Maybe he's getting careless. He looks Middle Eastern. There's supposed to be another one. I wonder where he is?* He finished his wine.

Next morning dawned fair and bright. Early in the day Berwick left an ordinary matchbook in baggage locker 218 at the *Bahnhof,* along with what his bosses in the Firm quaintly called a "shopping list." In the afternoon he strolled on along the lake, sucking in great lungfuls of the Alpine air, still chilly in this early spring, watching the circling, shrieking gulls. At last he found a café with tables on its modest flagstone terrace.

He settled at a round table, instinctively choosing a chair

with its back against the café's front wall. Just to the right of the terrace was a park filled with playing children and vigilant mothers and nannies, drinking in the first pale sunlight of the year.

Berwick watched an elfin blond girl, playing gently and delightedly with a fuzzy shepherd puppy. Her mother, slim, grave, and immaculate, watched the little girl fondly. Behind them an old stone fountain gurgled happily to itself, and sparrows pursued tidbits among the rustling leaves.

My God, thought Berwick, *look at this picture of peace. These lovely people, and this incredibly clean, beautiful, peaceful, orderly, picture-postcard country. It's as if there is no danger in the world, nothing ugly, nothing dirty. No American traitors or KGB goons or bastard terrorists with bombs.*

He smiled wistfully at the little girl's soprano laughter as the puppy bounded about her, and her mother's alto chuckle as she watched her child play. His reverie was broken by the waiter, a small, round, middle-aged man with a shiny pate, a huge smile, and a brilliantly clean white apron.

"*Guten Tag, mein Herr. Ein Wunsch?*"

Berwick returned the smile and ordered, suddenly very hungry.

The waiter bowed gently, and smiled still wider. "*Sofort.*"

Berwick attacked a plate of fresh sausage, rich cheese, and crusty white bread. He savored the rich Swiss coffee, half hot milk, and watched the little blond girl and her puppy. The dry leaves chattered and danced across the tiny park, the little girl laughed, the puppy barked. Berwick ordered a second pot of coffee, sucked in the cool lake breeze, and thought again about another child, a little blond boy, and the slim woman who had been his heart. A thousand years ago.

As he mused, sipping the rich coffee and watching the hypnotizing blue of the lake, he was suddenly conscious of movement close beside him. He looked down to find the elfin blond child standing at his knee, the fuzzy puppy cradled carefully in her arms. The little girl's huge blue eyes were grave.

"Sir," she said in clear, lisping German, "sir, you looked so sad. I thought maybe you would like to talk to someone."

Berwick smiled into the huge blue eyes. "Thank you. You are very kind, but no, I am not sad. I was just thinking of some things far away and long ago."

The little girl nodded gravely, as if that explained everything. "Do you have any children?"

Berwick shook his head. "No. Once I did, though. I had a little boy. He was blond, too, very much like you."

The girl frowned. "Don't you have him anymore?"

Berwick could feel his eyes growing misty. "No. Not just now, anyway. I will see him again one day, I know. But we must be apart for awhile."

"I hate that," said the little girl. "My daddy has to go away sometimes, too. Sometimes we have to be apart for a whole *week*!" And then she flashed a proud smile. "He's an officer in the army."

Berwick returned the smile. "That's wonderful. What's your name?"

"Heike," said the little girl.

"That's a pretty name."

A low, melodious woman's voice interrupted; the little girl's mother calling from her park bench. "Sir, I hope Heike is not annoying you. She loves to talk."

Berwick smiled at the woman. *"Gnaedige Frau*, with your permission, I was just thinking of having a small *Eis.* Perhaps Heike also, if you do not mind?"

The woman chuckled. "You are very thoughtful. Perhaps a very small one."

And so Berwick watched the blond girl savor her dish of ice cream, and sipped his coffee while the fuzzy puppy snored softly in his lap. The breeze from the lake was cool and rich on his face, and for a little while he was at peace. He did not think about the job ahead.

Twilight was falling over Lucerne when Berwick walked back along the lake to the *Bahnhof.* He stood for an instant across the street, in the shadowed doorway of a closed drugstore. *No point checking for surveillance*, he thought. *Too many people, too many places to wait. Not likely, anyway. Right, walk in like you belong here.*

Locker 218, empty before, now held two suitcases, non-descript, brown leather, somewhat battered. They bore initials that were not his, a couple of tattered hotel stickers from Venice, where Berwick had never been, and tattered baggage tags from Air France, on which he had never flown.

Berwick hastily walked the fifty meters to number 15 *Einsteinstrasse* and put the heavy suitcases in the trunk of the middle-aged, forest green Mercedes with the Frankfurt plates. He drove slowly southeast out the lake road toward Lonergan's chateau, feeling the beginning of the rush of nerves, watching the rearview mirror, rehearsing again every move of his strike.

He drove easily through the falling night, aware of the increase in his heartbeat and breathing, of the preternatural awareness and alertness of his mind.

He passed the chateau without slackening speed. Nothing unusual apparent: lights in the downstairs windows, dark upstairs; lighting inside the stone boundary walls, but apparently indirect and not very bright. Gates closed.

He drove on into blackness, until bright lights broke the gloom ahead. *Ah,* thought Berwick, *there it is.* Strings of red and green Chinese lanterns announced it first. Then he saw the long stone building with its steep chalet roof, and the enormous sign in very black Gothic letters. Named for the lake, of course: *Gastof zum Vierwaldstaetterzee.*

It was a lovely spot in spite of its jaw-breaking name. The big, rambling *gasthaus* was framed by a long line of fir trees, its terrace overlooking the lake and a floodlit sailboat anchorage. The far end of the crowded parking area was dark, its last few spaces tucked away under a thick belt of firs, black as the pit. He headed that way.

Berwick parked the Mercedes as far as possible from the lights of the *gasthaus*, backing into a parking spot against the stone wall next to the lakeside. He sat quietly, the windows down, listening. His eyes traveled steadily across the lot. There was no movement and no sound but distant music from the *gasthaus* and the gentle lap of waves on the edge of the lake.

He sat perfectly still for five minutes, careful to keep his foot off the brakes, so no taillight would break the darkness. He watched one car leave and a brown Opel arrive. Two laughing couples left it and entered the restaurant, and the chilly silence returned.

Berwick's watch glowed softly when he pressed the illumination button: 8:30. Time to go. He reached up to the dome light, pried loose the plastic cover, and felt for the lightbulb. It was gone. He smiled in the darkness. *MI6 thinks of everything,* he mused, *so their stupid agent won't light up the night when he opens the door.*

He locked his wallet and passport in the glove box and left the car. Still watchful, he quietly pushed the door shut, and opened the trunk. He removed the two battered suitcases and moved swiftly through the line of firs and over the stone wall, walking hurriedly into the deep shadows of the water's edge.

He stripped in the shadows, pulling on a lightweight wet suit from one of the cases. From the same case he pulled fins and a waterproof bag. He unzipped the bag and checked the contents by feel. Military load-bearing harness; silenced Uzi submachine gun with three magazines; small British air pistol; big Gurkha *kukri* in its sheath; two grenades; four pounds of plastic explosive; caps and two clockwork timers. Tucked along the edge of the bag was the flotation chamber, which would give it buoyancy. He closed the bag, satisfied.

He pushed his street clothing into the empty suitcase, shut it, and opened the second bag. He pulled out a single scuba tank and regulator, replaced the cases in the trunk and climbed over the wall. Finally Berwick slipped into his scuba gear, opened the oxygen valve, and disappeared like a shadow into the cold and gloom of Lake Lucerne. He turned toward Lonergan's chateau.

Berwick surfaced very slowly, easing his head above the surface only to eye level. He turned his body slowly through 360 degrees, checking for danger from the lake and seeing only darkness. The chateau looked like a Swiss postcard, nearly every window brightly lit. *Good,* he thought, *the brighter inside, the tougher to see out. Now, to find the goons and the doggies.* He made certain of his bearing to the darkened dock and sank beneath the surface.

He surfaced again under the dark edge of the dock and moved to land. Deep in the shadow cast by the tall garden wall, he crawled ashore, shed his tank and flippers, unzipped the waterproof bag, and slung over his shoulders the military harness, web suspenders, and belt.

Cradling the Uzi, Berwick moved swiftly around the corner of the wall, his eyes searching the gloom until he found what he had seen from the little knoll: three tall young saplings close together. Sure enough: the right size, the right place. He glanced again at the brightly lit windows of the house, slung the Uzi across his back, and then, with infinite care, began to climb the sapling nearest the wall. When the young tree trembled under his weight, he grabbed the sapling nearest it and kept on inching upward.

Now the whole garden was visible, and the ground floor windows, as well. He froze as the squat bodyguard passed one of the downstairs windows. But the man was deeply absorbed in what appeared to be an enormous sandwich. He was chewing with enthusiasm and he passed out of sight without a single glance into the darkness outside.

Berwick returned his scrutiny to the garden itself. Where were the Dobermans? The garden was still. *Well,* he thought, *got to try it sometime.* He measured the distance to the wall with his eyes, climbed a few feet higher, let loose the second sapling, and pushed off. He rode the bending sapling toward the wall and stopped his descent with one foot against the outside edge of the wall top. He let loose of the sapling, then stepped high, over the jagged glass and the beam of the electric eye to the inside edge of the wall top, and jumped down into the garden.

He remained frozen in a crouch where he landed, his senses reaching out across the hedges and flower beds for sound and motion. He drew the air pistol from its soft leather holster and rose to one knee so he could just see above the neatly clipped ornamental hedges that rimmed the formal flower beds flanking the brick walk leading to the house.

He saw the Doberman before he heard the silent hunter. The dog seemed to know someone was in the garden, but it could not tell where. Whining, it quartered nervously across the lawn in the garden's center, then moved down a path toward Berwick. Cradling the air gun in both hands, Berwick let it come closer until the dog was ten feet or so away. When the Doberman raised its head to sniff the air for the intruder, Cooper shot it in the throat. The dog tried once to bite at the tranquilizer dart, took two drunken steps, and collapsed.

Cooper smiled in the darkness. *Good night, doggie, sleep well. You'll be up and about in time for breakfast. Now, to find your partner, if it's abroad.* But the other dog did not appear, and Cooper moved toward a set of french doors opening into the central entry hall of the house. At the doors, he holstered the air pistol and slung the strap of the silenced submachine gun over his right shoulder. He stood quietly in the shadows just outside the french doors and waited, listening intently, hearing only an insistent chirping insect somewhere in the garden.

There was plenty of light from inside, and he could see no sign of an alarm system. He hesitated. *Doesn't mean there isn't one, but maybe the system on the perimeter wall is all there is.* From a pouch on his harness he took a glass cutter and cut a neat circle on the glass just above the door latch. Replacing the cutter, he dug again into the pouch and found a tiny roll of tape. He covered the circle with the tape, then pushed firmly against it, snapping the circle out with a barely audible click. He peeled tape and glass circle away from the window, reached through the opening, and slipped the latch.

He stood stock-still again for a moment, listening intently, but all was silence except for the monotonous chirping in the garden and a snatch of music somewhere upstairs. *The Prelude to Act III of Lohengrin,* he thought. He slid the *kukri* from its sheath, eased through the door into the entry hall . . . and met the squat bodyguard face to face.

The man froze, his mouth full of sandwich, his eyes huge with surprise. And then, as the guard's right hand groped for the heavy revolver under his left armpit, Berwick struck sidearm with the *kukri*, swinging the half-moon blade horizontally across his body, left to right, the heavy curved blade biting deep into the right side of the man's neck with the sound of a butcher cutting steaks.

The bodyguard's hands stiffened, and the sandwich shot out of his mouth like a cork from a child's popgun, followed by a rush of crimson blood. The fat man's knees sagged, and he reached blindly for support with his left hand. His groping fingers seized an ornate French walnut curio shelf bearing a pair of baroque ebony-and-ormolu vases. He pulled the shelf toward him as he sagged into the deep rose carpet.

Berwick bent, dropping the *kukri* onto the carpet. He caught one vase with his right hand, and blocked the fall of the curio shelf with his right shoulder, but he could not grip the other vase with his left hand. He batted it desperately, keeping it in the air, then struck it again with his open hand, knocking it into the corner of the next room onto a couch. It did not break. He froze, holding his breath, the thumping of his heart slamming in his ears like kettledrums.

But there was no sound except the same distant music, the ticking of a tall clock in the hall, and the soft gurgling and moaning of the bodyguard, who lay facedown in an enormous puddle of blood, his body shaking with a last spasm of departing life. Berwick eased the curio rack upright and set the remaining vase on one of its shelves. *Good God*, he thought, *what else can go wrong? Where in hell is the other bodyguard? Where is the other bloody dog?*

He hastily checked the first-floor rooms, but there was no movement, no sign of recent use, no warm coffee, no burning cigarettes, no half-eaten meals. He gave the fallen bodyguard one more brief glance. He was still, unmoving. Finished. Berwick walked to the hall drapes, wiped the blood from his *kukri*, and sheathed it. He lifted the Uzi and tucked it under his right arm, safety off. Ready.

Upstairs, then, he thought. *Lonergan's either somewhere up-stairs or he's gone out without his goon. Not likely. He wouldn't leave the muscle behind. Follow the music.* He mounted the broad front stairs, keeping to the inside of the stairway to minimize the chance of a squeaking step. But there was no sound on the thick carpet, only the music, getting louder, and the ticking of the clock, receding behind him. The music had changed now; this time the Beatles, "Yesterday."

Berwick moved silently down the dark carpeted hall, controlling his breathing, straining for any sound or movement, the Uzi held level and ready. There . . . the music came from the door ahead, the one with the thin strip of light showing beneath it. And now he could hear more, a soft moaning mingled with the music.

He paused, checked the empty hall again, and with his left hand cautiously tried the door handle. *Softly, Simon, ever so softly; very slow, very easy.* The handle pushed down without sound until he could feel the latch disengage. He pushed in, eased the handle back, and swung the door into the room

It was a bedroom, huge and high-ceilinged, decorated in what Berwick could only think of as Early Empire Brothel. The rugs and drapes were a sort of crimson brocade, and so were the fittings for the enormous bed, but most of the rest of the room was mirrors. Lonergan was stark naked on the bed, writhing about in a complex embrace with a tall young man who had over-developed muscles and very long, very bleached hair, also quite naked. Neither man, intent on whatever it was they were doing, had heard the door. The tall young man was on top of Lonergan, and could see nothing except Lonergan's private parts.

Then Lonergan saw Berwick standing in the doorway, reflected in one of the mirrors on the far wall. Lonergan's head jerked up from the young man's groin, and he tried to reach back toward the white oak nightstand, either for the intercom or for a weapon. But he could not get free of his ecstatic partner, who continued making love to Lonergan, unaware death stood twelve feet away.

Lonergan knew. Berwick saw it in his eyes as the turncoat strained to reach the nightstand.

Berwick smiled and methodically put half a magazine into the two men as they thrashed on the bed, still locked together. Utter silence followed the subdued coughing of the Uzi and the choked, cutoff cries. Berwick stood still, coldly watching the bloody bodies. He thought fleetingly he ought to feel some remorse. He had just killed three men he didn't know. But there was no feeling except satisfaction. "The world's cleaner," he said aloud, and backed silently into the hall.

He checked the other upstairs rooms, finding only empty opulence. *The other guard's gone,* he thought. *So's the other doggie. Time to create the accident.* He moved swiftly downstairs, hurrying through the kitchen to find the cellar door. At the bottom of the cellar steps he found what he sought, the big steam boiler that heated the huge house.

He nodded in satisfaction. The old wooden chateau would burn fiercely, and a boiler explosion would be a logical cause. Shame to burn such a pretty place, but the Firm wanted an accident, not an obvious assassination. He planted his *plastique,* molding it quickly against both boiler and oil tank. He set two clockwork timers for five minutes, and slid them into the *plastique*. He stepped back and paused, checking the installation. *Right. Time to go.*

He moved upstairs and onto the terrace fronting the lake . . . and froze. A man stood on the dock where Berwick had landed, a man he had never seen before, a narrow, swarthy face illumined suddenly by the glare of a flame when the man lit a thin cigar. Berwick stood silently, although he knew he was all but invisible. The man had destroyed his own night vision by using the lighter.

Another Middle Easterner probably. Looked it, anyhow. Shoulder holster, too-tight Italian suit: the other goon. No dog.

Berwick stayed deep in the shadows that shrouded the rear of the house, then moved swiftly toward the trees at the end of the building. From there it was only a few steps into the water. The man on the dock had not moved. Berwick could see the end of his cigar glow orange in the night.

Berwick crouched deep in the shadows, dropped his gear next to the waterproof bag, and pulled on his flippers and tank. He turned on his air, put in his mouthpiece, sank beneath the surface of the lake, and resurfaced under the dock. Looking up through the cracks in the planking, he could just make out the man's feet, black against the lighter dark of the night. The cigar glowed again. With infinite care Berwick moved to the edge of the dock, then surged out and up and grabbed the man's ankles. He kicked up with both feet, braced them against the edge of the dock, and pulled.

The man fell hard on his tailbone, cursing, the cigar arching into the water with a hiss. Berwick straightened his legs and surged backward, pulling the man farther over the edge. The bodyguard scrabbled for a handhold to save himself but found none. Berwick grabbed the man's shoulder holster and dragged him off the dock under the water.

The rest was easy. The bodyguard panicked immediately. Instead of trying to attack Berwick, he flailed madly with both arms. Berwick slid behind the man and shifted his hold to a full Nelson. Now the bodyguard could not reach either Berwick's air hose or his genitals, the only points at which he was vulnerable underwater. Berwick tightened his hold and hung on grimly against the bodyguard's desperate, spasmodic heavings. He kicked deeper; there would be no sign on the water of the death beneath, even were there anyone to see.

It did not last long. The bodyguard died in a cloud of bubbles, and the body sank away from Berwick as he swam far out into the black water. He made sure he had at least three hundred meters between him and the shore before he surfaced. He was in almost complete darkness.

The explosion was not loud. It was a muted thumping sound from the deep basement, and it took several minutes for the yellow and orange flames to show through the first-floor windows. Then they ran swiftly through the old wooden chateau, fed by the tank of fuel oil in the basement, and within five minutes the fire was roaring through the first floor and racing up stairways to the second.

Berwick realized the fire was lighting the lake far from the shore; the lurid glare was reaching out to his dark sanctuary. No power on earth, not even the highly efficient Swiss *feurwehr*, could stop the fire now. The bodies would be so charred that an effective autopsy would be very difficult indeed. Not impossible, of course, but not promising. Furthermore, he doubted the authorities would waste much time on the demise of foreigners of dubious reputation. He sank below the surface of the lake and turned for home.

Berwick surfaced far out in the lake beyond the glow of the lights from the *Gastof zum Vierwaldstaetterzee*. He raised his head above the water only far enough to watch the *gasthaus* and its parking lot, and remained motionless for more than ten minutes.

He was desperately tired and horribly cold, the adrenaline from the action at the chateau drained away, but his days in the SAS had taught him the time of greatest danger was the time of deepest fatigue, when the normal precautions were often forgotten or neglected. He was beginning to shiver, but he forced himself to remain still and vigilant.

But there was nothing out of the ordinary to see. The lot was still crowded with cars. He could just see the Mercedes at the dark end of the lot and hear the music and laughter from the *gasthaus*, louder and happier now, as the evening progressed. There was music, the sort of oompah sound everyone associated with Alpine Europe.

As he watched, an old Borgward sedan chugged out of the parking lot. A Ford and a Mercedes arrived, and another two men on bicycles. It was a big evening, and no one would notice the departure of another car. He sank beneath the black water once again, and swam toward the shore.

KENSINGTON, LONDON, ENGLAND
JUNE 1966

OUTSIDE BERWICK'S APARTMENT WINDOW THE THAMES rolled majestically past, unhurried, indifferent to the doings of mere humankind. There was little river traffic this time of day—a couple of small pleasure craft and a long diesel tour boat, its curved-glass windows crowded with people gawking at the shoreline of Chelsea and Kensington as the craft chugged downstream toward the city. Through the open window of Berwick's flat, a cool, light breeze blew off the river.

A gentle evening was coming softly down across the west end of London, and the broad street below his flat looked slick and clean after the afternoon rain. The streetlights were coming on, and their friendly yellow glowed on the wet street. The traffic was still heavy, as it always was at the close of the day, but if he leaned back in his chair, his windowsill shut out the street, and he could see only the everlasting river. It had always been his favorite scene.

He glanced again at the wide, placid expanse of the Thames *My old friend*, he thought, *heart of my homeland.* He smiled wistfully. *Heart of my heart, Sarah. You and our boy, who wanted to be an officer like me. My God, my Sarah, how I miss you.*

The sad smile remained as he savored the memories. Even after their son arrived, even then, the wanting never went away. *And when I came back home from training or a mission, we made love, frantic for each other. Sarah met me at the door once wearing absolutely nothing. I can still see her. Pieces of my uniform were scattered all the way from the door in here; I still had my muddy boots on when we were locked together on the floor.* He chuckled aloud.

My God, we made love everywhere. — when I was in Hereford, we lit up the night in our little flat. And I banged Sarah in the grass when we walked through the countryside of a weekend. There was that clump of trees — wonderful cover, that; you could see forever, no chance of anyone walking up and surprising you. Only the occasional bird . . . wondering what on earth these two big creatures might be up to.

And then there was the time in Germany we traveled on the night train to Bremerhaven. We were right in the middle of making love when that damned conductor stuck his head into the compartment to ask for tickets. Berwick's smile broadened. *Bitte, entschuldigen Sie!* the man had said about eleven times in quick succession. *He disappeared like the genie back into his lamp when he saw my hairy bottom and Sarah's bare legs locked around me and realized what we were up to. And Sarah giggled.*

He shook his head, pushing the memories back into the private, quiet place where precious and lovely things were cared for and stored for another day. *Don't dwell on it. Don't dwell on it, Berwick, you know you won't see Sarah again until the Lord calls you home. Live in the present. Get some back for her and our little guy.*

He went back to his book, Tolkien's *The Two Towers.* He had read it twice before, just as he had read all three books in the trilogy of Middle Earth, but he never tired of Tolkien's heroic prose and his graceful word portraits of a lovely world that never existed and never would. Berwick wished it had been real once, somewhere, and he wished it would come again.

He read King Theoden's plaintive lament for days departed, savoring the music of the words:

> Where is the hand on the harpstring,
> And the red fire glowing?
> Where is the spring and the harvest
> and the tall corn growing?
> They have passed like rain on the mountain,
> Like a wind in the meadow;
> The days have gone down in the West
> Behind the hills into shadow.

Like my own life, he thought, *passing like rain on the mountain, behind the hills into shadow: my bride, my son, my duty, and my regiment, the only things that ever mattered much to me besides my country.*

Now he had only country and duty . . . and memories. Those would have to be enough.

Berwick looked up from his book when the telephone rang, the distinctive double chime of British phones. He did not move from his comfortable chair, listening and counting. Six rings.

Then silence, then six more rings. When the telephone rang again, he picked it up.

"Yes."

"Sullivan. How about a drink?" The voice had absolutely no inflection, as if it were somehow generated mechanically, like the voice of a battery-powered toy robot found in toy stores.

"Good idea," said Berwick. It wasn't really a good idea at all, but he had to give the required reply. He did not want to leave home and his book and his memories this quiet evening, and he thought with regret of the cold beer and the chicken waiting for him in the refrigerator. He didn't mind doing what he had to for his country, but he'd never enjoy this cloak-and-dagger stuff—stilted code phrases, the sort of nonsense seen in a bad spy movie. He felt like an idiot mouthing the required words, but it was part of the job these days.

"Twenty minutes," said the voice, and the line went dead.

Berwick sighed and pulled on his shoes. The meeting place he knew, a quiet pub several blocks away in Chelsea, near the river. He brightened a little. At least the food was reasonably good, and he could order a beer. In fact, he remembered the pub made quite a good shepherd's pie, and the walk would be pleasant. He would stay off the heavily traveled streets and enjoy the peace after the day's rain.

The Coachman was beginning to fill up when he arrived, mostly businesspeople eager to let down after a long day. There was a sprinkling of lorry drivers and cabbies, too, equally eager for a drink after a harried day navigating the crowded streets of the metropolis. *I wonder who Sullivan is this time.* When he received his orders in the past, it had never been the same man twice, although whoever it was approached him like an old friend. He was always called Harry. More cloak and dagger.

This Harry was, indeed, someone he'd never seen before, a small man with a tidy grey mustache and a dark blue blazer. They shook hands like old friends, ordered a beer apiece, and carried them to a corner table.

"Another job," said Berwick. It was not a question; there could be only one reason for the meeting.

Harry nodded. "Aye."

Berwick pulled at his beer. "Where?"

"Place in Germany. Called Ansbach. In Franconia. Know it?"

The man talks like a telegram.

"Yes. A baroque town west of Nürnberg. Very pretty, as I remember it. Haven't been there in years, not since I was stationed up at Minden. The town wasn't much damaged during the war, and I remember a couple of very beautiful churches there."

Harry nodded. "You a churchgoer?"

"Yes," said Berwick. "God is the only abiding thing in this miserable, mucked-up world of ours. What's the job?"

Harry hesitated and looked around them. "Need to kill a person."

Christ. Another one of those.

"Who?" Berwick asked aloud. "And why?"

Harry pulled again at his beer. He looked embarrassed, Berwick thought, even hesitant.

"The target is very rich—supplies a great deal of money to a couple of neo-Nazi causes. Need to cut off the source of their funds as much as we can. The target is also virulently anti-American and anti-British, and has a considerable upper-class audience. People with some influence, and more money. They don't have the guts to go out and take chances in the street, but they're plenty willing to finance the hoodlums who do. We're reluctant to go through German intelligence to deal with this, or, believe me, we would. We think the target has extensive connections at Bonn. Besides, the Germans would have to arrest the target. We want to send a message, as well as cut down the money tree."

Why, thought Berwick, *why does he keep calling him the "target"?* But he said only, "Who is he?"

"Not a he. A woman."

"What? You want me to kill a woman? For Christ's sake! You know that's way beyond what I signed on to do, and our leaders know it, too."

"I know, and so do they. That's why I'm authorized to tell you the organizations she helps fund have murdered several people: opposition political leaders and a couple of German coppers. Worst of all, they've twice kidnapped and brutalized family members of people who've threatened to expose them or haven't come up with enough *Deutchmarks.* They even snatched a couple of children and knocked them around."

Harry paused to take a drink of beer. "Please understand, these people are a kind of terrorist Mafia; they're a menace, absolutely without conscience, and they're getting stronger by the day. Lots of money helps bring in lots of recruits. The worst of the lot is a group that calls itself the *Vaterlandpartei.*"

"The Fatherland Party," said Berwick. "I've never heard of

them."

"You will," said Harry. "That I promise. Anything we can do to stunt their growth will save lives—undoubtedly more innocents. And it may well avert massive political trouble later on. That's why we've asked you to do . . . this. I know it's distasteful as hell, but trust me, it's absolutely necessary. Still, you can back away from it, you know."

He leaned back in his chair. "So, what do I tell the boss?"

Berwick thought in silence. *Why do I hesitate at killing a woman? I guess it's some antique notion of chivalry, something learned from my parents, and in church, and all the books at school. But why hesitate? What bloody difference does gender make?*

He turned to Harry. "You say these Fatherland Party people have brutalized family members? Children? Look me in the eye, and don't feed me a ration of guano. Is that absolutely true?"

Harry met his eyes and nodded. "Yes. On two occasions of which we're sure. Others of which we have have only heard rumors. There may be more."

"And this woman funds them, Harry? Do you think she knows the extremes to which they go? Do you think she knows they kidnap kids and have 'knocked them around'?"

Harry shook his head. "I can't honestly say either way. Not for certain. But we think she probably does know, or at least she suspects and doesn't care. Anything for the cause, the noble end justifies any kind of dirty means, all of that claptrap. She is certainly cozy with the party leadership. In fact, we think the orator who does the warm-up speeches for the party leader is fucking her. Well, to be honest, we *know* he is."

"Okay," said Berwick. "I don't like it a bit, but I'll take the assignment. What's her name?"

"Von Kraus, actually von und zu Kraus-Wolfenburg. First name is Christiana; she's called Christa. There's a bunch of middle names, too. Too many to remember. You know, the string of family names nobility hangs on their kids. One thing, she lives alone, unless it's time for the *Vaterlandpartei* speaker to come and screw her. He generally stays overnight; sometimes he's there for a couple of days, but no more. Very busy running around Germany rousing the rabble."

Harry finished his beer. "A couple of servants, but they're banished to a cottage out behind the main house every night by ten. She's alone after that."

"Surveillance system?"

Harry nodded. "Oh, yes. We don't know, but we think it's manageable. I've got such details as we have."

"Give me the gen; you have it with you tonight?"

Harry nodded again and slid a fat sealed envelope across the table. "All in here. Everything. Tickets, map, photos, lots of *Deutschmarks* for expenses. Emergency numbers if you need them, as usual. There's also a dead-end credit card in the name on your passport and driving license, which are also phony, of course. When this is over, you and your cards will all magically disappear. Also as usual. Some other cards there, too. In the same name, just for protective coloration. Club over on Pall Mall, veteran's pension card, British Legion membership. That sort of thing."

Berwick listened in silence, picked up the envelope, and slid it into the inside pocket of his tweed jacket.

"By the way," said Harry. "There is just one other thing."

Oh, good. Here comes the really bad news.

"You've got to make this look like an accident, or maybe a death from natural causes. Heart attack, perhaps. We can't have the German police and their intelligence people getting too interested. Remember, we think she's got friends in high places."

"Tall order. How about a criminal act? A robbery, say. If the target is that wealthy, there must be something lying about to steal. Jewelry?"

Harry reflected. "Maybe so. Let me check. If I don't phone you within twenty-four hours and simply say 'no,' you may use your own judgment." He looked at his watch. "Time for me to go. Enjoy your dinner. *Ciao.*"

And he was gone.

My God, thought Berwick. *We've sat here in this warm, friendly place for half an hour, drinking beer and coolly discussing the murder of a woman I've never seen and don't know. And I agreed.* He sighed. *I wonder, I wonder, if maybe I've lost my soul.* Then he shrugged.

To hell with it; they started this, the sons of bitches, and they took away my girl and our son. Fuck 'em all; they're all the same breed of scum. Screw them and the horse they rode in on.

He walked to the bar to get another beer.

ANSBACH, WEST GERMANY

JUNE 1966

THE HOUSE WAS HUGE, A MASSIVE PILE OF OLD STONE, THREE stories tall and capped by a lichen-crusted grey slate roof. A black wrought-iron fence encircled it, topped with vicious-looking spikes like spearheads. Behind the iron gates a cobblestoned courtyard stretched back to a massive, forbidding porch, also closed off by iron grillwork. Berwick smiled, watching the place from the small park across the street. *God-awful front yard*, he thought. Looked like a barracks square, a parade ground, the sort of place he spent hours bashing when he was at Sandhurst.

He studied the building. What an edifice. A castle. But not one speck of color about the whole place. No flowers, no shrubs, no bright paint, nothing to relieve the dreary grey. It looked like an oversized mausoleum, a crypt, a house of the dead. There were five, no, six chimneys rising high above the slate. The house was ringed with mature linden trees, and behind it he could see tall old pines. There were garages back there, too, he knew—stables once—and a cottage, also of the same dingy stone. That, he thought, must be the servants' quarters.

He shifted his weight on the hard iron park bench and sighed. The whole neighborhood seemed to be made up of the same kind of grim, grey stone houses, apparently of roughly the same vintage. Not a bit of color about any of them, either. He wondered what sort of sour, scowling, unhappy trolls lived in those places. Nothing moved. *Do you suppose they are all dead inside but just keep staying on?* He smiled at the fantasy.

Berwick took another bite of his *Leberwurst* sandwich, and then pushed his plastic fork into the disposable container that held the remains of his potato salad. *Not bad,* he thought; anywhere in Germany, in any *metzerei,* the butcher could saw you off a chunk of the world's most delicious sausage, and sell you a bit of salad, made fresh that day. Top that off with a couple of crusty *bröchen,* and you had a lunch fit for a king. He took another pull at his bottle of *König Pilsner,* ate the last of the salad, wiped his mouth with his paper napkin, and sighed.

He reached for a cigarette, one of his omnipresent Players, lit it, and sucked luxuriously at the fragrant smoke. *Don't dare hang around here much longer,* he thought. *Been here an hour, and you can only stretch out a bag lunch so long.* Besides which, there was absolutely nothing going on around the house worth watching.

He reflected. She was home, all right; he saw her at the front window half an hour ago, and then again a few minutes past. She pulled apart the curtains and looked out. *Waiting for someone?* He wondered, as he picked up the remains of his lunch and shoved it and his empty beer bottle into the plastic bag, if she could be waiting for the Nazi rabble-rouser to come and give her her periodic screwing.

She was. He recognized Müller immediately from one of the excellent pictures Harry had supplied. The man drove his big BMW to the gate perimeter and honked, and the heavy iron gates slid open almost instantly. Worth remembering, Berwick thought. Electric controls from the inside. Smooth. Motor must be in the stone pillar that anchors the gate.

Müller parked in front of the grim house, and the woman came out to meet him on the drab, grey porch. *Attractive*, he mused, *slim, fine legs, good breasts. Good facial bones, but a very tough face, very hard, a bit in the concentration-camp style. Predatory. Carnivorous. Hair looks dyed, but a good job of it.* He watched as she flung her arms around her visitor's neck and the two vanished inside.

Nothing more to see, at least for awhile. From the appearance of the greeting, she was busy tearing off his clothing. Or vice versa. Or both. Berwick walked slowly on down the deserted street. He had left his rented Opel two blocks away, in a theater parking lot. Time to plan some, and prepare. If the woman and Müller ran true to form, they'd be hard at it for the rest of the day. The man would not leave until tomorrow. Then she would be alone. He thought he knew enough of the surveillance system to penetrate it. The big danger would be the cameras covering the yard and the fences around the house. They would be connected to a recorder inside the building, and probably to a security company monitor, as well.

Bad. He thought he could disable the security alarm, but before he could do that, the cameras would pick him up, record a nice photo of him, and almost surely advertise him to security people somewhere. Which would produce a quick visit from the *Polizei*. Could he get to her outside the house, and still make it look like an accident or a casual robbery? The answer to that question was also no. Or at least probably not. Not without following her around, maybe for days. Or watching the house. Both dangerous exercises.

He decided watching the house was the least dangerous course, but sitting in the park wouldn't do. Not in the evening hours, anyhow. Way too obvious. Maybe the soccer field just down the block. It had lights, so they played there at night sometimes. He nodded to himself. As long as there was a game, no one would notice him. Even without a night-vision device, he could see if anyone left the house. And follow. *Fair enough.* If there were a soccer game tonight, he could begin.

On the way back to his hotel, Berwick stopped at a department store. He bought a pair of heavy wool boot socks in one department, then walked downstairs to the hardware department, where he bought a box of heavy bolts. He was careful not to touch either the bolt box or the label on the socks with his fingertips.

Ready.

NÜRENBERG, WEST GERMANY

JUNE 1966

THAT NIGHT THERE WAS A SOCCER GAME TO COVER HIS surveillance, and Müller and the woman gave him the chance he needed even before full dark. He watched them come out of the great grey mausoleum and get into the man's BMW. The gates opened, and the big car moved out into the traffic and headed for the center of town. Berwick walked casually to his own car and followed.

He stayed well back, holding the Opel three or four cars behind the BMW. He could feel the adrenaline rising. To make it look right he'd have to take out Müller, too. *Fair enough.* He was the big voice for the Nazis; the warm-up man who got everybody excited before the main speeches. Like Göbbels did for Hitler in the old days. *He's just one more bastard.*

He followed the BMW down the road to Nürnberg. Off to the bright lights of the big town. Precious few bright lights in quiet little Ansbach. The shadowing job was easy. Several times other cars passed Berwick, until he had four vehicles between him and Müller. Berwick had to pass only once to keep

69

his quarry within view. He was only one more set of headlights in the gloom.

In Nürnberg, Müller parked in a three-story parking garage, and Berwick followed him to the second floor, parking five or six spaces away. *Not now*, he thought. *Too many people coming and going. Later.* He slouched down as the two walked past the Opel, down toward the exit from the garage. They did not even glance his way, both of them talking at once. *Not wary. Good.*

He sat up, rolled down the window, and lit a Players. He sighed. This would be a long night. He reached beside him for his purchases and shoved one boot sock inside the other. Then he broke open the boxes of bolts and filled the socks. He tied a knot above the cluster of bolts and hefted the improvised cosh. Plenty heavy enough to do the job with a single blow, and the sort of thing a professional robber might be expected to use.

His quarry did not reappear until after 1:00 a.m. He heard them laughing loudly together as they walked up the ramp toward their car, Müller's rich baritone a sharp contrast to the woman's shrill, abrasive cackling. *A little drunk, clinging to the man's arm.* She laughed again. *Like someone dragging fingernails across a blackboard. Nasty sound. Maybe a lot drunk. All the better.*

His heart rate had increased, and he took several deep breaths to steady himself. *Careful, Berwick. No hyperventilation.* And then, as the two walked past him, he took one more glance around the silent garage and slid out of the Opel. He had unscrewed the bulb in the dome light, and his rubber shoe soles made no sound on the concrete. He was no more than a step behind the couple when Müller sensed something and half-turned to look behind him. Too late. Berwick struck hard, swinging the bolt-loaded socks in above the man's right ear. The crunch of the blow startled even him, and Müller went down without making a sound. There was only the sodden sound of his body crumpling onto the concrete.

The woman turned toward Berwick, frozen in fear and surprise; her mouth was open as if to scream, but no sound came out. He looked into the wide, frightened eyes, almost hesitated, then struck hard again, smashing in the frontal bones of her skull.

It was done. Feeling a little sick, he glanced around him, then bent swiftly, pulled the man's wallet from his hip pocket, and snatched up the woman's purse. He did not strike again, confident there was no life left in either of them. *Quickly, quickly, Berwick. Get to your car and get out of here!* He felt nauseated, ready to throw up. *That was the worst, sweet Jesus, that was the ugliest thing I've ever done . . .* But now the imperative was flight.

The Opel started instantly, and he wheeled away from the two motionless figures, over onto the down ramp, then down halfway to the next floor before he turned on his lights. He had seen no one, and the Opel's license plates were false, thoughtfully furnished by a helpful MI6 man from Nürnberg. Still, he knew this was the most dangerous part of the whole operation. There were very few cars left in the garage, but someone coming late could see the Opel and remember enough to describe it to the police. Even information about an ordinary black Opel could be a problem, even though there must be thousands of them in Germany. He pulled out of the almost vacant garage, glanced in the rearview mirror. The street behind him was empty as far as he could see.

He drove sedately back to Ansbach, and on the outskirts of the silent town pulled into an alley, stopped, jerked the plates loose from their sticky-tape mounting on top of the real plates, and threw the fake ones in the second trash can from the right against the peeling wall of a tired brick building.

The wallet and the purse went in with them, along with the gloves he had worn. Someone would retrieve them well before daybreak. He didn't know who would do it, and he didn't want to know. He drove on down the alley, turned sedately into a major street, and drove to his hotel. He had kept the hotel key with him when he left that evening, and no one would see him return.

Suddenly he was very tired, drained of all energy, the adrenaline gone, feeling empty and melancholy. He crossed himself. "Dear God," he murmured, "may I be forgiven for what I have done."

Please understand why I did it.

FRANKFURT AM MAIN, WEST GERMANY
A SUNDAY IN NOVEMBER 1966

THE FRANKFURT SUBURB OF NEU-ISENBURG IS QUIET AND orderly, its neat stucco houses well-kept and handsome beneath their red tile roofs, set back from the streets behind tidy lawns, with iron fences and gates along the sidewalk edge. There is the occasional discrete shop, perhaps a neighborhood *gasthaus* or small, chaste hotel, but the area is generally residential, the home of good, law-abiding, hardworking citizens. It is green and soothing and peaceful. It is unthinkable anything unpleasant or ill-bred could happen there.

The Germans take great enjoyment in their lovely land, and one of their favorite pastimes is walking in the fresh air and the verdant greenery of their parks and squares. The citizens of Neu-Isenburg are no exception. Their favorite walking place is their own town forest, a large and beautiful grove of many acres, laced with broad, well-tended paths between evergreens and shrubbery. Through the verdant days of spring and summer, its well-tended flower beds are brilliant with blooms.

On Sundays, especially, the paths are filled with well-dressed,

73

courteous, orderly people. There are elderly couples, lovers hand in hand, giggling groups of teenaged girls, families complete with well-behaved children and grandchildren and equally well-behaved dogs, trotting sedately beside their masters.

Now the summer was gone, and the afternoon was grey and cold, with a light breeze ruffling the leaves of the shrubs and the needles of the trees. It had rained earlier in the day, and the well-drained paths were still damp and shiny with water. Occasional drops still fell, pattering down from the sodden trees to the carpet of brown and yellow leaves beneath. Even so, the walkers were out in force, complete with dogs and children.

Among the groups of walkers on their Sunday *spaziergang* strode an elderly man, dressed in a dark suit and snap-brim Bavarian felt hat, both well-worn but carefully maintained. Although he walked with a cane and a slight limp, his step was firm and regular, his back straight and his head high. As he passed a woman, he raised his hat and inclined his head to her in a courtly bow of gentle, old-world courtesy. She smiled in return: "*Guten Tag, Herr General.*"

Finally, as the bleak light began to fade into dusk, the old man left the *Stadtswald*, crossed the busy ring boulevard that bordered it, and walked briskly two blocks up *Schillerstrasse*, a quiet avenue lined with tall, old trees. He turned in through the wrought-iron gate of number 20 and applied his key to the heavy oak door of the small, neat, grey stucco house sheltering beneath a huge, ancient pine.

The old man entered, turned on the hall light against the coming darkness, and hung his overcoat and hat on two of a series of polished wooden pegs to the left of the door. He turned, rubbing his hands together. He had not thought it was so cold today. Ever since Russia, he mused, ever since Stalingrad, he had felt the cold so easily and so deeply. He shivered a little, remembering the ghastly, endless whiteness and the contorted corpses in the snow. A brandy would go well today. He turned into the dark living room, flipped on a wall switch, and stopped dead.

Three men stood facing him, still wearing their overcoats. The man in the center was in his midthirties, tall and blond, with high cheekbones and pale eyes, eyes of a blue so light they looked almost colorless. He was smiling at the old man, but there was no friendliness or warmth in his eyes.

The men who flanked him could have been brothers: dark-haired, thin-faced, scrawny, both wearing straggly, inadequate beards that did not quite cover the skin of their chins. Both were slightly stooped, both were smiling at the general, and both held automatic pistols.

Without a word, the man to his left struck the general back-handed across the mouth with the pistol barrel, breaking out his front teeth and driving the old man to his knees, coughing and gagging on his own blood. As the general knelt, helpless, the second young man kicked him methodically in the right kidney, and the old man bowed to the floor in agony.

Still in silence, the two men caught the general under the armpits and dragged him retching back into the hall, then through an entry opposite the front door and down a narrow flight of stone steps to the cellar. There the two held the old general erect while the blond man handcuffed his wrists over a water pipe running horizontally just below the ceiling. One of the young men ripped off the general's necktie, tore open his shirt, and jerked the old man's trousers and underwear down around his ankles. He stepped back, and began to clip and light a long cigar. He was still smiling.

The leader sat gracefully on the top of an old steamer trunk tucked neatly against the wall of the cellar. He smiled again, that horrible empty smile, opened his fur-collared black overcoat, and steadily regarded the old German officer. The general's eyes were clearer now; they showed his pain, but still glared a hawk's defiance. The general spat a tooth and a mouthful of blood toward the elegant blond man and stood without speaking, only his toes reaching the floor, the handcuffs cutting into his wrists. The old man's labored breathing was harsh in the chilly room.

"So, Herr General-Major von und zu Baltheim. The old eagle cornered, eh? You are in a very bad place, you know, my friend. I need some information you have . . . just a few very simple things, and then you can die in peace, easily."

He paused. "But I do not think you will be eager to tell me. You are a real *Junker*, eh? An aristocrat to your toes, with the *Junker*'s archaic code of honor. You are an anachronism, old man, a throwback to another time. A time past."

The blond man paused, and gestured to the young man holding the cigar.

"Kurt, here, is a sadist, Herr General. He is sexually aroused by other people's pain. He is puffing on a big cigar, as you can see. He is doing that to make a big, hot ember on the end, do you understand? In war, I know, you have smelled burning flesh, no? And Kurt carries with him some needles, too, and a razor, and some other of his favorite little tools. Please, Herr General, you can save yourself much pain, just by talking to me a little."

The cold, mirthless smile broadened, showing a collection of wonderfully white, even teeth.

"Come, now, shall we speak together as gentlemen?"

The old general's blue eyes were hard and unafraid. He spat another mouthful of blood, licked his lips, and spoke very distinctly.

"*Fick dich!*" he said softly. "Fuck you, you Nazi bastard, you arrogant son of a bitch. I know you and your kind, even without your stupid armband, you beautiful Nordic asshole. You are no gentleman. You do not even know what the word means. There is no mistaking a pig, even a pig in a thousand-mark overcoat. Your little friend may do whatever he wants. I tell you nothing."

The blond man shook his head without anger. "Too bad, Herr General, you help nobody but Kurt, who will enjoy everything he does to you. Well, I will ask you one time anyway. You may begin answering anytime the pain becomes unbearable, and I will stop Kurt's play. So, then, what I wish to know about is simple: It is the birth of a child, up on the *Obersalzburg* in November of 1931. A long time ago, eh?"

He shifted his weight on the steamer trunk, crossed his legs, and adjusted the knifelike crease in one immaculate trouser leg.

"But I know you will remember as if it were yesterday. It concerned an Austrian girl who gave birth in Bavaria. That in itself seems a little unusual. What is truly odd, however, is that there are none of the regular records our methodical bureaucracy always made of such things. There is no birth certificate. There is no mention of the mother or of the father, or of the child. Not even of the birth itself. There is no christening record in the local church. Nothing. There is nothing at all to show a child was born, and that is unheard of in Germany.

"But a few people had to know something about it, and I think you are one of them. And I think you know about . . . certain things that came after."

The tall blond man leaned forward, the empty eyes suddenly alight, peering intently at the old officer. "You know!" he said softly. "Yes, you do! I see it in your eyes. But you will not speak about it, will you, *Junker*? Ah, well, we shall reason with you. Kurt?"

Thirty minutes later the old man was still silent. He sagged against the handcuffs, no strength left in his knees. His thin body was spotted with the angry scarlet of cigar burns, and slim runnels of blood trickled down his legs to gather in a pool on the concrete floor. Kurt was smiling vaguely and humming softly to himself as he delicately applied the tip of the cigar to the general's chest. Von Baltheim moaned softly and bit his lower lip, but still said nothing.

The blond man remained motionless on the trunk. Then he raised his hand. "Enough, Kurt. Much more of this and his heart will go. That is what the old man is hoping for. He is willing it to happen. He will not break this way."

He raised his eyes to the general. "So, old man, you have won a little battle, at such a terrible cost. The Leader said you would be very tough. But now we will try something different, something more—how shall I put it—modern."

He took from his pocket a flat leather case and opened it. He

78

removed a glass syringe and fitted a needle to it. He selected a glass vial from an array of neatly labeled containers, and expertly filled the syringe. He turned to the general, holding the syringe poised delicately, like a dart.

"In your day, the drug of choice was scopolamine, old man. *Very* crude by today's enlightened standards. This drug"—he gently waved the syringe—"this drug will reach anyone, no matter how tough, even one as hard as you. Soon you will speak to me happily and freely, and answer my every question like an old friend. Here, we simply shoot it in your behind, so, and wait."

He returned to his trunk, sat down with a sigh, and deftly put away the syringe and needle.

"This may take as much as an hour to work fully, Herr General. That is why we first try more, ah, direct methods. And, of course, to please Kurt also. We will take you down, and you may sit on the floor. Your color is not good, and I do not want to lose you before we have talked some more. The position you are in is very like crucifixion, I understand. It much impedes your breathing. Your heart must not fail yet, so near to our pleasant conversation."

He smiled, laced his fingers over the knee of the spotless grey trousers, and watched as the two younger men lowered the old man to the floor and seated him with his back to the wall.

"Now we wait," said the blond man. "Now we wait, Herr General, and soon, quite soon, we will talk courteously together like old friends." His smiled widened. "But you do not feel friendly, I can see. What a shame."

"Bastard!" gasped the old man. "You say you are the master

race, *nicht wahr?* Just like the party morons in the old days. Well, I tell you, Nazi, I was a soldier longer than you have polluted this earth. I can tell you, you lovely Aryan bastard, in the old army you would not make a pimple on a *Gefreiter*'s ass."

An hour later, the old officer sat slumped on the cellar floor, his chin down on his chest, the old blood dried to crusty purple-brown scabs on his chest and legs. The tall blond man was standing, looking down at von Baltheim in the gloom. He sighed softly, and nodded to the torturer. The young man smiled and lifted up von Baltheim's head by the sweat-soaked, straggly grey hair. The old man's eyes opened and looked at him, still fierce and defiant.

Kurt laughed aloud, then slashed von Baltheim's throat in one swift movement, jerked the general's thin body forward, and dropped him on his face on the concrete.

The three men walked up the cellar stairs to the first floor without so much as a glance at von Baltheim, lying in a growing pool of his own blood, trying to push himself up on arms without strength, gurgling horribly as he tried to breathe through the rush of blood that drowned his windpipe.

The general fell forward on his elbows as the three men reached the top of the steps and walked on to the front door of the neat little house. They did not see the old man dip his right forefinger in the pool of blood and begin to write on the concrete floor.

He managed the straggling letters *R A U* before the final darkness overtook him.

ST. JAMES'S PARK, LONDON, ENGLAND
JANUARY 1967

COOPER LEANED BACK ON THE PARK BENCH, WATCHING THE grey smoke of his third Camel whirled away by a cracking north wind. It was cold in the park, chilly even for his thick Harris tweed jacket and British macintosh. Only four o'clock, and already the long winter night was closing down.

Up and down the wide park walks, the hardy British walked briskly, apparently indifferent to the cold. A rose-cheeked nanny passed him pushing a perambulator, with a diminutive pink face peering happily out from beneath a blue stocking cap.

Marvelous people, Cooper thought. *Whether it was against hordes of enemies or just a miserably cold day, they simply pushed on. No wonder they ruled most of the world.* He shoved his hands deeper into the pockets of the macintosh.

Wish I'd worn gloves. Hope my man's on time. Let's see. Look for a slim man in his late thirties, duffle coat and tweed hat, carrying two books under his left arm, one black, one red. With deep blue eyes. Called Simon.

Please hurry up, Simon, before I turn into an ice cube.

Berwick was on time, striding up to Cooper, holding out his hand as if the two were old friends. "You'll be Thomas. I'm Simon." Cooper liked the smile.

"My friends call me Tom, Simon. Do you want to go through the recognition ritual?"

Berwick's smile broadened. "Okay. I suppose we ought. I'm looking for a good place to buy cabbages. Do you know one?"

Cooper smiled in return. "What about Harrod's?"

Berwick laughed aloud. "Bloody silly thing, all that gibberish. I guess it's some use if you're meeting a Romanian turncoat, but not when you know exactly whom you're talking to. It's bloody cold. Want to walk?"

"Before I freeze," said Cooper.

The two men walked side by side on across St. James's Park, then turned down Birdcage Walk toward Westminster Abbey. The wind was in their faces, whirling a few truant leaves past them and on into the park.

"They say you're very good, Tom. Hope we're not wasting your time on this one. There may be nothing to it, so don't be disappointed in the outline I give you. There is a great deal we don't know, and the mystery we have now may simply remain a mystery."

Berwick lit a Player's, cupping his hands against the wind. "You know we monitor the commo of the radical organizations as best we can, just as your people do. Lots of it is only drivel, political oratory. You know the stuff I mean. Some of it makes sense; most of it doesn't. Much of it we don't follow up on. Well, now we have some recent traffic that has raised a lot of hackles on our leaders." He grinned. "And that is why they have decreed that you and I go forth into far places and find out what this somewhat vague talk may mean, if it means anything at all. They attach some urgency to the mission."

Westminster Abbey came into view ahead, a soaring monument to a thousand years of faith. Cooper stopped involuntarily, taken with the beauty of the Abbey, as he had been so many times before.

"Lovely, isn't it?" said Berwick. "Someone once called it 'the hand of the nation reaching up to God.' I like to think of it that way."

Cooper nodded. "I'm a little awed every time I see the Abbey." He chuckled. "I'm also getting colder. Would it be safe to find a pub to talk in?"

"I think so. I happen to know a good one just down to our left, only a couple of blocks away." He smiled again. "As it happens, I know a good pub in most parts of London. I was raised correctly."

The Three Coachmen was warm and quiet, dark oak paneling and a burnished bar in service when Queen Victoria was only a girl. They found a booth near the rear, and Simon went to the bar and returned with two pints of beer. Both men shed their overcoats and lit cigarettes.

Berwick nodded at a tall case clock at the end of the room. "We have about half an hour before the evening custom starts coming in. Then talking can get a tad difficult. Ought to be plenty of time to tell you what we know before that happens."

His face grew serious.

"For a while, after the spate of war-crimes trials at the end of the war, there wasn't much official talk about the Nazi Party. Except in connection with the Israeli apprehensions of various death-camp criminals. Even the Russians don't like to talk much about the Nazi days, except in a general way. Among other things, it embarrasses the bastards to be reminded that until June of '41, they and the Nazis were the best of friends."

Berwick paused briefly and drank deeply of the dark amber beer. "These days, though, we hear more and more about neo-Nazis. Most of the publicity goes to the skinhead morons and their firebombs, and the crazies throwing rocks at the *Polizei*. As a rule, those people are more annoying than dangerous. They're street punks, mostly. Teddy boys, second-rate hoodlums. Some used to be communists. A lot of them are losers who have to blame someone else for their lack of talent. But . . ."

Berwick paused.

"There is a neo-Nazi organization we watch very closely indeed. They are called the Fatherland Party. They are well-funded and quite dangerous. Until recently, we had an ear inside the organization, and we heard some peculiar and disturbing things."

He lit another Player's from the butt of the last one.

"The Fatherland Party leadership has started talking about some long-forgotten names, names from the old days of the Nazi Party, even before Hitler came to power. That's disturbing. It's puzzling, as well, and in a couple of different ways. In the first place, we had not heard those names from anyone in years. In the second place, the people they seem to be interested in were small potatoes in the old party hierarchy. Finally, these people are either long dead, or long since disappeared. What conceivable reason would a neo-Nazi group have for caring about them at all?

"We became even more interested when the Fatherland Party leadership began to talk about 'progress' in inquiries about these very people. And the message traffic refers to other messages concerning these same names. It's also interesting that the information to which they refer was doubtless hand-delivered, because we never heard it."

Berwick crushed out the cigarette and grinned at Cooper.

"So you and I are going back in time. We are going to try to find out what interests the Fatherlanders so much, and *why* it does. Our masters are nervous about this one, and I can't blame them. I smell trouble, too. The Nazis are up to something, and they must think it is worth devoting a hell of a lot of resources to. They are very well-funded, Tom, and their leaders are very bright."

Berwick glanced quickly around the pub, still quiet. Though none of the other few patrons were close to them, he dropped his voice, leaning forward across the table.

"Anyway, here are the people whom the Nazis are interested in. Horst Lammers and Seppl Heide were veteran Nazi street fighters, early true believers, personal bodyguards for Hitler in the old beer-hall days in Munich. Lammers later rose to a cushy job in the party apparatus. We know he survived the war. He was investigated by the de-Nazification court just afterward, and then he dropped out of sight. Heide disappeared before the war, very suddenly. We do not know what became of him.

"Then there was Gertraude Mannheimer, who was a cook in the Hitler household in the early 30s. Trude Mannheimer was, by all accounts, an attractive woman. She was also an absolutely convinced Nazi, a true fanatic. She is said to have worshiped the ground Hitler walked on."

Berwick took another pull at his beer.

"Trude is long dead. She was killed in one of the bombings of Berlin in early 1944. But by then she had risen high in the hierarchy around Hitler. She ceased to be a cook and was moved to a sort of supervising secretary's job. She had no stenographic skills, but she was intelligent. In short order she moved up to a responsible job controlling correspondence and clerical personnel in the party chancellery under Martin Bormann. She was exceedingly well-paid and accorded substantial respect in the party. A meteoric rise from humble beginnings, wasn't it?"

Cooper took another deep drink of beer, silent and fascinated as Berwick went on.

"Along the way Trude acquired a lover. We're not sure when, but we think it was rather early on the '30s. Surprisingly, he was an aristocrat, an army officer, Baron Franz Ritter von und zu Baltheim. A bloody fine officer, apparently. He'd won the Blue Max, the *Pour le Mérite*, back in the First World War, when he was only a seventeen-year-old *faehnerich*, an officer candidate. He stayed in the *Wehrmacht* after the war, one of the chosen few, and in the early '30s, the general staff used him as a sort of unofficial liaison officer to Hitler.

"Anyhow, he commanded a battalion in Poland in '39, a regiment in France in 1940, and later a division in Russia. He was badly wounded and captured at Stalingrad. Surprisingly, he survived the war, although he did not return to Germany from captivity until 1952. What about another beer?"

Cooper jerked back to the present. "Yes, please. I'll go get it this time."

When Cooper returned with a glass in each hand, Berwick was lighting still another Players from the butt of the last one. He pushed the pack across the table to Cooper.

"After he came back from Russia," said Berwick, "the general worked for the German government until he retired in 1965. Since then, he's lived quietly in Frankfurt. He was strictly an old-style officer; honorable and upright, no hint of any Nazi-style atrocities. A de-Nazification court cleared him entirely after the war."

Cooper interrupted. "Nothing since? No neo-Nazi or communist connections?"

Berwick shook his head. "Not a sign. And he lived a quiet, solitary life until November of last year, when he was brutally murdered in his home. He was tortured first, and then his throat was cut. The house showed signs of a search, which I find curious. Enough hammer-and-sickle signs were spray-painted around the house to convince the bloody press the killing was some kind of long-delayed vengeance."

Berwick shook his head. "The trouble with this theory, Tom, is he simply never seems to have been involved in the sort of conduct that would lead anybody to kill him. More convincing, he had been living openly in Frankfurt since he returned from Russia. Why would anyone who wanted revenge for something wait that long?"

"Diehards in the KGB, Simon?" asked Cooper.

"Maybe. But why? It's possible the torture may have been

a crude attempt to extract information. No drugs showed up in the autopsy, but then no one was looking for any. The doctors could easily have missed a discreet puncture mark among the other scars on his body. Anyhow, there are currently substances that do not linger in the blood. You know about them. It's too late to look for anything now."

The landlord passed them carrying two plates of food to another booth, and Berwick waited until the man was back behind the bar before he went on.

"Well, even the killing might have been written off and forgotten, except for the sort of accidental intelligence break that comes along once in a long time. The general belonged to an association of old soldiers who met regularly to drink beer and talk about the old days. Absolutely harmless. These men were line soldiers, not politicals. Even so, last year some leftist newspaper whined about them and accused them of being neo-Nazi. Patent nonsense, I think, but the story was picked up by Mossad, the Israeli intelligence people.

"As a matter of course, the Israelis put routine temporary surveillance on the leaders of the group. That included old General Baltheim, who was the president. Mossad used a house owned by a Jewish doctor, across the street from the general's home. They watched the general for awhile, photographing anyone who came around. Quite thorough. And they came up empty. As Mossad expected, there was nothing suspicious about the old man and his few visitors. There was nothing at all . . . until the last day."

Cooper nodded. "The day he was murdered."

"Exactly. Late on that last afternoon, three men came out

of Baltheim's house. The Mossad man was startled, because he had not seen them go in. He would have had them followed, but because the job was so routine, he was alone. But he did photograph them. The next day, the old man was found in a puddle of his own blood by his *Putzfrau*, his housekeeper."

Berwick glanced around the busy, warm pub, beginning to fill with its evening customers, then drew a glossy photograph from his jacket pocket. He laid it on the spotless tablecloth in front of Cooper.

"Mossad takes marvelous pictures. Recognize anybody?"

Cooper shook his head.

Berwick rested a finger on the tall blond man in the tailored black overcoat.

"That's Franz Dessau. He is an important man in the *Vaterlandpartei*, the Fatherland Party, what they call a *Leiter* in party jargon—a leader. The two skinny youngsters are hatchet men for the party, enforcers. They are—what's your term?—minor league."

Berwick leaned back in the booth. "Which means this killing had nothing whatever to do with vengeance. Normally, Tom, Mossad would have furnished a courtesy copy of this photo to West German intelligence. They did not do so in this case because they, too, are worried about the Fatherland Party's interest in old Nazi names. It's not that they don't trust German intelligence. But the fact is, like us, they can deal more, ah, directly with the Nazi danger than the police and the courts can . . ."

Berwick pulled at his beer. "And Mossad thinks, as we do, that the general might have been Trude Mannheimer's lover. At

least, he would have had regular access to her when he worked
as liaison officer to Hitler in the Munich days. He had a room
in *der Fuehrer's* residence in *Prinzregentenplatz*. He was a handsome young officer; she was a pretty woman; both of them were
single. So there is that tenuous connection to one of the names
the Fatherlanders are asking about."

Cooper picked up the photo and held it out to Berwick, but
the Englishman waved it away.

"Keep it. You must come to know Dessau, and you may well
need to recognize the trash with him. We don't know who they
are, exactly. Local muscle probably, low-level party toughs. But
we could run into them again, and it would be nice to identify
them instantly."

Cooper nodded. "I'd like to meet them, after what they did
to the old man."

"So would I. I cannot think the world would mourn either
of them. Or Dessau. Especially Dessau. Well."

Berwick lit another Players and grinned. "Got to give these
up. Maybe tomorrow. Anyhow, to finish my tale. There was
one very odd thing about the murder of Baltheim. The old man
lived for a few seconds after his throat was cut. And he died
game. He died trying to leave some sort of clue in the only way
he could.

"He wrote on the concrete floor. In his own blood, Tom. He
got down the letters *R A U*, and no more. No doubt he did not
finish what he started to write. The papers speculated he was
trying to write *rauber*, or *rauben*—robber, or robbery. Nothing
else makes much sense."

Berwick paused for a moment, then shook his head.

"But I doubt it. The general was a very bright man, indeed, and he had looked death in the face over and over again. He would have kept his head even in his last agony, and he would not have been writing anything about a robber. He may well have known they were Nazis. Trouble is, there are lots of German words that begin with those three letters. It could even be part of a name. It may very well be."

Cooper finished the last of his beer. "The general certainly wasn't trying to write Dessau's name, unless he knew him under some alias. From what you tell me, even that is unlikely. And it's almost a sure thing he didn't know either of the punks. They weren't in his class. All three were pros, so they wouldn't have used anything but first names. And those wouldn't be their own, even though they knew they were going to kill him."

Berwick nodded. "Quite so. So the old man tried to write the name of someone, maybe some place, that would give us a clue. If it was not the name of one of his murderers, then it surely was linked closely to the reason for the killing. Well, it may occur to us as we get deeper into this thing."

"*Tempus fugit*, Thomas. Things march on apace. Only yesterday our wizards made the connection between the general and Trude, and between her and the bodyguards, the names in the Nazi messages. *Die Vaterlandpartei* is obviously ahead of us, and our leaders hear time's winged chariots close behind them. They ordain that we move at once. I have tickets for us, for Frankfurt, tomorrow morning."

He slid an envelope across the tablecloth to Cooper. "I'm

happy we're working together, Tom. I understand you have a personal score to settle, and that's good motivation."

Berwick stubbed out his Players. "We've that in common, as it happens. An airplane went down with my family onboard. It was a bomb. Probably Muslim fundamentalist crazies, in my case. It doesn't matter. The sons of bitches are all the same. I understand hating, too."

Cooper regarded Simon a long moment. Then: "It keeps me going. Thanks for telling me."

It was raining when they left the pub. There would be worse weather to come.

FRANKFURT AM MAIN, WEST GERMANY
MORNING, 10 JANUARY 1967

COOPER FLEW INTO FRANKFURT ON THE MORNING BAC flight from London. He traveled on an American passport in the name of a child who lay long dead in a weed-covered cemetery in Rock Creek, Wyoming. There was little chance of any hostiles noting both he and Berwick were in Frankfurt, but both men knew you survived in the cold-war jungle by never neglecting a possible precaution. Berwick would arrive separately later in the day on *Lufthansa*, also carrying a false passport.

Cooper watched the sprawling expanse of Frankfurt roll into view below him as the pilot banked left and settled in on final approach to the *Flughafen*. For once the city and the valley of the Main lay sharp and clear in the deep cold of this January morning, the usual smog blown away by a frigid, gusty east wind. Cooper watched the gentle, wooded hills of the Taunus pass by below him, the ancient high ground that had once marked the northern edge of the Roman frontier. There the legions had stood guard, watching the wild German tribes to the north and east.

The gentle curve of the river Main came into view behind

the wing of the aircraft, meandering southwest on its ancient way to its tryst with the Rhine at Mainz. Cargo barges crawled along the river downstream to the junction, or upstream to the old bishop's city of Würzburg and the spotless little river towns along the way. Then the steel and glass of the city's western edge came into view. The skyscrapers of the financial district gleamed in the bleak sunlight, and the black-armed octopus of the *autobahn* writhed all around the city's edge, crawling with thousands of cars and trucks.

The Main bridges swarmed with traffic, much of it streaming in and out of the huge *Flughafen*, hub of central European air traffic. Frankfurt, up from the ashes of war, flexed her new muscles in the chilly morning, bustling, confident mistress of the booming commerce of New Europe.

Then the soft, sexy very British voice of the flight attendant reminded the passengers landing was imminent, and would they be certain their belts were fastened and their seat backs upright, please. Moments later the aircraft bumped onto the tarmac with a single shriek of tortured rubber and began its long taxi up to the terminal.

Cooper reflected on what he would do at the terminal, automatically planning routine evasion measures to shake any surveillance on the ground. No matter how small the chances of the opposition watching foreign arrivals, following the book could save your life, and maybe other lives, as well.

He collected his bag and went through passport control, watching the impassive German customs guards appraising each passenger who approached their counters. Some passengers the

guards passed with only a courteous nod. Others they subject-
ed to questions and a complete baggage check. The customs
men called their instincts *fingerspitzengefuehl*, "fingertipfeel," the
mysterious ESP that reacted so well to smugglers, terrorists, and
fugitives. For Cooper there was only a courteous nod and a cur-
sory glance at his passport. *Must be my honest face.*

Carrying his light bag, Cooper walked across the crowded,
noisy hall outside the customs area, passing two pairs of green-
coated, hard-eyed *Polizei* carrying handheld radios and stubby
Hechler und Koch submachine guns. He scanned the crowd,
searching for any sign of scrutiny or interest in him. But there
was nothing. He went out into the blustery chill of the sidewalk,
shivering in the cold, to the cab rank at the curb.

He let two couples go ahead of him to claim taxis from the
column at the curb, watching the cabs behind to be sure no cab
crowded into line to pick him up. He took the third cab, a diesel Mercedes polished to a gleaming carbon black, and gave the
driver the address of the Hotel Mozart, near the American military headquarters. It was a logical destination for a newly arrived
American, a solid, middle-class hotel just to the south of the tall,
drab Abrams Building, once the prewar main office of the enormous I. G. Farben chemical trust, now the headquarters of the
American V Army Corps.

Cooper watched his backtrail through the rear window of the
cab, but he could see no tail in the crush of big-city traffic. He
knew there could be an expert tail back there, especially in this
mass of hard-driving, competitive German motorists. A really
good driver with another man to spot for him could be hard to

see in heavy traffic. A really determined surveillance team would use two or more cars, and would remain invisible.

Beyond the mass of the giant Abrams Building lay the trees and lawns and dormant flower beds of Grueneburg Park, where he and many other American soldiers had run during their noon break, where the German office workers, senior citizens, and mothers with little children had gone for the sun and the flowers. Cooper smiled at the memory. On fine days the young secretaries had sunbathed topless sometimes, wearing only bikini bottoms. He smiled again, remembering one of his running companions falling into a bed of pansies while watching two young secretaries so attired.

The taxi driver braked, and turned his head. *"Wir sint da, mein Herr."*

Cooper paused inside the front door of the Mozart. He turned to watch the street outside, but could see no sign of anyone following. He walked on across the lobby and out through the side door of the hotel, then stopped at the side of the hotel for a slow count to twenty.

He walked across the busy *Bremerstrasse*, away from the hotel, dodging through the heavy traffic, drawing irritated honking as he forced motorists to brake for him. He walked on down a quiet residential side street, turned left at the next corner, then a hard right again, constantly watching the street behind. It was empty.

Cooper walked on another block, then turned down the entrance to the *U-Bahn*, the high-speed subway link in Frankfurt's supermodern citywide transport system. He stood on the concrete platform above the tracks, watching the stairs down which he had come. No one followed in the four or five minutes he waited for the next downtown train. He boarded with the only other people on the platform, two garrulous older women carrying shopping bags, and a striking young blond woman with a cherubic daughter of five or six.

He rode to the *Hauptbahnhof*, the main railroad station, where he went upstairs from the *U-Bahn* terminal and boarded one of the fast electric trains that took him south across the Main and out into open country, studded with farms and red-roofed villages. Finally the sleek train pulled into the station at Neu-Isenburg, and he transferred to a sedate streetcar for the final few blocks through the modest town. Both the train and the streetcar were nearly empty, and cars were few. He had not been followed.

The Hotel Weissinger sits on a corner just across from the town forest. It is a pleasant, modern, neatly furnished hotel, justly proud of its superb dining room. When Cooper entered the bright lobby, he was surrounded by the wonderful smell of baking, streaming in from the adjoining *Konditorei*, and he realized he was ferociously hungry. Taking care of that would be the first order of business, and he began to feel the pleasant glow that always accompanied his return to Germany.

He returned the smile of the pretty blond girl behind the counter. He greeted her in German. "*Guten tag*, my name is Martin. I have reserved a single room."

Her fine blue eyes shifted across the neat series of cards that announced the status of the hotel's rooms, and returned to Cooper. "*Jawohl*, Herr Martin. You are in number 21, on the first floor." She handed him the key, secured in the German style to

97

a large block of polished hardwood with the room number on a brass plate riveted to the block. No one accidentally walked off with a German hotel key.

Cooper gave her his best smile, taken with the blue eyes, the pink-and-white complexion, and the young breasts pushing at the girl's black sweater. The clerk beamed at him. "I am Elke, Herr Martin. If you want anything, I will try to help."

He gave her a little bow, thanked her again, and headed for the stairs.

He reminded himself that "first floor" really meant the second floor in Germany, and went up the stairs two at a time. He turned right, found his room, and set down his bag. Following old habit, he looked in both directions, unlocked the door, and remained in the hall while the door swung wide open.

The room was empty, and neatly made-up. To his left was a tiny bathroom, no more than a basin, a toilet, and in the corner a drain in the tile floor with a shower nozzle above it. You could stand under the nozzle, or you could lift it down to spray yourself by hand. The whole room was, in effect, a shower, its walls completely covered by pale blue Delft tile. *Simple*, he thought. *I wonder why we don't build things like this?*

He locked the door behind him and walked to the tall windows. The room overlooked a broad terrace, deserted now in the frigid January weather. It looked a little woebegone, the iron tables and chairs stacked neatly in one corner, waiting for better days, the last tired leaves of the previous autumn scattered across the flagstones of the terrace floor.

The windows seemed secure enough, and there was no

balcony. Certainly an intruder could get at the windows from outside, but only with difficulty, and only by going through someone else's room. The locks were sound, and could be reached only by breaking the glass. He would be as secure as you could in a public place.

He opened his garment bag, hung his clothes in the closet, placed his shaving kit on the back of the toilet, and very carefully arranged a few items so he would know if they were touched in his absence. He left the lights on and went out, checking the hall routinely as he did so, and relocked the door.

Making sure the hall was empty, Cooper reached into his coat pocket, drew out a slip of plastic, one inch by three, and pushed it solidly into the crack between door and jamb, about four inches from the floor. It could not be seen in the dim light of the corridor, and would fall silently to the carpet if the door were opened while he was away. He walked on down the hall and took the stairs for the lobby.

NEU-ISENBURG
EVENING, 10 JANUARY 1967

COOPER AND BERWICK SAT AT THE FAR END OF THE HOTEL dining room, the empty plates gone, a final beer on the table before them. Cooper regarded the dark bottle with satisfaction, as he poured the golden beer frothing into a graceful tulip-shaped glass.

"I'd forgotten how much I love real German beer, Simon. I wonder why we can't make real beer in America."

"That is rather good," said Berwick, sipping from his glass. He studied the bottle. "Henninger Export. It's new to me."

"The biggest Frankfurt brewery," said Cooper. "A tall building on the left bank of the Main. There's a restaurant on top, and the whole floor revolves. The food's not *cordon bleu*, but there's a first-class view, especially at night."

Berwick glanced around them. The nearby tables were empty, and the only other patrons were out of earshot across the dining room. "To business, then. Tomorrow we start, Thomas, and I think we begin with the Baltheim house here in Neu-Isenburg. We know the blokes who killed the general must have searched the house, but no one's infallible. And just maybe the killers got everything they wanted from the old man and didn't search at all. I am now told there was indeed a puncture mark on one of his buttocks that could have been an injection."

The Englishman lit one of his Players. "But maybe they *didn't* get everything. There are people who can hold out against the drugs for awhile. And maybe the old man passed out before they could make him talk. He'd been very badly treated, and he was at least eighty. Anyhow, we try the house first. We will cooperate with Mossad on this one. Ever work with them?"

Cooper shook his head. "The Thais, the Malaysians, even the Chinese. Never the Israelis."

"I think you'll enjoy it," said Berwick. "They're good. Very professional, very experienced, very tough. They have laid on an entry into the house. I'm told it will be smooth and without risk."

"When do we go in, Simon? Surely breaking in after dark ought to be safe enough. But you can't see a damned thing, let alone do a really thorough search."

"Quite so. I don't like night entries, either, bumbling about inside with flashlights. No, this is a daylight operation, a gentleman's gig, as they say. We meet the Mossad people tomorrow morning, at a petrol station near here. We are to be pest exterminators, I'm told. Mossad has coveralls for us, and spray guns, and all the other paraphernalia bug killers use. Rather neat.

"We are going to walk in as if we belonged there. We will even have signs that warn passersby to be careful, lest they be poisoned by whatever it is we fumigators fumigate with. We shall also have papers that authorize us to seek out and destroy all manner of vermin, just in case a solicitous neighbor or a zealous policeman should ask."

He chuckled. "And even if someone hostile is watching, bug-hunting is a logical thing to happen in a house that must be sold after its owner dies."

Cooper smiled. "And I assume the coveralls will permit us to carry some hardware. I am a little nervous on a job without some weaponry. Is a handgun available?"

Berwick nodded. "Yes, it is. In fact, in my briefcase, leaning against my chair, is a Browning and shoulder holster for you. I think you might keep it by you tonight."

Berwick paused, his lean face grave.

"I cannot tell you what there is about this job that raises my hackles, Tom, but I simply do not like the smell of it. I liked it even less when I picked up a new kernel of information today. It may mean nothing at all, but it may also mean we are fishing in even murkier waters than we thought.

"It seems the old general and Trude were much more than casual lovers. We now know he had two children by Trude. One was a daughter, dead long ago in the 1944 bombing. The other is a son, Erich Ritter von und zu Baltheim. He is listed as an heir to the old man's estate. As a matter of routine, we ran him through the computer. And behold, he is a leading light in the Father-land Party, *the* leading light, in fact. He is called *der Leiter*, the Leader, the great woolly ram himself."

He finished his beer. "Let me give you a little more gen about the party. They're not large yet, but they want to be, and they're growing fast. And there's no question about what they really are.

Start with the party badge, and its flag. The emblem is the old imperial eagle, the one with two heads. They call it the Blood Eagle. It's framed in a white circle, on a bloodred background. What does that design sound like to you?"

Cooper nodded. "All it lacks is the swastika. And at any distance, it must look exactly like the old Nazi badge."

"Just so," said Berwick. "And the party philosophy, with certain minor cosmetic changes, could have come right out of *Mein Kampf.* The party faithful revere the old days, and the old places, and all that mystic racial claptrap."

He frowned. "Before it was torn down a few years ago, they used to meet in the *Buergerbrau Keller* in Munich, on the old Party Day. You remember the place. It was where Hitler started the 1923 *Putsch*. It was a sort of party shrine, fairly dripping with holy Nazi memories.

"I'm sure you know the Nazi Party is permanently banned in Germany. But the law permits free expression otherwise, so the *Vaterlandpartei* can meet and speak and recruit. They stay clear of calling themselves Nazis, or advocating the extermination of the Jews or the overthrow of democratic government. As long as they don't repeat the old Nazi line, they can function openly.

"Mossad watches them closely, and so does the German intelligence service. But they're secretive as hell. Mossad has even tried using sophisticated directional mikes to see what the party leadership talks about in private. That effort hasn't produced much."

Berwick rubbed his chin briefly, as if in thought. "Our ear inside the party, our informer, was our best source of information. Trouble is, the police fished him out of the Rhine last month—accidental drowning, they said. Maybe."

Berwick paused thoughtfully. He had Cooper's full and rapt attention.

"The Fatherland Party does a lot of public oratory about the Blood Eagle. The eagle will spread his wings again; he will rise to his eyrie again; that kind of mythic moonshine. But there's something more to it, Tom, something that may be far more deadly. On three occasions Mossad has listened in on Baltheim talking to his Number Two and using the term the *Blut Adler*, as if it were a personal title. Our inside man reported the same thing. We don't know what the Blood Eagle is, but we know it's important to the new Nazis. And that means trouble.

"Maybe it is meant to apply to Baltheim as the leader. Maybe it means no more than the party insignia. And maybe I am reading too much into it and imagining things, because I detest Nazis. Maybe. But I don't think so. In context, it sounded like Baltheim was talking about some image, some totem, some secret icon that the neo-Nazis will gladly fall down and worship. The whole lash-up bothers me."

Cooper made circles on the tablecloth with the bottom of his empty beer glass. "Me, too. Anything that smells of the old Nazi mythology has the potential for big trouble."

Berwick reached for the check. "Ah, well, there is probably no connection between the Baltheims, father and son. Our information is that they had a violent falling-out years ago, over Erich's neo-Nazi doings. They had not spoken since. And it certainly looks like the son's goons killed the father. Anyhow, we shall see whether our fumigating expedition tomorrow sheds any light on things. Come upstairs, Tom. I shall give you the automatic. We should have breakfast by seven. We meet Mossad at eight sharp."

In Berwick's room the Englishman handed Cooper a nylon shoulder-holster rig carrying the nine-millimeter Browning. Cooper was glad to be armed again. He slid the weapon from its shoulder holster and worked the slide, satisfied with the smooth action and clean, gleaming bore. There were two magazines, both fully loaded with thirteen rounds. He slid one home in the butt of the weapon with a flat, metallic snap, worked the slide again to chamber a round, and set the safety.

"Do you want more cartridges?" asked Berwick.

Cooper shook his head. "If a man in our business needs more rounds than that, Simon, he's going to lose the war."

Cooper removed his jacket and tried on the harness, slipping the elastic strap loops over each shoulder. Berwick made a minor adjustment where the straps crossed between Cooper's shoulder blades, and the harness felt secure. The automatic hung comfortably under his left armpit, butt forward and down, held in the holster only by the pressure of the spring built into the ballistic nylon.

Cooper put the jacket back on and walked around the room while Berwick watched. The Englishman nodded.

"Good fit. Nothing shows. Now let me show you my new toy."

Berwick reached into his briefcase again and pulled out a similar shoulder holster. From it he drew a heavy, brutal-looking pistol, the biggest automatic Cooper had ever seen.

"My God, Simon, it's a cannon. What is that thing?"

Berwick grinned. "This is my Dirty Harry pistol."

He deftly worked the slide to eject a stubby, flat-nosed brass cartridge. He tossed the round to Cooper.

"Clint Eastwood is my hero, Tom. Remember Dirty Harry carries the .44 Magnum revolver? Well, this is the automatic counterpart. It's Israeli-made, called a Desert Eagle. With wad-cutter ammo it's a little like hitting your man with a bowling ball. And it cracks engine blocks and all manner of other quite solid objects."

Cooper pointed the pistol at his travel alarm on the bedside table, liking the heft and balance of the gun, noticing both front and rear sights carried a fluorescent bead for sighting in poor light.

"I've read about them. It feels good and it points well. How many rounds?"

"Only ten," said Berwick. "But it's the first few rounds that count anyway. At least I'm sure anybody I hit will go down and stay down."

Berwick smiled again as Cooper handed back the heavy pistol.

"With this," he said as he tenderly reloaded the weapon, "with this Harry Callahan could have blown away half the crooks in San Francisco. Surely it will make an impression on a Nazi skin-head."

He slid the pistol back into its holster. "Good night to you, Thomas. Tomorrow we fumigate. Who can tell what curious insects we may find."

NEU-ISENBERG
11 JANUARY 1967

THE VAN WAS WAITING FOR THEM AT AN ESSO STATION TWO and a half blocks from the hotel, parked in a lot behind the station buildings, out of the view of passersby. Both Cooper and Berwick brightened when they saw the van.

It was a forest green Ford, two years old, with Frankfurt plates and just enough dents and scrapes to give it credibility. Gigantic yellow Gothic script across the sides announced the van belonged to *Schaedling-Schmidt, Frankfurt-Main*, and provided a telephone number for citizens anxious to be rid of troublesome vermin.

But the crowning touch was an enormous red-and-black plastic cockroach, complete with waving feelers and huge green glass eyes, squatting menacingly on the roof of the van, glaring with obvious malice at the public and their houses.

"Neat, eh?"

A small, scrawny man in coveralls stood by the rear doors. A full black beard almost hid his thin face, and his black eyes sparkled with humor. He shook hands with both men, speaking almost faultless English with a slight New York accent.

"I am Moshe. I am pleased you like my creation. It has always seemed to me that the more glaring and gaudy the cover, the more effective it is. I have always wanted to do a surveillance dressed as the San Diego Chicken. Who would suspect?"

Cooper and Berwick laughed as the man turned to the truck doors. "You will see how thorough I am. I have some wonderful coveralls for you, like mine. Across the back is also the name of our firm, Schmidt, and again my fine glowering cockroach."

He opened the two doors. "And I want you to meet my colleague. This is Lore."

Cooper found himself looking into a pair of large, level eyes, smiling and steady, eyes of a lovely violet shade he had never seen before. The woman was small and slim, her long ash-blond hair braided and wound up on her head.

Cooper realized he was still holding her delicate hand.

"I apologize," he stammered. "I was staring. It's just that, well, you are very lovely, and you remind me of someone I knew . . . I knew a long time ago."

Cooper felt as if he were blushing, but he did not want to look away from the enormous violet eyes, wide mouth, and snub nose. He thought he had never seen a more attractive woman, although he knew she was not beautiful by conventional standards. There were freckles scattered across the tanned cheeks and button nose. She would never be a model for Vogue. But he felt a stirring in his groin just looking at her. One slim ankle was visible beneath the baggy trousers, and two small breasts pushed at the white T-shirt under the coveralls.

She smiled, an enchanting, elfin grin, obviously well aware of the impression she had made. Her voice was low, almost husky, her English clear but plainly accented in German.

"*Shalom*, Tom. The pleasure is mine."

She shook hands with Berwick, then turned again to Cooper. "I know we shall enjoy working together. Here, let me help you in."

She extended her hand to him, her grip unexpectedly strong, her palm dry and cool. "Here," she said, "here are coveralls for you both, with the so-brilliant roach on them. You can change in the van while Moshe drives." She smiled that amazing smile again, and turned her back chastely on them both.

They parked directly in front of number 20 *Schillerstrasse*. The street was quiet and empty. They paused long enough to set up two large black-and-yellow signs, complete with scowling death heads, warning the world that *Schaedling-Schmidt* was filling this house with noxious vapors. Then they carried their gear up to the front door: an electric compressor, respirators, and canvas bags of other equipment. They crowded about the front door while Moshe squatted in front of the lock.

Cooper had never seen anyone use lock picks so quickly and efficiently. Moshe had the door open in seconds. He stood up and grinned. "So easy. A very ordinary lock."

Cooper stored that piece of information away as he helped carry the gear into the house. So it was not the kind of lock you'd find on the house of someone involved in any kind of illegal activity. No one expecting danger would tolerate a lock like that. Something more learned about the old general.

They divided up the house, the two Mossad agents starting with the living room. Cooper began with the general's den, and

Berwick trotted down the concrete steps to the cellar where the old man had died so hard. They had all done this sort of thing before, the painstaking, back-breaking, thoroughly dull search, covering the house inch by inch. They would carefully search, replacing every item precisely as it had been, watching for tell-tale threads or hairs left to tell some watcher the house had been searched. They wore surgeon's gloves and moved slowly.

Cooper had the most laborious of the tasks; the den walls were lined with bookcases higher than his head. He methodically examined one book at a time, flipping through the pages of each to make certain nothing had been secreted between the leaves, nothing hidden in a hollowed-out shell of a book, nothing—at least nothing obvious—written between the lines of the text. It took an enormous amount of time, but it had to be done. Two hours of steady, silent work went by, and he still had not come close to examining all of the books.

At last Moshe and Lore entered the room. The living room was finished, and they had found nothing. Berwick was finished in the cellar, and could be heard in the bathroom, moving the cover of the toilet tank to peer inside it. Moshe raised a bushy eyebrow.

"Where do you want us to start, Tom? The desk?"

Cooper nodded. "Yes, please. I'll stick with these damned books." The two Mossad agents began, and the patient search went on.

Another hour passed, and Cooper still had not finished all the books. He moved methodically down the last bookshelf, trying to focus, to concentrate on each volume, ignoring the nagging pain behind his left shoulder blade that told him he had stood tense and expectant too long. Cooper shut the pain out. You could strike gold in the most unexpected places. There was absolutely no room for haste or lack of system. You went by the book, no matter how tired you got or how long it took.

He was about twenty books from the end of the shelf when Lore suddenly sucked in her breath in surprise, the sound clearly audible in the silence of the house. Cooper turned.

"Something?" asked Moshe.

She raised her head and nodded. "Here, maybe." She was sitting cross-legged on the floor, and spread across her lap was a huge, black, old-fashioned photograph album, the sort with large pages in which the snapshots are contained by little pockets that hold the corners of the photos.

She had carefully removed an old photo, a large, faded picture of several smiling middle-aged people dressed in the style of the 1930s. Ordinary. But tucked away behind it was a smaller print, three children about seven or eight, all in miniature Bavarian peasant costumes against an Alpine background and a mortared-stone parapet about three feet high.

But what had prompted Lore to suck in her breath was the fourth figure in the picture. A man stood posing behind the three children, his legs spread wide, his hands on the shoulders of the two youngsters on the outside. The man was also dressed in ordinary peasant *Lederhosen* and an embroidered shirt.

But there was no mistaking the face. Adolf Hitler smiled out of the snapshot, the very picture of avuncular affection, a broad smile on the usually grim face. Cooper had never seen the tyrant's face so relaxed and happy.

Moshe reached into the pocket of his coveralls, pulling out a tiny Minox camera. "Hold it still, Lore, and I'll copy it." The Minox flashed, and Lore replaced the old photo. She slowly pulled out the next picture, a shot of deer in some Alpine meadow. Also ordinary. But behind it, too, was a surprise: a faded photo of the same four people, this time joined by a smiling, slim, blond woman, kneeling casually next to Hitler.

There were sixteen pictures, obviously taken at various times when the children were between five and eleven or twelve. The boy and girl on the outside in the first snapshot appeared in all the pictures. The third child, a very blond, husky boy, appeared in only four. The blond woman was shown in fifteen photos, Hitler in two. Moshe copied all of them, and Lore went on through the album. But there were no more concealed pictures.

The rest of the house had produced no surprises, nothing even remotely interesting. There were eight framed photographs sitting on the general's desk and the windowsill behind it. All but two were of the general and other officers, taken during the war. The remaining two were both old. One was probably a picture of von Baltheim's parents. The other was a family group picture, including the same elderly pair.

Cooper returned to the bookcase, relieved he had only a few volumes to go to finish his boring task. He had to work hard to concentrate on his job, his mind wandering to the pictures Lore had found. Maybe there was nothing to them; the old man had been no Nazi, so he had saved the pictures because of the woman or the children in them, of course. Maybe they were relatives, but if so, why hide the pictures? If they had sentimental value, why not just throw away the ones with Hitler in them, and keep the others openly? Or cut *der Fuehrer* off with a pair of scissors and keep the rest?

Cooper almost missed it. He was leafing through the next-to-last volume in the bookcase, eager to put it back and be done. The book was a large, prewar pictorial tour of Berlin, with nothing inserted between the pages or written in the margins. He was about to put it down when he realized the heavy back cover and its cloth lining had been separated, neatly slit apart where they joined at the spine, then re-glued. The slit was just beginning to work open after all the years.

He gently fit one little finger between cover and lining, pulled the lining further loose, and eased out a photograph. It was a glossy, eight-by-ten photo of a smiling blond woman and a handsome *Wehrmacht* colonel. The man was unmistakably von Baltheim, also smiling, in full uniform. From his collar hung the striking blue enamel Maltese cross of the *Pour le Mérite*, the Blue Max.

Cooper sat down in a straight-backed wooden chair next to the general's desk and stared at the picture. They were an attractive couple, the tough young colonel and the attractive blond woman. They looked happy and comfortable together.

Cooper turned the photograph over. A small, neat photographer's label was pasted on the back: "Theobald. *Breuckmanstrasse* 12, Berlin. 1940."

He turned the picture back face up and frowned. There was something familiar about the pretty blond. "Lore," he said, "please bring me one of those snapshots you found, one that has the young woman in it."

The slim Israeli woman knelt beside his chair. She chuckled when she saw the picture in his hands, and held one of the snap-shots up beside it. The women were the same, without doubt, although the pictures had been taken years apart.

"I would bet a lot of money," said Cooper, "that is Gertraude Mannheimer, onetime cook for *der Fuehrer*, sometime secretarial supervisor in the Chancellery, longtime lover of the General. Want to bet?"

Lore chuckled again. "No, I do not bet. Not when I know I will certainly lose. That is certainly the lady. We have already one very old picture from the Reich archives."

She handed the two pictures to Moshe and Berwick. "But I confess I am a little disappointed. The general made a real effort to hide these pictures. But why?"

Lore stood up and stretched prettily. "It is no secret he and Trude were lovers, even though at the time they were most dis-creet. And pictures of her with some children? *Nah und*? Why hide them? Even the ones with Hitler in them mean nothing that I can see. It is no crime to have a picture of that pig, so why hide them?"

Berwick stared at the picture. "Quite so. There must be an-other reason for hiding these pictures so well. He wouldn't have kept them unless they were precious to him. But he also felt a need to conceal them, even in his own house, even so long after the war."

Cooper cut in. "It is not Hitler he is hiding, Simon. That would not be logical. That leaves the children. I don't know what the hell sense that makes, but it has to be the kids. And maybe, just maybe, they are related to why Baltheim was killed. He didn't hide anything else that we can find, so it's at least arguable these pictures have something to do with the reason for his death."

Berwick nodded. "I think you're right, but I'll be damned if I can even guess at what these pictures have to do with Nazi interest in the old man." He shook his head. "Or with the letters *R A U*."

"Well," said Moshe, "whatever the answer is, we have—how do you say it?—come up empty here. I am very hungry indeed, and we have spent enough time here to fumigate two or three houses. Let us leave this place; suddenly it smells of death, and the air is stale."

They left the house together, carrying their gear, breathing deeply of the cold clean air outside. Cooper could still picture in his mind's eye the old Berlin photo of the handsome young officer and his pretty Trude. All the old man had left of her, he thought. The general must have loved her very much, to keep her memory green all these years. It must have been a wonderful love affair.

MUNICH, PRINZREGENTENPLATZ
APRIL 1932

TRUDE MANNHEIMER SAT POISED ON THE EDGE OF HER narrow bed, hearing the sweet lingering chimes of St. Josef's Church strike two in the deep silence of the night. She sat tensely, her head cocked to one side, intent on any sound from the hall outside her room. A single candle stub lit the softness of her light hair, long and loose down her back.

When the soft rapping came, she reacted instantly, pulling back the bolt she had oiled earlier that day, swiftly opening the door. She reached for the hand of the young *Wehrmacht* captain who stood there, pulled him into the room, and locked the door behind him.

He pulled her to him in the soft candlelight, and she sought his mouth hungrily, pushing her belly against him, feeling the hardness of the military buckle and then the hardness of his manhood, turgid against her body.

"*Ach*, Trude," he whispered, "what you do to me. I want you now, my love!" And he stepped back to tug at the belt of her thin robe. She was panting with want, but pushed him gently back to-

116

ward her only chair. "Sit, Franz; I will do the boots." And she knelt to pull off the high-topped officers' *Stiefel* as the man fumbled with the buttons of his tunic and pulled off his broad leather belt.

They rose together, and she moved back to watch him step out of his trousers and underwear, until he stood naked and erect before her. In a single motion she pulled loose the belt of the robe and shrugged the garment from her shoulders, standing slim and elegant, her head thrown back, the brown nipples of her small, taut breasts already erect.

Without a word the young man scooped her up and carried her to the bed. Before she could speak, he had covered her mouth with his, and her soft body with his hard one. Without preliminary, he parted her thighs and mounted her, already wet with wanting him. Trude arched her back, locking her slim legs around his flanks as he surged into her.

God, she thought, *this stallion is mine. Little Trude, the humble cook, and between her legs is this beautiful young nobleman with the marvelous cock. Now that he has been with me, he will never want another woman!* And she gave herself entirely to the moment, riding him until he threw back his head and cried out in the darkness. Trude could feel the pulse of him inside her body, and with arms and legs she held him fiercely to her.

Later, as they lay spent in the silence of the April night, she listened to St. Josef's chime three, the sweetness of the bell lingering long in the chill air. She would have to wake him soon, to return to his own room. He could not be found here in the morning. But there would be other nights.

Trude smiled in the darkness.

FRANKFURT AM MAIN
11 JANUARY 1967

THE EARLY AFTERNOON SUN POURED THROUGH THE BROAD window of Cooper's hotel room, turning the red geraniums in the window box a brilliant crimson. A soft breeze touched the thin curtains and swung them gently into the room. Berwick sighed and shut his notebook with a snap.

"Moshe and I will start looking for Lammers in *Berchtesgaden*. His address there is old, but at least it's postwar. Maybe he's dead, or senile, or long moved away, but it's a start. You can reach me at the *Berchtesgadner Hof*. I'll be a British major called Simon Ashe. I'm on leave from Minden. Moshe has a passport for one Herr Goldwasser. He's staying at the Hotel Hirsch. He's a Frankfurt generator salesman up for the skiing. Tom?"

"I've laid on the passports," said Cooper. "Lore and I are Mr. and Mrs. Morrison of Kansas City. We'll use our own first names and stay at a small hotel called *Haus Immel*. It's out in Berlin-Dahlem. We're told it's sedate and quiet, just the thing for a couple of tourists. The Morrisons are an American ex-officer and his German wife, looking up her family. It's good cover.

Ancestor-hunting is popular these days."

Cooper grinned. "If only the State Department knew just how easy it is to become anyone you want. No fee, either, no forms in triplicate, and no waiting for bureaucrats. Much more efficient."

Cooper went on. "Trude's trail is cold. We know she lived at 17 *Goethestrasse* in Berlin-Dahlem. At least, that's the last address we have. The area was flattened in the '44 raids. I don't even know whether there is anything left of the buildings that were there in '44. We'll start with whatever is left of the civil records, and then try the churches. If they weren't destroyed, the Catholic and Evangelical churches both kept good parish records."

He paused, and met the eyes of the other three. "That's it. It's almost plane time, and we need to get to the *Flughafen*. Please take care, everyone."

The four of them stood up together.

"Luck," said Berwick softly. "Don't take any chances. No unnecessary ones, anyhow. I want you all back. Moshe, your people have a fine word for times like this."

"Better than luck," said the little man, extending his hand, palm up. "Clasp your hands together, here, on top of mine, and say it together, everybody. *Shalom.*"

"*Shalom.*"

WEST BERLIN
12 JANUARY 1967

COOPER LEANED HIS TEMPLE AGAINST THE WINDOW OF THE TWA 727, watching the lights of Berlin winking on in the dusk below. As they turned onto their final approach to Tempelhof Airport, the great flaps on the wing below his window slid down with a whine of servomotors. The airspeed of the graceful Boeing slowed still further.

Below him he could see the long amber chain of beacons leading them into the runway. Then the beacons vanished below the wing, and the aircraft settled in to its last glide to the runway. Only the enormous expanse of the city's lights was visible, a sea of many-colored stars, stretching away forever.

He was acutely conscious of the faint sweet scent of Lore, sitting beside him, leaning toward the window as he was, her shoulder brushing his.

"No matter how many times," she said softly, "no matter how many times I see Berlin, I am moved. I don't know what it is, exactly. My family is part of it, at least ten generations lived and died here before the war. But there is more. It is so soaked in history. There is so much of greatness here, and so much evil."

Then, suddenly, she chuckled. "Listen to me, the famous philosopher! That is not my style."

She sat back in her seat and laid a cool hand on Cooper's, suddenly very young and eager. "Tom, may we go to Kempinski's? I have not been there in years. The food is superb, and well, it *is* Berlin, the Berlin of the old days. There is nothing to do tonight. May we, please?"

Cooper smiled down at her. "Of course, Lore. I've never been there. I'd love to go."

She squeezed his hand in delight.

The aircraft met the tarmac with a squeal of rubber, bounced once lightly, and settled in on the soil of ancient Berlin. The whole aircraft shook as the pilot reversed his engines to slow down, and they turned onto the taxiway for the terminal. In the distance, floodlit in the evening, the great white monument to the Berlin Airlift crews soared into the darkening sky.

Today the Restaurant Kempinski is in the Bristol Hotel, on the *Kurfuerstendamm*, the *Ku'damm*, the brilliant, bustling heart of West Berlin. Kempinski's has been a Berlin landmark time out of mind. Before the war it was on *Potsdammer Platz*, in what became the dreary drabness of East Berlin after the surrender of Nazi Germany.

Entering Kempinski's is taking a step back in time, to a day when life was surer and slower and meant to be enjoyed, when there was, or seemed to be, some certitude in life. It is one of those restaurants in which service is a profession, not a casual job. At Kempinski's a boy starts his apprenticeship early, serves long, and proves himself before ever he rises to be a waiter. Only if he works very hard, and is very good, may he one day aspire to be headwaiter, or even to the very apex of the pantheon, *maître d'*.

Kempinski's is a place of silence and well-bred conversation, where jukeboxes and Muzak are as remote as the moon. Cultivated talk surrounds the ceremonial serving of the best in food and wine. The dishes appear as if by sorcery, at precisely the correct time and temperature. No service personnel are obvious, but they appear instantly, like genies, about the time diners think of something they want. The fine china is spotless, the white napery glows, and cigarette butts disappear magically the moment they are extinguished.

Cooper had called the hotel from Tempelhof to say that they would be late, and they had taken a taxi directly to the restaurant. Cooper was certain they had not been followed, at least not by a single car. If there was a serious tail, it would use more than one car, and it would be almost impossible to detect.

They began the meal with oxtail soup, thick and strong, and followed it with smoked eel, served cold on a bed of lettuce with capers and pimentos. Cooper watched Lore eat with delight, smiling at her obvious enjoyment of the fine food. She raised her head, destroying the last of the eel with relish.

"Am I funny, Tom?"

Cooper's smile widened. "No. I am only enjoying watching you enjoy yourself. Where do you put all of that?"

She returned the smile. "What do you Americans say? I have the hollow leg. No, Tom; I am usually not a big eater, but when the food is as good as this, I make up for lost time."

She giggled. "That was only a good beginning. A very good beginning. Where is the rest of it?"

Cooper laughed aloud. "Be patient, it will be here soon. Here, have some more wine and tell me about Berlin. You know the city, and I don't."

He watched her slim, animated face, the violet eyes sparkling as she talked of the old Berlin her parents had known.

My God, he thought, *keep your distance, Cooper. You're getting too close to this woman. No more of that, mister; once was enough. Once was enough pain for two or three lifetimes.*

And then the waiter materialized with two tantalizing broiled chickens, the skin crisp and brown, tiny carrots and mushrooms swimming in the rich gravy. There was salad, as well, and a monstrous plate of *spaetzli,* the delectable homemade noodles. Lore's travelogue of the city ended abruptly, and they settled down to the meal.

As Lore sighed softly and neatly arranged her silverware on the empty plate, Cooper poured them both a second glass of the cool wine, a splendid *Niersteiner Doktor.*

"Tom, the wine is delicious. Am I in the presence of an expert?"

Cooper shook his head. "I wish I could say that. I like wine, but I only know a few basics. I know some of the fine vineyards, and some of the famous areas of the Rhine and Mosel. I learned that much, anyway. You can't go wrong if you choose from the best areas. In Germany, vintage is not nearly as important as area and reputation. I've learned a few of the so-called best years, but most of those are too expensive for ordinary people, and besides,

I can't always remember the so-called best years anyway."

He smiled. "There, now you know my secret."

Lore raised her glass to him. "The best things are often simple. How did you learn about growing areas?"

"Some reading, some trial and error. We used to drive through the wine country on weekends. The growers were always happy to sell you their wine direct, and to talk about wine. You could taste it and choose what you wanted to take home. We spent a good many weekends just driving. It's the loveliest country I know. We . . ."

We. Heidi and I. The weekends with Heidi. The travel and the sun and the wine. And love in the evenings in some little *gasthaus* along the road. He was silent.

"Tom? There is a shadow on your face suddenly. Did I say something wrong?"

Cooper shook his head. "No. I was just thinking about another time and . . . well, about some things that happened a long time ago." He raised the slender crystal glass.

"Here's to success."

They lingered long over coffee and sherbet, with a final glass of the golden wine to top off the meal. Plainly relaxed and happy, Lore talked of Israel while Cooper sat in silence, hearing the love of her homeland in her voice. She called up images of the incredible blue of the Mediterranean off Haifa, and the *kibbutz* where she had grown up, an orphan, over against Israel's eastern border. She talked of sweat and work and dedication, turning a hostile land into a garden, made fertile with blood as well as water. And war.

Lore gently turned the wineglass around and around, her eyes on the bowl of carnations in the center of the white tablecloth. Her voice was quiet and soft and musing, and then suddenly it went ice cold.

"The Syrians came through the fences of the *kibbutz*, Tom. It was in the first light of morning, and there was very little warning. They were mostly infantry, but there were four tanks, too. They crushed things, houses, livestock, people. They just killed and killed. Anything that moved, even the cats and dogs. We had only small arms, but when the Syrians got into the streets of the *kibbutz*, we could get close enough to rush the tanks.

"We threw our bombs from trenches and from the tops of the buildings—they were crude, but they worked. Jugs of about two liters, almost full of petrol and a handful of sawdust, with a wick made of rags taped into mouth of the jug. We used grenades, too. The tanks were Russian T-54s, and they had those long, round auxiliary fuel tanks on the back. Those caught fire, too, and then the crews tried to get out."

Lore's jaw set and her eyes seemed to go out of focus, seeing something in another time and place, a long way away.

"They came scrambling out of the hatches, Tom. They were terrified of the fire. Some of them were already burning, screaming and running. We just let those run until they dropped. The others we fired on with our Sten guns. None of them got away. I remember two who were wounded and slid back down into the burning tanks and fried. They screamed and screamed."

Her eyes cleared, and she met Cooper's. "And I laughed, Tom. I laughed."

Her huge violet eyes were vacant again, once more seeing something in the past.

"I have a hole in my shoulder from that day. And nightmares. They used to come every night—the children running from the tanks; the tank crew burning and screaming. I don't get the nightmares often anymore, but I have a great many memories. I tend them carefully, like a garden, because I do not want to forget. And that is why I do what I do. When I am tired or afraid, which is often, I think of my friends who are buried in Israel, and the children crushed under the tanks. And then I am not afraid any longer. Or at least I can control it, which is the same thing. At any rate, I am able then to do what I have to do."

She sipped her wine and looked up at him, pushing away her own phantoms. "So, enough of me. I know I am not supposed to ask, but I will anyhow. May I know what keeps you out in the cold, as Mr. LeCarre says? I am shamelessly prying, and I will understand if you tell me so."

Cooper shook his head. "I don't mind. It's simple in my case, and maybe when you work with someone it's good to know what makes them tick. For me, it started when I was in Vietnam. I led troops there for two tours—those are one-year periods of service. I believed in what we were doing, and I still do. But we were simply not allowed to win, although I believe we could have, had the civilian leadership turned us loose. From that time on I wanted to do more to fight the communists, but that wasn't enough to make me leave the army."

He poured the last of the wine. "Anyhow, I was finally transferred to Germany. I wanted to stay in 'Nam. But they wouldn't let me, and that was probably right. Looking back, I can see I was pretty close to terminal burnout. I might have gotten somebody killed needlessly, one of my men, or maybe myself"

"In Germany, I married. A wonderful marriage it was, with two beautiful kids. And then, on our last leave, just before we were to come home, my family was killed by a terrorist bomb. In Brussels." Cooper kept his voice very flat and matter-of-fact. "And so I turned to this . . . business of ours. I have a lot to pay back."

Lore put her hand on his. "Oh, Tom, I am so sorry! Now I understand the shadow on your face. I was stupid to ask. I went somewhere I did not belong. I—what is the word—trespassed."

Cooper rubbed his chin and attempted a smile. "No. You couldn't know. And it's not bad to talk about it sometimes. I don't want to forget it, but I have hugged it to myself in silence for too long. And you of all people will understand. Our reasons for being here are very much the same."

He drained his coffee and reached for the wineglass.

"Let's finish, Lore. This has been a fine evening, but there's a lot to do tomorrow. We need to get to the hotel and plan a little. I have a feeling tomorrow will bring some progress."

They touched glasses with a clear and pleasant chime, and their eyes met.

BERLIN-DAHLEM
EVENING, 12 JANUARY 1967

DAHLEM IN EARLY EVENING IS TIMELESS. IT IS, AND LONG has been, a quiet, private suburb, a place of substantial villas, surrounded by venerable trees, carefully tended shrubbery, and well-behaved flower beds. On this night a chilly grey fog crawled through the streets and shrouded the villas and the lawns, until the houses might have been cities of the dead.

But for the occasional well-groomed Mercedes or BMW at the curbside, the year might well have been 1929 or 1930, in those vanished days of artificial peace and hope, and the illusion of permanence and safety. The street lamps glowed a faded yellow in the fog, and pale ghosts timidly walked the old streets.

Cooper drove the brown Opel slowly between the ranks of grave tall trees that flanked the empty street. Only a few lights shone in the ghostly houses of Dahlem, little sparks escaping between heavy drapes, faint corpse-lights in the fog.

"This is spooky, Lore," said Cooper. "It's as if we were in a time warp. Suddenly it's 1930 again. I expect to see brown shirts and swastika armbands coming out of the fog. Maybe I'm a little fey, but I almost feel we're in a dead city, a dream city that will vanish if we look at it too long."

He furrowed his brow, embarrassed by his fantasy, and offered an apologetic smile. But Lore did not return it. Her expression was grave.

"That is exactly the way it feels, Thomas. It makes me feel cold, somehow, colder than this January night. I know what day and year it is, but for just a moment in time . . . I am not superstitious, but there are ghosts here. I am a Jew, remember, and many Jews lived here before the killing began. My own family had a villa here."

Cooper turned the corner into the broad *Bremerstrasse,* and at once the illusion disappeared. The fog was thinner, and the street was brightly lit, lined with shops and restaurants and respectable small hotels. They were back in the present. He saw their hotel instantly, *Haus Immel,* a newly painted, white five-story building on the next corner.

The trip from Kempinski's had been long, circuitous, and exacting. In Berlin, of all cities, there was a measurable chance of being recognized on arrival and followed by the KGB or even one of the terrorist groups. And so Cooper and Lore had openly taken a cab to Kempinski's in the best tourist tradition. But afterward they left by the rear door, into the parking lot where the Opel had been left for them, keys in the ignition.

They drove out into the roaring traffic of the *Ku'damm.* Cooper chose a long, indirect route to Dahlem, keeping to residential areas, where a tail would be most obvious. He was content. You could never be positive, but he was reasonably certain they had not been followed.

They registered at *Haus Immel* as the Morrisons of San Francisco, and the smiling middle-aged clerk complimented Cooper on his fine German. Thank you, he replied. It is kind of you to say that, but one forgets so much in the years away, *nicht wahr*? Yet it was wonderful to be back in Germany again. Yes, said the clerk; and a pleasure to have foreign guests who enjoyed one's country so much. A fine room awaited them. The boy would carry their bags.

The room was indeed fine, with ornate high ceilings in the old style, and a chandelier of tinkling crystal. It was furnished in beautifully tended old oak: a long polished dresser with a gilt-mounted mirror, two pink print upholstered chairs, and a monstrous double bed heaped with goose-down comforters. The walls were done in old floral wallpaper, a little faded, but still warm and welcoming. Four prints of old Berlin hung in polished frames, prints of baroque stone buildings long gone to rubble, and in front of the buildings smiling people, long gone to dust.

The wall facing the door held a graceful trio of tall double windows opening onto the *Bremerstrasse*, their heavy pale-blue drapes still open to the night and the fog. From somewhere below came the faint sound of waltz music—*Wiener Blut*, Cooper thought—but that was the only sound. The only light came from a small brass lamp with a dark-blue art-glass shade, subdued in the heavy shadow of the room.

Lore's hand crept into Cooper's as they stood side by side in the silence.

"Thomas, again I feel we are back in the '30s, perhaps back

in the last century. I am a twentieth-century woman, very practical, very much a realist. But there is something about this night, this city, this hotel. Do you feel it?"

"Yes. I have all evening. I don't want to speak above a whisper, for fear it will all vanish."

Lore stepped in front of Cooper, still holding his right hand, and reached up with her free hand to put her palm on his cheek. She raised the huge violet eyes to his.

"Tom, I am too old to be coy and elusive. I have seen too much to play maidenly games. So I shall say this right out, without preliminaries. I want you to make love to me tonight, on this wonderful mysterious night when nothing is what it seems. No strings attached, no obligations, no awkward tomorrows. I do not mean to trespass on your memories. I think you want me; I have seen it in your eyes."

Cooper ran his left hand up her slim arm to her shoulder, and cupped his hand behind her neck, feeling the silky wisps of hair there, beneath the coil of fair hair. He could feel the want inside him, feel the hardness and heat start in his groin.

"God, yes; yes, Lore!"

She turned her back to him. "Unzip me, Tom."

Lore raised her hands to the front of her black bra, unhooked it, and shrugged her shoulders, letting the bra drop to the floor. She stooped swiftly, pushing the black bikini briefs to her ankles with both thumbs, then stepped daintily out of them. Her hands went to her hair, and she deftly removed two small combs, letting it fall in waves around her shoulders and halfway down her back when she shook her head. Cooper fumbled with the buttons of his shirt.

Lore stood straight, arms by her sides, and Cooper's eyes ran over her pointed breasts, the nipples already erect, slender waist, and the fine reddish-blond hair deep between her thighs. Then she climbed onto the bed, into its center, and knelt there, facing him.

She held out both arms to him. "Come to me, Tom. Now, quickly!"

They knelt in the center of the big bed, belly to belly, her breasts pressed against the thick hair of his chest, mouths pressed together as their tongues sought each other.

Cooper slid his right hand down the smooth curve of Lore's back and cupped her buttocks, drawing her more tightly against him. His lips took in the erect nipple of her right breast.

"Tom!" Her voice was husky and urgent. "Now, do it now! Take me, Tom, do not wait. I want you in me now!"

Cooper raised her small, firm buttocks enough for her to straighten out her legs, then pressed her down on the bed, her hair spread in a wild tangle of red-gold around her face. Her breasts heaved with her panting.

"*Now*, Tom! Now! Now! Now!"

Cooper grasped her wrists and pinned them to the bed, holding her helpless as he drove into her, harder and harder. Her fingers contracted into fists and her lithe body squirmed beneath him as he drove deep into her again and again. And then, as he felt the first hot rush, Lore's huge violet eyes opened wide.

Cooper pushed his belly hard, hard against hers and pulsed inside her, holding himself deep. Her whole body shuddered and shook with the waves of orgasm, and then she went limp beneath him.

As his own spasms gradually subsided, he raised himself on both elbows and looked down at Lore's freckled face, her eyes now closed, beads of sweat standing out across her forehead, tangled hair wreathing her face. He looked at her for several long moments, then lowered his body gently onto hers, feeling the brush of her nipples against his skin, careful not to put his full weight on her petite body.

Cooper kissed the round, white bullet scar on her right shoulder, then reached over and turned out the art-glass lamp. Softly, the distant ghostly music played "Tales from the Vienna Woods." But for the spectral music, and their quiet breathing, there was no sound in the soft darkness.

BERLIN
MORNING, 13 JANUARY 1967

THE MATRONLY, GREY-HAIRED WOMAN IN THE CENTRAL record office had tried to help, but her records showed nothing. Yes, of course, she said, the records went back to the war, and before, but there was absolutely no record of a Gertraude Mannheimer at number 17 *Goethestrasse* in Dahlem. Not in 1944, and not earlier, either. The entire area had been destroyed in an air raid in, let us see, March of 1944, or perhaps it was April. But the records remained, and the records were accurate.

She would like to help, she said. She would like to help them find the Frau's family roots in Germany. And the Herr spoke such fine German; almost no accent. But there it was. There was simply no such person shown at that address, or for that matter, at either of the next-door addresses on either side.

Cooper thought quickly. "Frau Meyer, as a great favor, if such a thing is possible, could you tell us the names of those people who *did* live at number 17? It is just possible that my wife's relative used another name. She was twice widowed. The war, you know. And her father had been in opposition to the, ah, regime of those days, do you see? She might have been afraid to call herself Mannheimer."

The motherly woman paused, her mouth set in a disapproving line. Such things were irregular, and took more valuable time. But then she smiled. For them, so interested in Germany and the family, why not?

And she left the long, polished mahogany counter to return with yet another huge black-bound ledger. She carefully turned the pages, patiently scanning the painfully handwritten entries in Gothic cursive, many of them well over a half-century old.

As her finger slowly traced each entry down the page, Cooper's mind raced. If they drew a blank here, they could only try to canvass the old neighborhood where Trude had lived. But after all the years, and the bombings, and the shelling and the evacuation, what real chance was there?

Then the woman found what she sought, and turned the big book around on the counter so they could study the names in it, those names from another time, real people, long since dead or scattered. Cooper had trouble reading the crabbed Gothic script, now fading with age, but there was no mistaking the thirteenth entry. There it was: *v.u.z.Baltheim, Frau G., Nr. 8.*

Cooper kept his face serious and calm, and did not react to the entry. He shook his head finally. No, he recognized none of the names. What a pity. No doubt she lived elsewhere, and their information was incorrect. So many people disappeared in those last days, and no one knew what had become of them. Terrible, was it not?

The older woman nodded in sympathy. Yes, it was dreadful.

And she was so sorry she could not help. But she hoped they would enjoy their time in Germany.

Cooper gave her his most winning smile, and Lore beamed at the woman as they shook hands. They had certainly appreciated all she had done. A thousand thanks, and *auf Wiedersehen.*

But the woman held on to Cooper's hand for just a moment, her forehead wrinkled in thought.

"It is odd, mein Herr," she continued. "Do you have other relatives traveling now in Germany?"

Cooper shook his head. No, they did not. And then he guessed, and asked as casually as he could, "Were there then other people inquiring after Frau Mannheimer?"

"Yes," said the clerk. "Only a few days ago. A man. I must say I do not think he could possibly be related to you two. He was German, I'm sure, but he was crude, and he had shaved off all his hair." She grimaced. "He was trash, that one. I think he was one of those hoodlums who cause so much trouble on the streets these days. He was, I think, one of those skinheads. That is what some of the newspapers call them, anyway. Awful people."

Cooper and Lore agreed that the visit by the unknown man was most peculiar. Had he also asked to see the roster of people who lived at number 17? No, the clerk said. She did not like the man. He had not asked, and she had not offered. They again thanked the woman for her help, and left as quickly as possible.

"So," said Lore, as they walked down the long hallway outside the record office, "the Nazis have been here, too. We are very close to them, Tom. I wonder if they know?"

As they left the massive records building, she took Cooper's arm. "Let us look as much like tourists as possible. Perhaps they are still watching the record office. Would they cover it for so many days, with so many people thronging in and out?"

Cooper forced himself to smile down at her.

"I think not, but this is a big show for them, whatever it is. Now, when we get in the car, I will drive sedately away and take us far from Dahlem, out along the Havel, where the roads are less crowded and we can see a tail. You watch our backtrail. As soon as we're sure we're clear, we'll trade the car for a new one and pick up some weaponry. I feel the need for a gun."

The road behind them remained clear as they drove out along the Havel, the lovely long lake of Berlin. Cooper stopped at a *gasthaus,* a gingerbread house that looked as if it belonged in the Alps. While Lore ordered coffee for them both, Cooper went to the pay phone at the back of the room and dialed the panic number he had memorized before they flew into Berlin. It was answered on the second ring.

"*Ja, Mertzgesellschaft.*"

"Herr Steiner," said Cooper, using his code name.

"Borkum," said the voice. The recognition signal was correct.

Cooper spoke hastily in German. "I need to turn in a car, and get another. German plates, preferably Berlin. And I need standard tools for two. I am at *Gasthof Kaiserpfalz*, on the Ziller road near the Havel. How long?"

"One hour, maybe a little less. Look for two women in a dark green Mercedes 220. Both will wear brown cloth coats and red scarves. Both are blond. Clear?"

"Clear. I will come outside to the parking lot in front. Grey suit, black raincoat, no hat."

"*Verstanden*," said the voice. "Understood." And the line went dead.

Cooper walked to the front of the room, past neatly ranked wooden tables, lovingly scrubbed until the tops were white and a little concave. The dining room was empty. Lore had taken a table in the front corner of the room, with a view of the door and the parking lot. She smiled when he walked up to the table and flicked her little pink tongue at him.

Cooper grinned, and sat down beside her. "Wanton woman. You look good enough to eat. And that's not a bad idea."

Lore's smile widened. "I'd love it, but I'm afraid we'd attract some attention right here in the middle of the room."

Her smile faded. "Tom, about last night. I promised no postmortems, no entanglements. And I meant it. But I did want to say one thing. You are a wonderful person, my friend, a stallion, and a real man. You made me very happy in that big bed. You pushed the shadows back for me."

Cooper started to speak, but pressed his lips together when a young woman in a spotless apron appeared with the coffee. *Just as well*, he thought, as the waitress unloaded their cups and a steaming pewter pot, pouring the first cup for them. *Just as well the waitress interrupted. She's lovely, and she strikes a chord you haven't heard in years. But we're ships that pass in the night. Don't even think about getting serious. Don't say anything stupid.*

Lore was ordering an egg, *broetchen*, cheese, and marmalade.

"My God," said Cooper lightly, as the waitress turned away. "I thought we had breakfast already."

Lore smiled demurely. "That, sir, was three whole hours ago. One cannot live without fuel."

Cooper chuckled. "I seem to recall you eating two eggs, several *broetchen*, and all manner of other things at the hotel. That would hold the ordinary person for days."

"But I am not the ordinary person. Besides, you exhausted me. You are a dreadful man, and my famine is entirely your fault. Will you share the breakfast with me?"

"Well, maybe a little. Just to help you out, understand."

"Liar. You'll eat most of the food, and we'll have to order more."

And they did.

The car exchange went without a hitch. Fifty-five minutes after Cooper's call, a nondescript dark green Mercedes pulled into the parking lot. Just right, he thought. Not too shiny, not shabby, either. Like a thousand others in the city. He glanced at the plates, noting the number began with *B*. Berlin. That was right, too.

Their bill already paid, Cooper and Lore left the *gasthaus* and walked to the Mercedes. He handed the Opel's keys to the driver as she and her companion got out of the car.

"The brown Opel," said Cooper. "In the corner of the lot."

The woman nodded. "Your tools are in the bag on the front seat. *Auf Wiedersehen.*"

"*Wiedersehen,*" said Cooper, and slid behind the wheel. He pulled the Mercedes into the Ziller road, turning back toward Dahlem. As he drove, Lore opened the blue Pan Am flight bag on the seat between them.

"Very nice," she said.

Cooper heard the metallic snap as she worked the slide of one of the pistols. Lore chuckled. "Two Walther PPKs, just like James Bond carries. Two magazines apiece, and shoulder holsters. The cartridges are wad-cutters; no ball ammunition, thank heaven."

She dug into the bag again.

"And there are knives. One is a heavy-duty gravity knife; the other looks like a hunting knife; very heavy blade, built to slash."

"Fair enough," said Cooper, pushing the car fast along the Havel, looking icy and forbidding in the January morning. "I'd like something a little heavier than the PPK. I carried the .45 so long it became an old friend. But the PPK is reliable, at least."

"You do not need a howitzer," said Lore, "like that cannon that Simon carries. It is where you place the bullet that matters, Tom, is it not?"

Cooper grinned. "Of course it is. And I'll bet you're one of those Annie Oakleys who can put a bullet exactly where you want it, any light, any range. But I can't always surgically place a bullet. I want a slug that will knock a man down no matter where I hit him. At the least, I want it to ruin his aim."

"Excuse me," said Lore. "Annie Oakley? Who is that? She was never in any of my English lessons."

"Sorry. She was a famous performer in Wild West shows. She was a trick-shot artist. You know, stand on a running horse and break small glass balls with a .22 rifle, shoot over her shoulder with a mirror, punch holes in playing cards, that kind of thing. So we call any fine female shooter Annie Oakley."

"Ah. I feel better, now that I know you paid me a compliment."

They rounded a curve and approached a turnout next to the lake, deserted and forlorn in the cutting wind of winter. Cooper pulled the Mercedes to a stop.

"Please watch the road both ways, Lore."

He took off both raincoat and jacket and pulled the elastic harness of one shoulder holster over both shoulders. He made two swift adjustments, then put his jacket and coat back on.

"Better. That's a wonderful confidence builder." He pulled back onto the deserted road. "Now for *Goethestrasse*."

"Tom," said Lore. "It seems to me the Nazis may have people watching the area where Trude lived. They will want to see who else is interested. They may not know we are on the trail, but they will take no chances. We must be very careful in Dahlem this afternoon."

Cooper nodded. "They'll be watching, of course, or they're a lot more careless than I think they are. But we simply have to take the chance. We'll take extra pains to break contact on the way to the hotel. I don't think there'll be danger on the street in daylight. If there's trouble, it will come tonight."

BERLIN-DAHLEM
AFTERNOON, 13 JANUARY 1967

GOETHESTRASSE WAS AN AREA OF QUIET APARTMENT BLOCKS, built mostly in the dreary, featureless, flak-tower style of all buildings put up just after the war. In those desperate days, the nation's whole energy concentrated on feeding its people, and providing any kind of adequate shelter. Aesthetics did not matter. The apartments were graceless concrete cubes, drab and ugly, but they kept people alive.

A few of the old prewar brick buildings remained, however. They stood solemnly, morose and grey, dinosaurs among the newer, sleeker animals around them, built with the stolid middle-class permanence of peacetime. The older generations of Germans traditionally did not move much. If Cooper and Lore were to find anyone who had lived here during the war, their best chance would be in one of the old buildings.

Old number 17 was long gone, first to the smoldering rubble of 1945, then to a flat, empty lot, laboriously cleared by hand in the grim days after the war. Now the site was occupied by one of the postwar concrete apartment blocks, sterile, ugly, and faceless

142

like most of its neighbors.

They tried new number 17 first, speaking to the manager and then to a few of the older occupants. They drew a blank. Everyone tried to be helpful. But then, it was so long ago, was it not, *mein Herr,* and they had all lived someplace else in those days. They were sorry.

Cooper and Lore learned nothing in the two neighboring buildings, either, tramping the stairways and knocking on doors through the long, cold, dreary afternoon. The chill darkness of evening was coming swiftly down when they came to number 30.

The manager was an elderly woman, hard of hearing, with a cane to help a dragging, stiff-legged walk. She was reserved and suspicious at first. But then she smiled and invited them into her modest living room, hung with pictures of prewar Berlin, and the smiling people of those days.

Ach, she did not need to refer them to any of the tenants. No. For she herself had lived at number 17 during the war, at least until that awful day when the bombs had hit the old brick building and brought it down on them. *Herrgott!* So many people dead, so many! And some who survived the falling of the building were caught by the fire that followed.

She shook her head sadly, and Cooper caught the glint of a tear on one wrinkled cheek. But then the gentle smile returned.

Who were they seeking?

"Frau von Baltheim," said Cooper. "Gertraude von Baltheim, born Mannheimer. A few questions only."

The old woman smiled in remembrance. "Trude. Oh, yes. Trude lived just down from me, in number 8. I knew her, of course, and her children. We were friends."

The smile faded. "Trude and her pretty daughter both died that night. She got the children out, to the door of the shelter, and then she went back for something, I never knew what. The little girl ran after her, and they were both caught by the bombs. We never found any trace of them. They were just gone, like so many others in those days."

She raised her head, the faded blue eyes suddenly very alert and suspicious.

"But, please, *mein Herr*. Why do you ask? This is not . . . official, is it?"

Lore interrupted, speaking her quick, clear, hard-edged Berliner Deutsch, flashing her dazzling smile.

"No, *Gnaedige Frau*, it is personal. Very personal. You see, General von Baltheim was my mother's cousin. I am trying to learn more about the family. I have been away from the homeland with my husband for a long time. Now the trail is hard to follow. My mother has been dead for many years, and the rest of the family is almost gone. I am trying to assemble some kind of history while there is still time. One's roots are so important, *nicht wahr?*"

The old woman nodded vigorously. *Ach, ja*, of course. Her own family was dead or scattered. Now no one would know most of its history. The Frau was so wise to search out her background while she could. Did the Frau know the general was dead? She had read it in the papers. So tragic. Brutally murdered. Probably by the godless communists.

"Yes," said Lore. "And I never had the chance to meet the

general. That is why it is so important to learn something of Frau Mannheimer. Anything at all about her background, and about her children."

The old lady nodded. "There is so much, and it has been so long. There were the children, of course. Monika was born in 1934, I think it was, late in the year. And little Erich must have been born in '33. That was before I knew Trude and her man. She moved here just before the war, I think, in '38 or '39.

"The general I met only a few times, when he had brief periods of leave. Then he disappeared at Stalingrad in early 1943. It was thought that he was dead, although Trude never stopped hoping. I did not know he had survived until I read about his death in the papers."

She shrugged her thin shoulders sadly.

"He did not return here, or if he came back to Berlin I never saw him. What was left for him here, anyway? There was not even a grave to visit; not even a building with memories in it. I wish I could help more; I knew so little about Trude's people. I remember she came from a farming family, somewhere down in Franconia. Ansbach, I think, or somewhere near there. But the details. *Ach*, it has been so long."

The old woman suddenly brightened perceptibly. "*Wunderbar*! Why did I not think of this before? Please wait." She rose slowly from her chair and hobbled from the room, leaning heavily on her cane.

Lore looked at Cooper, and he could see the shadow in her eyes. She did not like lying to this decent old lady about her dead friend. Cooper patted her hand in reassurance. He hated the deception, too, but there was no help for it.

The woman returned carrying a hatbox. It was one of the old-fashioned round ones, with a ribbon for a handle and a picture on the side of a stylish woman of the 1920s. It bore the name of a Berlin couturier long dead in the rubble of his fashionable shop.

She handed the box to Lore.

"I have taken the liberty of keeping two pictures of Trude—for my memories. But the rest of this you may have. It is your right; you are family. There are photographs in it, letters from her man, medals, that sort of thing."

The old woman's eyes were misty.

"I think this is what Trude went back to the building for. I found it where the staircase had been. I understand why she went back for it. In times like those, one clung to any link with normalcy, with the old, good times. Memories of good things were sometimes more important than food and warmth.

"I know. I carried a picture of my Ernst with me every time I went to the shelter, and he had already been dead more than a year, fighting the English in the desert. It is more than thirty years now, and I am an old woman, but I have that picture still. It is faded, but the memories are still green."

She fell silent, her eyes on something far away. A silvery tear crawled down one cheek. She wiped absently at it with one wrinkled hand.

Lore rose and went to the old woman, putting her arm around the thin, stooped shoulders. They stood quietly side by side for a moment in the darkening room. The manager raised her head, patted Lore's hand, and smiled faintly.

"I am so glad I gave you the box, my dear. Now go, please, before I do something stupid and cry for days long gone and people long dead."

"May we take you to eat, *Gnaedige Frau?*" asked Cooper impulsively. "We are so grateful. We would like to do something for you."

She touched his hand. "*Nein.* Thank you. You are very kind, but suddenly I wish to be alone with my memories. I want to spend a little time with my Ernst."

BAVARIA. THE BERCHTESGADEN ROAD
EVENING, 13 JANUARY 1967

IT BEGAN TO SNOW AGAIN WHEN BERWICK TURNED OFF THE *autobahn* at the foot of the Alps below *Berchtesgaden*. Moshe slumped against the door on the passenger side, sleeping soundly, as he had for the last two hours. Berwick hummed softly to himself, and smoked one of his ubiquitous Players.

They had driven through foul weather all the way from Frankfurt. First it had been a mixture of snow and freezing rain, packing and sticking in the corners of the windows, clinging to the wipers in thick chunks. It had turned to a gentle swirl of fine snow as they crossed the Danube at Ingolstadt. It had thickened when they passed Munich, finally dwindling to the occasional lonely flake as Berwick pushed the big Mercedes hard across the broad, placid Inn at Rosenheim. Now it was snowing again, big lazy, sticky flakes drifting in ordered ranks out of the black void above.

The Alps loomed ahead of them through a somber, misty, lowering sky. Berwick felt his mood lighten despite the gloom. He could not remember a time when he did not catch his breath at the sight of the Alps. He had climbed everywhere in them.

They were ancient friends . . . and enemies.

He had known some bad times in them. There was the freezing day on *Piz Badile,* in the Upper Engadine of Switzerland, when he thought he would not live to see the morning. And there had been the awful early morning on the Walker Spur of the *Grandes Jorasseses* at Mont Blanc. He shook his head, remembering. LeMastre had come unstuck only two or three meters below him. Berwick, on belay, grimly set his climbing boots against the miniscule ledge as the rope smoked through his gloves. LeMastre bounced twice off the sheer face, trying desperately for purchase with the climbing hammer he still clutched.

Berwick could still feel the bruising shock when LeMastre hit the end of the rope. Berwick had only held his companion because he had driven two pitons instead of one into the fissure just above his head. One piton popped out with a ring like a crystal chime; the other one shuddered, slipped, and then held. But Berwick was jerked up against the remaining piton so tightly he had to fight for every breath.

He hung that way, panting, only one toe on the ledge, while LeMastre revolved helplessly, unconscious, in the windy void below. And finally, working very slowly, Berwick had managed to drive two more pitons above his remaining original one. Then, gasping for oxygen, he ran a rope from the new pitons to the line that held LeMastre, tied it off, and cut himself loose from the piton.

After that there was the single-handed climb down the face until he could swing LeMastre in against the rock, get the injured man into his sleeping bag, and secure him against the face.

Berwick took all of LeMastre's pitons and rope, and started the long climb down for help. Climbing alone in the swirling snow, he had to save the pitons for the worst pitches, knowing he could not retrieve them to use again.

He had climbed, exhausted, down through a hostile white shadow land that cut him off from the world of warmth and safety and people. He could see no more than ten or fifteen meters in any direction. But he had gone grimly on and on, making almost 1,000 meters of bad rock. At last he had come upon a party of four veteran Austrians. And with the generosity of the mountains, they had put the tired Berwick into third place on their rope and climbed to LeMastre.

Berwick smiled in the darkness of the car. LeMastre had survived. They had climbed again; they had conquered the Walker Spur. And now LeMastre was gone, dead on the north face of the Eiger, knocked off the Hinterstoisser Traverse by a rockfall. *That is one mountain that is still left for me,* he thought. *When this operation is over, maybe I can take the time.* He sucked hard on the cigarette. *Maybe I can do something clean again.*

Bad Reichenhall loomed suddenly out of the darkness and snow ahead, a spa for the ill and the tired and the elderly. Its streets were lamplit in the dusk, cold as death and almost empty. About now they would be serving dinner in the rest homes and sedate hotels. Berwick swung the big car smoothly through the quiet streets, and on up the curving blacktop through the forests, into the snow swirling into the headlights and building up in heaps at the windshield corners.

Moshe stirred and raised his head. "Simon, where are we? It

is dark, and I have slept too long. I have not done my share."

Berwick shook his head and cracked the window beside him to let out some of the cigarette smoke. "*Bad Reichenhall*. And not to worry, Moshe. I'm not tired, and we're close now."

Berwick pushed his body back against the seat, twisting to ease the ache in his buttocks.

"Moshe, one thing we need to talk about. About tomorrow. I've heard your German, and I can't hear any accent at all. But at the risk of being overfussy, I've got to ask. We can't afford to muck up the mission tomorrow. Are you positive the bureaucrats won't hear something non-German in your voice?"

Moshe grinned. "Not a chance, Simon. I'm a *sabra*—you know, born in Israel—but my parents came straight out of Nürnberg, by way of the camp at Mauthausen. I learned German at home, from them. German is as native to me as Hebrew. And the papers are perfect. It will be a piece of pie."

Berwick chuckled. "Cake, Moshe. A piece of cake."

"Whatever. Some kind of pastry. Trust me, Simon. I shall surely get the information. They will think I am the very model of a fat-assed bureaucrat and suspect nothing. You must see me in action one day. It is pure magic the way I inspire the most complete belief from all sorts of people. My beautiful plastic cockroach is only a small example of my expertise." A light flickered in Moshe's eyes.

"I am especially good with women."

"Okay, Moshe. I believe. One day I shall take lessons from you." Berwick swung the car deftly through two tight turns, through gloomy canyons of darkness, snaking through the black of the massed pines that crowded in on the road like monstrous ogres in the night. Snow whirled in heavy sheets through the beams of the headlamps.

"We'll be in *Berchtesgaden* in another ten or twelve minutes. Call me at the *Berchtesgadner Hof* in the morning when you've got the gen. I'll meet you."

"Roger," said Moshe. "I'll be there just after the city offices open, so I should call before 9:30."

The gradient of the road was flattening out. Ahead a light gleamed in the night and was gone. And then the darkness began to lighten, they turned again, and *Berchtesgaden* lay ahead. The town was a festival of lights, a glow of warmth and peace through the curtain of snow.

They passed the first houses of the town. Berwick had always loved the little Christmas-card village, all immaculate wood-and-stucco houses and bright shops. Over the curving streets hung wonderful wrought-iron signs, gilded and enameled in brilliant colors. Colorful murals of the mountains and their people covered house walls. And out there in the wild night, looming protectively over the picturesque town, stood the tremendous granite bastion of the Watzmann.

The streets were busy, mostly people in bright ski clothing. Many shops were still open, and the restaurants were full. Berwick suddenly realized he was tired and hungry, and eager for the warmth and light of a busy restaurant. He knew the feeling of old. It came from more than ordinary fatigue and hunger. It had its roots in the endless isolation and danger of the job. *I've got to be careful,* he thought. *Even here I've got to be careful. I'm*

152

vulnerable when I feel like this.

He forced himself to remain fully alert as he found Moshe's hotel in the *Donaustrasse*, just off the main street. He could see nothing suspicious near the modest, modern inn, built in Alpine style and flanked by tall pines. Nevertheless, he drove completely around the square in front of the hotel before pulling in under the hotel's portico. But there was no movement on the short, quiet street. The square was empty except for a statue of a bearded man in a cocked hat, carrying a sword and standing sturdily in the cold, hat and caped shoulders covered with wet, new-fallen snow.

Moshe left the car with a casual wave, and pushed through the door of glowing oak. Berwick turned back into the main street, and drove on uphill toward the *Berchtesgadner Hof,* still watching the road behind him.

By the time he parked in the lot across from the hotel, he was beginning to let down. He regarded the Hof with pleasure. It had long been the jewel of the town, from the days when Hitler had come to *Berchtesgaden* before the war. It was still an imposing, beautiful hotel in the old style, set high on a ridge above the town.

Once it had welcomed Nazi party chiefs, high-ranking *Wehrmacht* officers, and others of the Third Reich's anointed. Now the Hof was part of the complex of American armed forces recreation facilities scattered around the town.

He checked in as Major Ashe of her Britannic Majesty's Army of the Rhine, accorded the hospitality of an ally's facilities. "Number 213, Herr Major," said the elderly clerk. "Will you require a bellman?"

"*Nein, danke,*" he answered. "*Ich kann alles selbst machen.*"

He trotted upstairs to the spacious, ornate lobby. At the top of the broad staircase he dodged a laughing pair of tiny twins in red parkas, chasing each other across the lobby. He grinned. Not quite the old days of the great party gatherings, he thought. But the laughing children were a vast improvement over the crowds of Nazi stuffed shirts.

He found number 213 and dropped his bag on the bed. He stretched long and slowly. God, he was tired! And hungry. He would not eat at the hotel. The dining room was a real disaster these days. Once it had been *cordon bleu*. Now it was a sort of McDonald's with tablecloths and napkins. But there was a place down the hill that did wonderful things with venison and *steinpilzen*, the slightly bitter mushrooms that went so well with game. He would have a good dry Mosel to go with it, and let down a bit.

Then he would come back to the room, stand under the shower for a long time, put the automatic on the bedside table, and drive his wooden wedge under the door. And sleep. He could get a good eight, maybe nine hours.

The real work would begin tomorrow.

BERCHTESGADEN
MORNING, 14 JANUARY 1967

MOSHE CHECKED HIS APPEARANCE CRITICALLY IN THE plate-glass window next to the record office. He winked at his reflection, entirely satisfied with the image. *The perfect bu-reaucrat. I could have been a great actor. I can imitate anybody.* Moshe's neat black beard and mustache were topped by a pair of heavy, dark horn-rimmed glasses. He wore a new charcoal fedora, respectable but inexpensive, like the rest of the clothing. He wore nothing you could not buy over the counter in one of the large mass-sale department stores like *Kaufhof,* which was precisely where Moshe had found his wardrobe.

His plain dark overcoat covered a crisp grey suit, white shirt, and modest dark grey tie. The crowning touches, *the things that make me an artist.* His left hand gripped a furled black um-brella, well-worn, and his shiny black shoes were covered with rubber overshoes. He mentally patted himself on the back. No self-respecting minor functionary would be caught dead with-out either item.

The snow had stopped, and a freezing mountain wind

hurried through the streets, chasing a newspaper page across the slick, wet blacktop of the newly cleared pavement. Dirty clouds huddled close over the valley, hiding the great brooding crag of the Watzmann high above the town. More snow coming. There would be no sun this day. Moshe pushed open the gleaming plate-glass door of the record office and stepped into the warmth.

His forged credentials identified him as a representative of the federal census bureau. They got him past the long, glossy wood counter that separated mortal souls from the guardians of the city's sacred records. *Thank God for German thoroughness*, thought Moshe. *There is virtually nothing that is not recorded someplace. All you have to know is where to go and what to ask for.*

A pert young woman, obviously an apprentice and eager to please, led him past a dozen desks of assiduously working clerks to the *sanctum sanctorum*, far in the rear. There sat the supervisor in her office, like a troll in a cave. Moshe recognized the type instantly: a dragon, a forbidding middle-aged woman with an enormous bosom and too much rouge of a peculiar orange color.

Moshe greeted her most formally, with a little bow, presenting his imposing identification, calling the woman *Frau Colleagin*, mixing formality with esteem. He had come, he said, to inquire whether three citizens still lived in the town. They were well-known in the, ah, old times. His inquiry was quite confidential. There was no question of trouble, of course. Quite the contrary, it was all routine, really. But important. A very discreet question from elsewhere in the government. Surely the *Frau Colleagin* understood?

She nodded knowingly. Of course; and her office was entirely discreet. Always. She insisted upon it. And she would personally procure whatever the *Herr* wished, to insure confidentiality.

Moshe thanked her. He knew she would understand, and he was sure that he could count on her experience and discretion. He gave her a neatly typed slip of paper bearing Lammers's name and two others, false but plausible. She waddled off into the nether regions of her domain to consult the files.

Moshe sighed quietly. He had been slightly apprehensive that she might have wished to check his credentials by telephone, but she was obviously entirely convinced. He must remember to thank the people in the greeting-card shop in Nürnberg. They made such awful, sugary, maudlin greeting cards, and such marvelous false identification, of legitimate paper and legitimate ink, if you needed it. They had made both of Moshe's passports, all three of his driver's licenses, and the identification he had used this day.

The supervisor returned with surprising speed. She was disappointed she could not help the *Herr* more. Two of the names she could not trace at all. Perhaps during the war they had been here and gone again. That happened rather a lot in those days. But afterward, no. Did he wish her to check another spelling?

Moshe shook his head.

But she did have one address, at least. The man Lammers. Herr Lammers had, indeed, lived here these many years, and still did: down in the *Sonnengasse*, at the foot of the hill near the *Bahnhof*. Number 12. Occupation retired, although he had worked for the American recreation area for many years. Could she do something more?

Moshe gave her his best smile, businesslike but cordial. No, he needed nothing more. He would perhaps check with his superior about the other names and return. But for now, thanks again, and *auf Wiedersehen*. He repeated his correct little bow, and they shook hands. She escorted him back to the front of the office, and he walked out into the biting Alpine wind, well content.

He met Berwick at the *Wienerwald* restaurant on the main street overlooking the valley. The snow had begun again, a thin patter of flakes out of the south, driven by the cutting wind. There would be much more snow before sundown, a wet, persistent fall that would coat the steeples and roofs and streets, and crown the slopes above the town with a glistening blanket of snow and ice crystals.

Berwick was seated at one of the windows overlooking the valley, methodically destroying a roast chicken. He smiled benignly at Moshe, motioned to the seat opposite his, and raised a chicken leg in salute.

Moshe sat down and looked at Berwick's plate in mock horror.

"My God, Simon, do you eat all the time? Is this breakfast or lunch?"

Berwick mumbled around a mouthful of the succulent chicken.

"Neither, actually. It's a sort of *elevenses*, I suppose. Do you know the word? It's one of our excellent British inventions. A little something somewhere between breakfast and lunch. Must keep one's strength up, mustn't one? Have some?"

Moshe raised his hand toward an expectant waitress. "Why not? But only because I don't want you to be embarrassed by eating this obscene great meal alone."

Moshe had stopped at his hotel to call Berwick and change before coming to the restaurant to meet the Englishman. The glasses, the hat, the galoshes, and the business suit were gone. He was currently a tourist: red nylon parka, black turtleneck and slacks, soft après-ski boots, wire-framed glasses. Had the *Frau Colleagin* forsaken the gargantuan homemade lunch tucked away in her briefcase and come to the *Wienerwald*, she would not have glanced twice at this smartly dressed skier.

"How did it go?" asked Berwick. "Obviously no trouble."

Moshe shook his head. "No. A piece of . . . cake. And some *very* good luck. Lammers is here still, after all the years. He lives at number 12 *Sonnengasse*, which is down below, between the railway station and the mountain we are sitting on. Our information was correct. He has been here ever since the war, working for the Americans. The recreation area. I don't know what he did for them."

The waitress arrived, and Moshe ordered a whole chicken, with potatoes and salad.

Berwick raised one eyebrow. "What was all that you said about *my* obscene appetite?"

"As you said, Simon, one must keep up one's strength. I like your *elevenses* custom very much. And I, at least, have been working this morning. Well, when do you want to call on Lammers?"

"I think it is safer to wait for night, Moshe. What do you think? I am impatient, but I would feel better with darkness for cover. And it will be quite cold tonight. That sky says snow is coming, lots of it, and a wind all the way from Siberia. It will keep most people indoors. I would rather not be seen, especially if he is hostile and does not want to talk to us. We may have to reason with him a little."

The Jew nodded. "Yes. I worry that the other hunters may be close. But surely we can wait at least until this evening."

"All right," said Berwick, "then it's agreed. It will be full dark by six. We go then."

THE SONNENGASSE, BERCHTESGADEN
6:30 P.M., 14 JANUARY 1967

THE TOWN WAS CRUSTED IN CRISP NEW-FALLEN SNOW, TWO inches and more, luminous white on the housetops and the parks and yards, a glutinous dirty-brown slush in the streets. Even the workaday shabbiness of the *Bahnhof* was softened and made beautiful for a short while. The tracks were empty: there would be no more trains this night, and the snow was still falling, starting to cover the rails. It was as if fifty years had melted away, and the old houses were new again, in an older Germany, a Germany gone forever.

Berwick and Moshe stood motionless at the head of the *Sonnengasse*. The gentle curtain of fine snow continued to fall, speckling their hair with flakes, gradually whitening the shoulders of their ski parkas. Down here there was no brightness. The street was wearily silent, drab and old and tired like its neighbors, pushing back toward the foot of the mountainside and ending there. It was almost too narrow to drive a car into, no more than a cobblestone alley with a shallow gutter on one side.

Berwick shivered beneath his nylon parka and heavy sweater.

The old alley was bitter cold, cold as the ages, cold as the grave. Its mouth was lit by a single inadequate bulb, suspended in an old-fashioned lantern-shaped shade on a wire stretched above the street. The houses were genteel-shabby, all needing paint, beginning to settle at the corners, their plaster walls cracking with years and dampness. There were six two-story buildings in the narrow *gasse*, dozing in the icy gloom. There were no trees, no sidewalk, only the dark, slick cobbles.

Berwick did not like the look of the place. If the Nazis were also in town looking for Lammers, this would be a bad place to meet them. *Maybe we should have come in daylight*, he thought. *Well, no turning back now.*

He unzipped his nylon parka, took off his gloves, and put them in the right-hand pocket. He reached up under his left armpit and loosened the big Desert Eagle in its nylon holster. He touched the heavy Bowie in its sheath inside the waistband of the parka, over his right buttock. He laid a hand lightly on Moshe's shoulder.

"As we agreed," he whispered. "Take the right side. I'll go left. Watch the doorways and the spaces between houses. I think number 12 is the last one on the right. Ready?"

Moshe nodded in silence, and raised a clenched fist with the thumb up.

With a last glance down the empty *Bahnhofstrasse* behind them, they walked into the gloom of the *Sonnengasse*. There was no sound in the shabby alley, only the faint crunch of their boots on the dirty patches of ice and snow scattered across the slick, wet cobblestones. They walked on slowly and steadily, each man watching the opposite side of the alley, watching for movement, for the lifting of a curtain, for the sudden gleam of light at one of the dirty windows.

But there was nothing, nothing but the dark and the bitter cold and the melancholy whine of the wind. The front windows of several of the old houses showed dim light, faintly glowing behind tightly drawn curtains and heavy drapes. There was no other sign of life.

Berwick paused on the crumbling stone stoop of number 12 and stood stock-still, back to the door, listening intently, straining to catch any small sound in the night. But the silence was intense, broken only by the honk of an automobile horn in the town high above, and the faint barking of a dog somewhere far away to their right. Then even these sounds were gone, and the silence came down again, palpable as cold steel in the moldering alley.

At last he was satisfied. He eased the automatic from its shoulder holster, thumbed back the hammer, and slid his hand in the pocket of the parka, the pistol in his fist. Moshe stood watching the alley behind them as Berwick knocked softly once, and then again.

At first no sound marred the profound silence. Then there was a faint stir inside, and a gruff voice from behind the door. *"Ja, wer ist da?"*

Cooper answered instantly, his voice commanding: *"Polizei! Sofort aufmachen!"*

There was a rumbling and clicking of bolts, and the shabby door swung inward. A pale wedge of anemic light lit the stoop and the cobblestones and the dirty snow. Berwick pushed inside, and Moshe backed in beside him, still watching the dark alley. He swung the door shut, and the alley returned to its primordial murk.

Moshe did not see the leather-coated man standing in the shadows at the mouth of the alley, at the corner of the *Bahnhofstrasse*.

Horst Lammers was tall and bearlike, with a large twisted nose and an old scar winding through the stubble of white beard on the left side of his face. He was stooped with the years, and very grey, but still tough-looking, and now wary and alert. The three men stood together in Lammers's kitchen, furnished only with a scarred, round table and two plain wooden chairs. Behind Lammers stood a gas stove and an old refrigerator. The room was empty of decoration, but it looked spotlessly clean.

Two brightly scoured cheap aluminum pots hung on nails over the stove, and the old table had been scrubbed so often its finish was entirely gone, its top smooth and white. A single bowl of soup steamed on the table, flanked by a half-full bottle of beer and a gnawed chunk of coarse dark bread.

Berwick watched Lammers ease away, obviously trying to put the table between him and his visitors.

"Please do not back away any further, Herr Lammers. Just sit down. Believe me, we mean you no harm."

"You are not police," said Lammers. He stated it as a fact, his voice deep and gruff. He remained standing.

"No," said Berwick. "Quite so. But we are nevertheless not your enemies. We want some information you have, that is all." He paused. "And we are quite willing to take it in confidence and pay for it. Pay *well* for it, Herr Lammers. Then we will leave you alone as if we had never been here. Now, please sit down."

Lammers lowered his lanky body into one of the plain chairs, never taking his eyes from Berwick's face. At last he nodded.

"You are not German, although your German is very good. There is no Slav sound, so you are probably an American or Englander."

He picked up his beer bottle, and Berwick's right hand tensed around the automatic in his parka pocket. Lammers saw the faint movement and the bottle froze halfway to his lips. His seamed face cracked in a wintry smile.

"I drink, that is all. I am not crazy enough to start anything, Herr whoever-you-are. You are one of the dangerous ones; there is something about the eyes. I have seen it before, in the old days."

He shrugged and tilted his chair back, still holding the beer bottle.

"But God knows I can use money, and if you had wanted to kill me, you would have done it before now. So, ask me, and I will try to answer."

"How much?"

Berwick remained on his feet. "I think we can pay five thousand marks, perhaps double that, if the information is right. You understand the price will depend in part on what you can tell us?"

Lammers nodded. "Then we can do business. Ask."

Berwick paused, carefully framing his questions. He wanted Lammers to talk freely. He did not want to use drugs on this old man.

"You were one of Hitler's bodyguards during the '20s and

'30s, were you not?"

Lammers's grizzled eyebrows rose, but he nodded in silence.

"You and Seppl Heide?"

Lammers nodded again.

"How long did you continue as bodyguard?"

Lammers shrugged. "Until the Boss kicked us upstairs, us Old Comrades. *Alte Kameraden* were all very well and good in the early days, the street-fighting days. But later there were all the lovely pure Aryan types in their pretty black suits—the SS, you know. With the SS around him, he didn't need us as body-guards. So we became dinosaurs, a kind of icon maybe, with no real function except to be petted and praised on Party Days."

Lammers took a long pull of his beer, and sighed.

"In the first years, in the old days, we were in the vanguard, believe me. We were plenty good enough to fight it out with the Red goons in the street, and we left a lot of our blood on the cobblestones. But later we were something of an embarrassment. Horst Wessel died in time to go from pimp to legend in one easy jump. You know the marching song named for him? He was supposed to have written it, but I don't think he was smart enough. I knew him, mister. He was a real asshole, but he died at the right time. We who survived were just relics."

Lammers stared into the neck of his bottle, as if he saw some-thing else inside, something other than beer. "But, oh, the days that were! When we were all together, all of us as one man!" He paused and looked up again. "But I will say Hitler did find jobs for us all. Oh, yes. Nice jobs. Well-paying jobs. I even wore a suit and tie every day. And I stayed out of the fucking war."

Faded blue eyes pierced Berwick sharply.

"But that is not what you came to hear, is it?"

"No," said Berwick softly. "No. I want to hear about the incident that involved you, and Seppl Heide . . . and Trude Mannheimer."

He was not prepared for Lammers's reaction. At first, the old man did not speak or move. His face was ashen, and both hands were clenched so tightly around the beer bottle his knuckles showed white against the dark glass. Berwick let the silence drag on. For the first time he was aware of the metallic ticking of a cheap blue plastic alarm clock on top of the old gas stove.

Finally Berwick spoke, his eyes locked on Lammers's, pushing his sudden and apparent advantage. "You know what I want, Herr Lammers. I can see it in your face. You are assured of money and confidentiality."

Lammers continued to stare fixedly at Berwick. He licked his lips twice, and finally shook his head.

"No," he said, so softly Berwick had to strain to hear. "No, it is not that. My God! How did you guess?"

"That does not matter," said Berwick. *Lord, the man couldn't tell how little they really knew.* But he smiled at Lammers.

"All we want is the account in your own words. We will protect you, if that is what you want."

Lammers nodded. "I do not know how you found out, but somehow I think I can trust you." He shrugged. "I *must* trust you. No, what is hard is just talking of it after all these long years. Maybe, maybe it will be good to speak to someone about it at last. I have done a lot of things, and I have no particular regrets about them. But this one thing is different."

He still gripped the beer bottle tightly in both hands.

"Please understand, I did this thing, we all did, because we believed in something. *Der Fuehrer* said . . . we were told . . . we thought that it was necessary for him, for the Movement. He said Germany needed us to do it. But, God! I cannot forget what we did, of all the things I did in the old days . . ."

Lammers finished the beer in one swallow.

"So then, sit down and I will tell you. And please, drink a beer with me while I talk, and tell me your name—*a* name, at least. I cannot speak about this thing without some . . . some understanding, some fellow feeling. Do you understand? I cannot say it to a man whose name I do not even know."

For the first time Berwick was touched. "All right," he said. "Open me a beer then, and one for my friend. And call me Simon."

He set a cassette recorder on the tabletop before him.

Lammers nodded, eager now, and produced three bottles of warm beer from the top of the old refrigerator. He opened them all, and passed two across the table to Berwick and Moshe. He sat down again at the scarred, scrubbed table, cupped his hands around his bottle, and sighed softly.

"All right . . . Simon. This will take a little while; it has been a very long time ago now. God above, so long ago. But I shall remember it all for you. For it is printed in my mind, on my heart, maybe, as if it happened yesterday. Turn on your little machine."

MUNICH
LATE AFTERNOON,
18 SEPTEMBER 1931

THE HUGE APARTMENT AT 16 *PRINZREGENTENPLATZ* HAD BE-
longed to Hitler since early September of 1929. It was a model of
ponderous, *bourgeois* luxury, a stodgy place of massive furniture,
heavy drapes, and monstrous gilt-framed pictures, including
some of Hitler's own work. It occupied the entire second floor
of the building.

Before 1929 he had lived in two drab, crowded rooms in
the *Thierschstrasse*, but as the National Socialist Workers' Party
slowly grew in numbers and power, its leader chose to move to
quarters more fitting to the future master of Europe. The *Prinzregentenplatz* flat was supposed to be paid for out of the proceeds
from *Mein Kampf,* and from fees for interviews with the press.

But Hitler's turgid book did not sell well, and journalists were
not yet interested in him, at least not enough to pay to listen to
his ranting, interminable monologues. Instead, the money for
the ostentatious flat came out of substantial gifts from industrialists and noblemen. These donations were simply investments,
policies that insured their future in case this noisy, vulgar upstart

ever amounted to anything in the politics of Germany.

The library, reception room, and dining room of the flat overlooked the Prince Regent Square. There were six other large rooms, including the bedroom occupied by Hitler, and a second bedroom for his niece, Angela Maria Raubal, called Geli. These two rooms were separated only by an ornate bathroom with gold-plated fixtures.

Another bedroom was occupied by the elder Angela Raubal, Geli's mother, Hitler's half sister, who kept house for the brother she idolized. The other rooms were occupied by household servants and bodyguards.

This day the windows stood open to the loveliness of the classic German September, balmy and sunny, with just a touch of early-morning chill to warn of the coming of autumn. The laughter of playing children and the bark of an excited dog drifted in from the grassy square. Three men and a woman sat close together around the inlaid game table in the ornate library. They were oblivious to the beauty outside.

The woman was petite, young, and pretty, with a pale oval face and long ash-blond hair done up in a severe bun. The high collar of her black servant's dress framed a stubborn chin and tightly pursed mouth. She sat bolt upright, rapt as the others were, her eyes glowing with worship.

For across the table Adolf Hitler was speaking, his voice low and intense, hoarse with anger. He turned to the larger of the two men, a hulking brawler with massive shoulders, a badly broken nose, and a long, stark white scar from left ear to chin, souvenir of a razor in a Hamburg bordello years before.

"Horst,"—Hitler used the familiar *du*—"Horst, she will not be quiet; she *will* see him no matter what I say. I will try to convince her one more time, this night, but I do not think she will listen to me. To *me*! She has no sense of what is necessary for the future, for the Movement, for Germany! No, I am sure she will talk. She may even talk to the newspapers, even to the foreign press! We can wait no longer; do you understand? If she will not listen to me, it must be done *this night*."

His voice dropped to a soft, caressing whisper.

"My friends, I must go to Nürnberg, and then on to the North. She demands a decision immediately. Otherwise she will make it all public. We must do what is necessary for the Movement and for the Fatherland."

His intense gaze shifted to the other man, a slim hatchet-faced man with receding blond hair. "And you, Seppl? Will you remember the whole fate of Germany is in your hands? My fate? The party's?"

Finally Hitler turned his burning eyes to the woman. "Trude? Are you also willing to dare for me?"

All three nodded, their eyes fixed on Hitler.

The hoarse, intense, cajoling voice went on.

"Remember, there must be no one to accuse or protest, no one to make trouble. There can be no obstacle to the future of the Movement. It will be our secret, my good friends. No one else must ever guess."

He paused. "And you all know my memory is long. I never forget old comrades who have given of their souls for the party, for me, for Germany. And so I shall remember you three."

It was silent in the small, elegant library. Outside in the square, the children still laughed, playing in the warm sun of September.

MUNICH
EVENING, 18 SEPTEMBER 1931

THE BITTER ARGUMENT IN THE BEDROOM HAD LASTED AL-
most an hour. The rest of the household could not understand the
words, for both walls and doors were thick. But everyone knew
Hitler and his niece were angry, shouting at one another so loudly
they could be heard even through the thick bedroom door.

Angela Raubal fluttered nervously in the hallway, anxious
for her daughter but unwilling to risk the wrath of Hitler. Her
half brother was not only her idol, but the benefactor on whom
she depended for the entire welfare and future of herself and her
family.

Finally the door opened suddenly, crashing back against the
wall, and Hitler strode from the bedroom, his face dark and
flushed in anger. Geli Raubal was close behind him, tall, lovely,
her long dark hair tousled, her face streaked with tears.

"Adolf," she cried, "Adolf, please! I must know! I shall not
change my mind. You must remember what I told you!"

Hitler did not so much as turn his head. He strode swiftly
to the stairwell and trotted down to the street, headed without a

backward glance for the long black Mercedes touring car, wait-ing to take him to the Nürnberg road. Sobbing, Geli ran into the library and out the french windows onto the balcony.

"Adolf!" she screamed. "For the last time, you must do it for me!"

Hitler was already at the door of the Mercedes. He turned completely around to face the balcony, feet spread, hands on his hips as if he were about to address a crowd. His eyes were abso-lutely cold. His anger was gone, and his voice was flat and even, calm and icy. *"Zum lezten Mal, zum allerlezten Mal, nein!"* He turned on his heel and entered the car.

Geli stood in silence on the balcony, tears running down her cheeks, until the taillights of the Mercedes disappeared down *Prinzregentenstrasse.* Then she slowly, haltingly, walked back into the apartment and into her bedroom, ignoring the outstretched hand of her mother. The door shut behind her, and the lock snapped sharply.

Her mother knocked once, twice, anxiously asking whether her daughter needed help or company. Geli's voice in response was measured and firm. She wanted to be left alone, *Muti,* no more. She sounded, her mother said afterward, like one who has decided something, whose mind was made up at last. Her mother, wondering, shook her head and went about her house-hold duties. *A terrible thing,* she thought; *another argument with dear Adolf, who has done so much for us all. Ah, well, there had been arguments before, and they had passed. So would this one.*

The house settled into its evening routine. The apartment was soon quiet, as it often was in the absence of the master. Hitler frequently kept the household agitated far past midnight, insisting everyone share his insomniac hours, filled largely with his endless monologues. This night the residents of number 16 would be spared the late-night harangues they had heard so many times before: Hitler's destiny to lead the German people, the evil of the Jews, the Slavic menace, the manifest destiny of the Aryan race, and so on. They would not have to listen—again—to the legend of Siegfried and the *Niebelungen* and the rest of the mystical nonsense in which *der Fuehrer* reveled.

This night, free of his presence, the apartment slept early. By midnight, the staff had long since retired, leaving only a night lamp glowing in the broad hall leading from the front of the house to the long line of bedrooms at the rear.

The permanent servants lived at the far rear, former Army Sergeant Winter and his wife. Next to them lived Angela Raubal, then the pretty young cook, Trude Mannheimer, and across from her the two bodyguards, bigimposing, craggy Horst Lammers and slim, quiet Seppl Heide. Just after two, in the chill of the morning, Trude Mannheimer's door opened noiselessly, her room already darkened so no light flooded into the hall. The severe bun was gone; her fair hair hung loose down her back almost to her waist; she wore a robe and her feet were bare. She stood motionless in the hall listening, a hunting animal, her head raised and cocked, her eyes shifting from door to door. She stooped, checking for light under any door up and down the hall. There was none.

Certain the house was asleep, she rose and rapped softly on Lammers's door. It opened instantly, also into darkness, and the bodyguards stepped onto the carpet. Both were barefoot, and wore only trousers. Without a word the three moved to Geli Raubal's door, where Trude produced a key and slid it into the lock. The door opened without a sound, and the three entered, easing the door shut behind them.

They turned on the ceiling light as the door clicked shut, and they moved to the bed. Shocked by the sudden light, Geli Raubal sat bolt upright in bed, bewildered with sleep. She was naked, and instinctively reached for the thick down comforter to cover her body. She had neither time to gather it about her nor time to speak. Trude closed her right hand hard over Geli's mouth and grabbed the girl's thick, lustrous hair with her left.

The burly Lammers pinned both of the girl's wrists with his hamlike hands, pulling her arms high over her head. The comforter dropped away, leaving Geli again naked to the waist. As she thrashed, helpless, the lean man drew a 6.5 millimeter Walther automatic, cocked the weapon, and wrapped a thick, wet towel around it. He pressed the muzzle of the pistol between the girl's heaving breasts, bent over, smiling, to look directly into her terrified eyes, and squeezed the trigger.

Geli Raubal's body jerked convulsively at the muffled report of the pistol. Her eyes glazed, and her chin tipped forward on her chest when Trude released her. Lammers dropped her wrists, and she flopped back against the pillow, her mouth and eyes open, blood welling over her breasts and the comforter.

Heide forced the pistol into the girl's right hand, and wrapped her fingers loosely around it. Trude briefly bent to rest the thumb of her right hand against Geli's throat, feeling for the beat of the carotid artery.

Trude raised her head, nodded reassuringly at the two men, and all three moved quickly around the room, gathering up two recently written letters from the dresser and smoothly and efficiently searching every drawer and the shelves of the closet. Horst Lammers suddenly raised his hand for attention, and showed the others the black diary he had found tucked beneath the mattress. Trude and Heide nodded, and all three moved to the door without a second glance at the dead woman in the bed behind them. Trude turned out the overhead light, and opened the door. She tripped the latch to lock behind them, and the three slipped soundlessly into the deeply carpeted hall, empty and silent.

The house on *Prinzregentenplatz* slept on.

THE SONNENGASSE, BERCHTESGADEN
7:00 P.M., 14 JANUARY 1967

THE ROOM WAS UTTERLY SILENT, EXCEPT FOR THE TINNY ticking of the clock. Berwick turned off the Sony recorder. The snap of the switch was clearly audible in the silence of the dreary kitchen.

"So . . . Simon," said Lammers hoarsely. "There it all is, the whole dirty little story. Not the worst thing anyone did for the *Fuehrer* and the cause, but bad enough. Bad enough for me, in any case. No one has known all these years, nobody but Trude, and Seppl, and me. And Hitler, of course, and he is long since dead. And you two now, and you have promised the past will remain buried."

Cooper nodded. "And we shall keep the promise. Only a few people in our line of work will know. They will not bother you. As to the money, it will be paid when and where you wish. In another currency, in another country, if that is what you want."

He paused and licked his lips. "Another question: Captain von Baltheim, the *Wehrmacht* liaison man to Hitler. Did he know of the killing?"

Lammers shook his head with a wry grin.

"Never! That man was a Prussian of Prussians. You know, the *Junker* class has its share of assholes, but the best of them were real men. They never lost their sense of honor; they never kissed anybody's ass, including Hitler's; they never gave up. They could be arrogant beyond belief sometimes, but they had principle and guts."

Lammers reached for his beer bottle. "No, von Baltheim was kept out of it entirely. God knows what he would have done if he knew. He supported Hitler because he thought Hitler would lead Germany back to her place in the sun. But down inside, I think, he despised the *Fuehrer*. And I do not think he would have tolerated murder in any case."

Lammers took another drink. "And there was another reason. Little Trude had a thing for the *Junker*, a big thing. He was screwing her even then, you know. She was terrified that he would hear of her part in the killing—there, I have said it plainly—because she did not want to lose him."

Lammers leaned back in the wooden chair, obviously relieved by telling his story, and eager to talk more. Berwick felt the twinge of pity again. He turned on the Sony once more.

"And now we come to the major questions, Herr Lammers. You must know whom Geli Raubal was referring to when she said, 'I must see *him*.'"

Lammers shook his head. "No."

He saw the disbelief in Berwick's face and his voice became urgent.

"I swear it, Simon! He was in a cold rage, and he rambled from one thing to another. You do not know what he was like when he was angry! Everyone was afraid to ask. Sometimes it's better not to know some things, and that was one of them. We just knew it had to be done for Hitler, and for the party. That was enough."

Berwick's voice was soft and cold. "So you killed Geli Raubal without knowing why?"

Lammers nodded miserably. "Yes. We all assumed she had been playing around. Hitler could not afford the embarrassment, not with the party so young and fragile. And not with his ego, either. My God, his arrogance was as big as Munich. Have you a cigarette, Simon?"

Berwick shoved the battered pack of Players across the table. Lammers dug out a wrinkled cigarette with shaking fingers, and lit it with a kitchen match.

"You see, people gossiped a lot about her. There was one story that she had been caught in bed with Emil Maurice, Hitler's chauffeur. And then there was also talk she had been fucking somebody in Vienna, or Graz, or even Munich. There was even a rumor the man she was screwing was a young Jew. You can imagine what that story would have done to Hitler.

"Now, Geli had left Munich for about five months not long before we . . . before she died. The party line was that she was studying something-or-other, music I think, in Vienna. And that's when we heard the rumor a Jew was fucking her there. There was even talk that he got her pregnant."

Lammers shook his grey head. "But I never believed that crap. Hitler was far too calm during that time. If it had *really* happened, our leader would have gone completely crazy.

Knocked up by a Jew! My God! You can imagine!"

He chuckled unexpectedly. "I don't think she was in Vienna at all."

Berwick lit a cigarette of his own. "Why not?"

"Well, during that same time Hitler drove to *Berchtesgaden* a lot, always with Seppl Heide driving. And usually his half sister went along, too; Angela, Geli's mother. They went down very often, even though Hitler was working incredible hours building the party. And they did not stay in the south very long, usually just overnight. I think they went to see Geli."

The clock ticked away in the momentary silence.

"No, I never believed that shit about Geli sleeping around or getting pregnant by a Jew or anyone else. She was a flirt, and not very bright, but she was fascinated by Hitler. And afraid of him, too, like the rest of us. God! I have broken all the commandments between morning and night, but that man was not human! He would kill you without the slightest—"

"Stop!"

It was Moshe, his voice a harsh hiss. "Quiet! Listen!" He pointed at the outside door, his other hand already reaching inside his coat. Then Berwick heard it, too, the faint crunch of ice under a shoe sole, close to the door. He pointed at the light switch on the wall behind Moshe, and pulled the Desert Eagle from its holster.

Moshe never reached the switch. As Berwick pointed, the door flew in toward them with a rush of foul black smoke, a flash of orange-and-crimson fire. Gritty grey plaster dust rained from the ceiling as the explosion shook the old house and hurled the beer bottles from the table. The two shiny pots fell clanging onto the stove top, and the wall cupboard doors flew open, flinging a torrent of plates and glasses into the room.

Berwick slammed the table over on its side, dropped to his knees behind it, and rested the automatic on the edge of the table, pointed at the doorway. Moshe dove away from the open door, scrambling for the corner of the room.

Three men crowded into the open door, so alike they might have been brothers. All three were tall, young, and blond, and all wore a sort of uniform, dark pants and black leather jacket zipped to the neck. They were bareheaded, and the first two carried Uzis, the short, stubby submachine guns made grotesque by long tubular silencers screwed to the muzzles.

The first two men opened fire without aim into the room, swinging the ugly weapons from side to side, simply hosing sprays of bullets at random across the kitchen. Ricochets screamed off the old stove and the refrigerator, and Berwick felt the thumping of bullets slamming into the solid oak of the table in front of him.

Berwick filled his front sight and squeezed his trigger. The automatic boomed, a crashing explosion in the small room, and bucked hard against his hand. The .44 Magnum slug took the leading man in the center of the chest, knocking him backward, his mouth going slack, his eyes glazing, dead on his feet.

The shock of the massive bullet threw him into his companions, and before the muzzle of the second Uzi could come up again, Berwick shot the second man in exactly the same place. The second man slid down the wall beside the door, head lolling, leaving a bright smear of crimson down the plaster beside the front door.

But Berwick could not swing onto the third man fast enough. He had no gun, but as Berwick turned the Eagle toward him, the black-jacketed youngster half-knelt, and rolled a grenade across the floor just to Berwick's right where the table could not protect him. Berwick grimly ignored the grenade, framed the man in the automatic's sights, and blew him backward through the open door into the gloom outside..

Berwick turned his head to see the whole room frozen in slow motion. The deadly missile, an egg-shaped American fragmentation grenade, rolled gently to a stop not four feet from him, just out of arm's reach.

As Berwick tensed his legs to jump away from the green metal egg, Horst Lammers's big body dove past him. The old German clutched the grenade with both hands, and cuddled it under his belly, covering it with his massive body. His face was turned to Berwick, and his craggy face split in a wide, almost childish smile.

"*Auf Wiedersehen*, Simon," he said softly, and then Berwick dove away and the roar of the grenade shook the room.

Berwick rolled swiftly and came to his feet in a crouch, his ears ringing, the automatic leveled at the doorway. But there was no movement there, only the empty rectangle of darkness and the two leather-coated dead men crumpled on the threshold. Berwick motioned to Moshe, then pointed at the nearest corpse.

"Moshe! Quickly, the pockets; take whatever you can find. I'll cover!"

As Moshe began to turn out the pockets of the corpses, Berwick moved to the empty, splintered frame of the outer door, the automatic out in front, ready, head cocked, alert for any sound. But there was neither sound nor movement outside, nothing but the chatter of excited voices from the neighboring houses, and splotches of light suddenly thrown across the dirty cobblestones as windows and doors opened up and down the shabby alley.

Moshe was beside him. "Got the wallets, Simon. There are yards behind these houses; must be a back door!"

Berwick nodded, and the two men turned back through the old house, through the kitchen, a smoking shambles splashed with scarlet. Berwick glanced once at Lammers's crumpled body, a red ooze spreading out from under the old man's belly.

Thanks, Horst. Last time pays for all. I wish I had called you by your first name at least once.

And then they were through the sitting room with its worn carpet and heavy old-fashioned wood furniture. Berwick gulped at the biting winter air as they ran through a miniature garden, desolate now in the winter chill. They jumped the sagging back fence, and began to claw their way up the steep slope behind, up through the blackness of the close-packed firs, slipping on the carpet of old needles.

Until at last they could no longer hear the excited cries of the neighbors, only their own ragged breathing and the faraway two-tone braying of a brazen police horn.

BERCHTESGADEN
8:00 P.M., 14 JANUARY 1967

THE ADRENALINE RUSH OF FIGHT-AND-FLIGHT WAS GONE, and Berwick was beginning to feel deeply tired. He shook his head like a man emerging from deep sleep, pushing himself to concentrate on the street behind them. He and Moshe walked easily for half an hour through the crowded streets of the town, mingling with the brightly dressed tourists and skiers, window-shopping, stopping once for coffee and schnapps. At last, when he and Moshe were sure they were not followed, they walked up-hill through the light snow to the *Berchtesgadner Hof* and up the broad staircase into the majestic old hotel.

Tired as he was, Berwick smiled when they entered the Hof. He had always loved the severe splendor of the old hotel, all dark-wood paneling and stucco, chandeliers glittering from the high ceilings. These huge, sedate rooms were full of memories. There were ghosts here, shades of days long gone, days of pomp and ceremony, the comings and goings of the elite of the Third Reich, generals and pompous party functionaries, plump wives and sleek mistresses, champagne and string quartets.

The bar in the cellar was busy this night, full of vacationing American military families. Across the room a pianist played "Memories." They found a quiet table in a dim corner of the bar and ordered beer.

"No real chance anyone saw us clearly, Simon?" Moshe drank from the tall glass, leaving flecks of the thick foam on his neat black beard.

Berwick shook his head. "No, I think not. It was pitch-black in that alley, and any light from inside was behind us. That was the only time any of the neighbors could have seen us. And we left nothing behind. No, I think we're safe enough, but I don't want to stay past early morning. I think we could attract attention to ourselves if we left tonight."

Berwick wearily fished a crumpled Players from his shirt pocket and snapped his battered Zippo. He sucked deeply at the fragrant smoke, filling his lungs, feeling his heart still beating well above normal. With the exhilaration of combat and flight ebbing away, he felt the coming of profound fatigue. It was always the same. He had known the feeling again and again in war, and in the silent, ceaseless, back-alley struggle with the Russians.

He sucked again at the cigarette, and took a long drink of the beer. He forced himself to concentrate on the problem at hand. "So, Moshe, what did you get? Nobody is close to us. I think we can risk a look at the wallets."

Moshe nodded, sliding from his pocket the two slim, expensive wallets he had taken from the leather-coated men. He held them in his lap, below table level, out of casual view.

"I see nothing extraordinary, Simon. Let's see, some paper

money, driving license, identification card, a picture or two. There are a couple of membership cards, a soccer club, a . . . ah!" He sucked in his breath, glanced around, and pushed a card across the table to Berwick.

"See, Simon, here is our enemy, an enemy both new and old. Both men carry these cards. They are members of VAPA, the *Vaterlandpartei*. Remember their lovely Nordic looks, the kind Hitler loved to collect for the SS?"

Moshe's quiet voice oozed contempt. "Different party name, same old scum. The same hoodlums who were storm troopers in the old SA, only probably better trained, and certainly better armed. Those expensive leather jackets cost a lot more than the old brown shirts and riding breeches, but otherwise they are the same breed of bastard. I am so sorry I was out of position to shoot. How I would have loved to kill one of these pricks." The Jew's usually smiling face was stone-hard, his eyes angry and glowing with hate.

Berwick pocketed the card. "Easy, Moshe; I shot for us both. Now let us reason together. Why were they after us? Or was it Lammers? After all these years, there was surely no reason to kill poor old Lammers over some ancient party grudge. It seems pretty clear they were afraid Lammers would tell us something."

He sipped his beer. "And it must be something that goes back to the old days. They were willing to take big chances to shut his mouth for good. Ours, too. In case the old man had already told us something."

Moshe nodded. "The key has to be the very thing he told us. That was what they feared. It must be. All these years go by, then suddenly the neo-Nazis are interested in von Baltheim, Trude, Lammers, and Heide. It cannot be coincidence; it simply cannot. But what the hell is it that is so important? That time in Hitler's life is extensively documented."

Berwick shook his head. "That's true. But remember that up to now, everyone generally agreed Geli Raubal committed suicide. Remember Hitler made a tremendous public show of mourning, then and later. She was treated by the party press as his personal saint. There were rumors in later years that maybe it wasn't quite suicide. There were rumors at the time, for that matter. But there was never any proof."

Berwick's forehead furrowed. "Maybe that's it, then. It doesn't do *der Fuehrer's* image much good if the public learns he ordered poor Geli killed. His own niece, right? His great passion. Remember all that carefully prepared party mythology. So *R A U* meant *Raubal*. It must have. Old General von Baltheim just didn't live long enough to finish the name."

Berwick motioned to the waitress, all blond curls and enormous breasts beneath a bright Bavarian *dirndl*. He held up his right thumb and first fingers in the German style as she approached. *"Bitte, Fraulein, noch zwei bier."* He gave her his best smile, and she beamed back at him, bridling prettily, giving him a little bow that revealed nearly all of both creamy breasts, braless beneath the green cotton of the blouse.

Moshe smiled. "What is your mysterious power, Simon? I think she's ready to leap upon you right here. You should take advantage of that opportunity. She is certainly lush."

Berwick shook his head. "Maybe later. First I have got to

reach Cooper and Lore. If VAPA has people out after Lammers and anyone who talks to him, they may have done the same in Berlin. They may have covered the logical places Cooper would start his search, including Trude's old address. I know Cooper will be careful. But I want to tell him there's another player in the game. What the hell was that place in Dahlem?"

"*Haus Immel*," said Moshe, swallowing the last sip of beer. "On the *Bremerstrasse*."

"Thanks," said Berwick, rising. "I'll leave the building to call. There's a pay phone down the street, downhill to the right of the front door. Damn all this track-covering we do. Some time I'd love to make a telephone call from a phone inside a building, like real people do. And maybe someday there'll be a telephone you can carry around with you and call from anyplace. Ah, well, shan't be long.

He rose from the table and stretched, then strode toward the stairs up to the lobby, grinning at the buxom waitress as he went. "*Bis naher*," he said with a wink, "until later." She beamed in return, and Berwick took the stairs two at a time. He felt the urgent need of a woman, as he always did after violent action. He hoped the waitress really meant what her eyes had told him.

She had.

Berwick could feel the cool of the breeze from the narrow opening in the window, drying the sweat on his naked back. He slowly thrust deep into the panting woman as she knelt on the bed, her head and shoulders bent down to the sheet as he rode her from behind. The waitress with the blond curls and the creamy skin was lost in her own faraway world of ecstasy, her breath coming in gasps, mewing softly to herself as Berwick thrust into her again and again, his belly pushing hard against her full buttocks.

He glanced to his right, watching them both in the dresser mirror: her eyes were tight shut, her whole body shaking as wave after wave of orgasm surged over her, her hands clenched on the bottom sheet.

Berwick could feel the moment coming for him, and his hands pulled back against the woman's hip bones, holding her buttocks against his belly while he drove into her. Her cries rose higher and higher, and she began to shake, her whole body trembling beneath him. And then the rush came over him, and he pulsed into her, and their cries rose together.

Later, in the quiet darkness of the big room, Berwick lay on his back, smoking in silence, warm within the deep caressing comfort of the goose-down comforters. The woman lay beside him, one smooth thigh against his, her soft curls brushing his left shoulder. She slept deeply, her breathing slow and regular, aglow with warmth and fatigue and satisfaction. Berwick's cigarette glowed. The hotel was absolutely quiet, deep in the silence of the black Alpine night.

My God, he thought, *it has been so long since anything so good happened to me. I wonder if it is a combination of killing first, and a woman afterward. I'd hate to think it is, but. . .* There was the time in Lucerne when he took out the American fairy, the turncoat, the one who sold out the CIA agents to the Russians. *And the girl afterward, the little redheaded whore. Lord! That was just as fine as this lovely great blond mare.*

Berwick shook his head a bit sadly, and lit another Players from the butt of the last. He stared into the darkness. *It is what it is, Berwick, and you are what you are. Do what you must do, and no more, and remember why you do it, and just maybe you can keep your soul.* He pulled at the cigarette, and turned his attention to the problem.

He had reached Cooper, thank God, first try, at the hotel. He had been prepared to use the code words that were such a pain in the ass to memorize. But Cooper had gotten the booth number, and then left his Berlin room to call him back from a pay phone. Cooper also had news.

"It was in the hatbox, Simon, an old leather address book, full of erasures and changes. Under *H* I found the initials 'S.H.' They are followed by the name Kurt Mann, and a farm address clear out on the East German border. It's near a town called Hof. Simon, this S.H. sure could be Seppl Heide."

"Very possibly," said Berwick. "Although it could be a lot of other people, too."

"It could," said Cooper, "but it's suggestive that the initials appear before somebody else's name. This Kurt Mann could have known Heide. Hell, he could even *be* Heide. And through-out the rest of her address book, Trude used people's full names, not initials."

"All right," said Berwick. "It's only a guess, and the gen's over forty years old, but it's all we have. The VAPA people came bursting in before I finished talking to Lammers, but he had lost track of Heide long ago. I don't think he could have helped any more than he did. At least we know what happened in the flat on *Prinzregentenplatz.* Moshe and I will drive to Hof tomorrow early and see what we can find out."

"Okay," said Cooper. "Is there anything else? I'm running out of ten-*pfennig* pieces for the phone. I'm glad you two are in one piece, Simon. Watch your ass. There'll be more of the bastards."

"I know. We've shaken them for now, I think, but I'll keep looking over my shoulder. We'll leave here early and see you in *Fischbach-Au* as planned. And be careful yourself. You may have VAPA sniffing after you, too. And keep our central number in Frankfurt posted, Tom. I'll do the same. *Auf Wiedersehen.*"

"*Wiedersehen.*"

Berwick had the distinct impression that he had interrupted something with his call. His instincts had been right; there was some chemistry there, some magic between the lovely *sabra* and his American friend. "Christ, Tom, be careful," he whispered aloud. "For God's sake don't let your balls overload your brain. There is something very ugly loose, and it's sniffing at the door."

Beside him the buxom woman stirred sleepily, and her smooth hand slid across his belly and sought his groin. Berwick rolled toward her, cupping one large, pointed breast, and found her mouth and tongue waiting for him.

Outside in the chill silence of the night, a single bell struck two, marking the passage of the hours; two sweet lingering chimes, echoing briefly in the icy gloom, and then gone forever. There was no other sound but the ice-cold little river down the hill, chattering happily to itself in the night.

BERLIN-DAHLEM
MIDNIGHT, 14 JANUARY 1967

COOPER STOOD NAKED IN THEIR HOTEL ROOM, LIT ONLY BY the dim light from the street lamp outside the hotel. He looked fondly down at Lore, her body curled into a ball, her tousled ash-blond hair tangled on the pillow, the nipple of one breast just visible outside the sheet. She was half-asleep, smiling faintly.

Their lovemaking had been intense, almost frantic. She had wanted him to dominate her the first time, and he had taken her almost roughly, mounted her as a stallion mounts a mare, and driven into her hard until the moment came for them both.

Their second coupling had been entirely different: She sat astride him, infinitely gentle, infinitely slow, tormenting him, holding him just short of orgasm for long minutes, then finally closing around him, moving smoothly up and down around him, faster and faster, until his belly heaved up against her buttocks and he exploded into her.

He put the warm memory aside. Now the need was to be ready for trouble later in the chilly night. He looked around him.

The door was already securely closed and locked. Solidly

pushed home under it were the two wooden wedges he carried with him always. He propped a straight-backed chair under the door handle, shoving the chair hard against the door, making certain the rear legs were well-rooted in the carpet. He nodded in satisfaction. So much for the door.

He went to one of the closets and lifted the clothes rod from its brackets. It had been there for many years, several times repainted, made of heavy, solid hardwood about three and a half feet long. He laid it on the floor beside the bed on his side.

He walked to the windows, double-paneled and opening out like doors, in the European fashion. They were secured by a simple latch, a hooklike device that would keep out no one. Worst of all, four feet below the windows ran a broad ledge, doubtless accessible from other windows on the same floor and easy for an active man to negotiate. Cooper shook his head. An assassin could even stand on the ledge and shoot inside without entering the room at all.

He pulled all the drapes shut on both the right and left windows and pinned them securely shut with safety pins from his bag. He left an opening about two feet wide in the drapes on the center window. Through the gap shone the pale yellow light from a street lamp some twenty meters to his left. Beneath the right and left windows he set the bedside tables, and loaded each with glass ashtrays, drinking tumblers, and two jars of Lore's makeup. Under the glassware he tucked a fold of the drapes.

Cooper then went back to his bag and produced what appeared to be a flash attachment for his typical-tourist's Canon. Attached to it was a long, slim insulated cord that looked like a recharging attachment, complete with European wall plug. A sleepy voice came from the vast bed.

"My dear Tom, surely you're not going to take photos. I need to refresh my makeup first."

Cooper chuckled. "No, though you're quite a lovely picture. This little gimcrack is an electric eye. It's the kind of thing James Bond would love. Very simple. Watch, my sexy wench."

He propped the flashgun up on the floor with his carry-on bag and aimed it at the center window. Then he pushed the "on" switch on the flash, ran the cord to the bedpost, tied it off, and led it on to his side of the huge double bed, nearest the window.

He stepped back and checked his work. His automatic and the heavy K-Bar hunting knife lay on the floor next to the pole from the closet, easy to grab. Lore's weapons lay in the same position on her side of the bed. The room was as secure as he could make it.

He could not be sure an attack would come this night, or at all. But he had to sleep. You did not last long in this business if you went out into the jungle tired. He slid into the bed and kissed sleepy Lore softly. He moved his wristwatch from his left wrist to his right, and slid under the watchband the plug on the slim, insulated cord to the flashgun.

He sighed and wriggled into the warmth of the bedclothes. Midnight. If trouble came, it would probably come between three and five, when the streets were deserted and the old city slept its deepest, in the cold, empty predawn hours when sick people died. He closed his eyes and was asleep almost instantly.

The tingling on his right wrist jerked him wide awake, heart pounding. Something had broken the beam of light between the drapes in the center window; it had triggered the light cell in the flash, and the alarm under his watchband had begun to vibrate. Cooper dropped his hand to the PPK and sat up cautiously. A shadow of something or someone lay in the pool of yellow light on the carpet at the foot of the bed. And as he looked at the shadow, it moved.

He pulled the alarm cord loose from his wrist and gripped Lore's arm with his left hand. She was instantly awake. Cooper transferred the pistol to his left hand and picked up the clothes pole in his right. He rolled silently across her naked body and stood upright on the floor next to the bed.

The shadow was more distinct now, the silhouette of a man against the window, working with some tool to push back the ancient latch. Behind him, Lore slid out of bed, picked up her automatic, and knelt behind the bed, the Walther pointed steadily at the window.

Cooper moved across the carpet, keeping near the wall farthest from the window, breathing deeply to control his hammering heart. He was careful to stay out of the pool of light from the window. He moved soundlessly next to the center window, some three feet to one side of it, invisible to anyone entering until the intruder was fully in the room.

He leaned forward. One man was working, patiently, on the lock with a knife, a second man just behind him on the ledge. As Cooper watched, the latch gave with a soft click, and the window swung silently open. Cooper laid the PPK on the floor next to his right foot, and set himself, feet solidly planted, the hardwood clothes rod in both fists.

The intruders stood motionless on the broad ledge, waiting to see whether the click of the latch produced any reaction inside the room. Then the first man eased the windows apart. *He's done this before,* thought Cooper. *These men are professionals.* Slowly, ever so slowly, the man who had jimmied the window eased his way into the room, sliding one leg over the windowsill, then starting to bring the other leg in. The second man was close at his back. Cooper could see the dull sheen of knives in the right hands of both men.

He waited until the first man began to draw his outside leg across the windowsill. *Now, now while he's straddling the windowsill.* And he struck, his feet wide apart, swinging the clothes rod with both hands like a baseball player swinging at a head-high pitch.

The heavy hardwood rod struck the intruder in the face squarely, with a crunching sound like a butcher chopping meat, knocking the man back outside the window, his head snapping back, his body sagging. Cooper set his feet and lunged, using the rod like a fixed bayonet, smashing the tip hard into the man's chest, putting his shoulders and legs behind the thrust.

The attacker fell into the man behind him, and for an instant Cooper could dimly see the second man's face, bone-white under a black watch cap, eyes wide in fear, mouth open as if he were shouting, without a sound coming out.

The second man tried to keep his hold on the window frame, but the weight of his comrade and Cooper's strength behind the thrust broke his grip on the icy brick. Suddenly the resistance to Cooper's drive was gone, and with a shriek of pure terror both men disappeared. Cooper leaned against the windowsill, breathing hard, and distinctly heard the heavy, sickening thump of flesh on concrete four stories below.

Cooper shivered, suddenly aware of the chill draft on his naked body. He did not look outside. Let any casual passerby guess from which story the men had fallen. He stepped back from the window and called to Lore.

"Turn on the light on your side." The end-table lamp instantly flicked on, bathing the room in a yellow glow from its place on the floor. "It's over," said Cooper. "Two men. Both of them fell all the way to the sidewalk." He smiled at Lore, still kneeling naked at the side of the big bed, PPK gripped competently in her right hand.

"Before I lose my concentration watching you, let's straighten up the room and put the furniture back where it belongs. The *Polizei* will surely call on everyone in the rooms above where our friends landed. Get a robe on, and set the door back in order. I'll take care of the furniture."

Lore nodded and rose to her feet. Cooper hurriedly returned the end tables to their customary places. There was blood on the end of the clothes rod, blood and what looked like a tiny scrap of flesh. He dipped the rod under the faucet in the bathroom, scrubbed it clean with his hand, then went back to the room and rubbed the end hard with his T-shirt. He replaced the rod, its damp end in the darkest corner of the closet, and moved their clothing onto it from the other closet.

He put on his robe, already hearing excited voices in the corridor and on the street outside, and the brassy two-tone horn of a police car tearing at the night, coming steadily nearer. The night clerk was obviously alert, and the German police were as efficient as always. It would not be long. He looked at his watch. 3:45. No more sleep tonight.

He opened the window and looked out, as any hotel resident would do, to see what the excitement was about. Below him on the pavement lay two dark-clad forms, in the ugly, broken, tangled postures of the dead. On both sides of Cooper's room hotel guests leaned out to watch the excitement. Cooper exchanged comments with both couples, reassured to find they had obviously heard nothing from his room. He turned to Lore.

"It wouldn't be out of character for a tourist to walk downstairs to see what's going on. I'm going to do it, and see if I can catch a glimpse of their faces."

She was perched daintily at the foot of the bed, her expression serious. *She looks about sixteen,* Cooper thought, *and oh, so vulnerable.* He pulled on a shirt and trousers. "I'll knock in three series of three. I shouldn't be long."

She nodded. "Be very careful, Tom. Even with all those people milling about, be careful."

He was back in less than five minutes. He had joined other anxious hotel guests, gathered in the lobby in the garish light of the police floodlight and the unearthly flashing blue of the emergency lights. And he had seen the faces of the dead.

"One man was a stranger, Lore; he could be anyone. But the other one I knew. Oh, yes. The second man at the window was one of the skinny goons who killed von Baltheim in Neu-Isenburg. No mistake. Our callers tonight were VAPA boys. Nazis."

Lore had produced instant coffee with an immersion heater. She handed Cooper a steaming cup.

"So the Nazis know exactly where we are, Thomas, and who we are. Or at least they know we're hostile. I can't imagine them trying anything more tonight: too many people nearby, too many police. And they know we're ready, or they have to assume we are. But they may try again tomorrow, even in daylight. Our airplane takes off when, eleven?"

Cooper nodded. "Yes. We have to get to Templehof not later than ten. I think we ought to get there a lot earlier. I can call in from a pay phone there without being overheard. The waiting areas will be full of people and reasonably safe. We'll have some breakfast there and stay together. Better still, I'll call our local number and get some help to stick close to us until the airplane leaves. What do you think?"

Lore sipped at the steaming coffee. "We can leave here as soon as there are lots of people up and around. And, yes, I would feel more comfortable with some friendlies near us at Templehof. Frankfurt will make certain we break contact with any tail on the other end."

She paused. "Tom, I feel a terrible sense of foreboding about this whole thing. There is something big on when the Nazis take chances like this. This is out of character for them; they like the sure thing."

They heard the heavy footsteps outside in the corridor before the knock came. Cooper spoke softly to Lore.

"Go to the bathroom; keep the PPK in your pocket, just in case this turns out not to be the *Polizei*."

But it was, two courteous young officers in police green, who apologized first, then asked a series of clear, businesslike questions, and examined all the sills of their three windows.

Had they heard anything before the scream?

"No," said Cooper. "All the commotion awakened us. Were the dead people burglars or some other criminals?"

"*Natuerlich,*" said one officer. "They were surely criminals, perhaps even terrorists. Both had weapons."

The questioning was over quickly, and the officers departed, apparently satisfied. Cooper smiled faintly. Policemen were the same all over the West, he thought. When scum die, especially scum with weapons, law and order is not terribly curious how it happened. It's enough that the streets are cleaner.

"So," said Lore. "Now we have only to wait for daylight. Let us pack, Tom; I love Berlin, but this time I shall be more than happy to leave this city. Now it is only a place of fear."

PANTON STREET, LONDON

MORNING, 14 JANUARY 1967

In Panton Street stands a narrow building that was newly built when Victoria was a girl and not yet queen of England. Standing in the heart of London, just off the Haymarket, it has survived dozens of coats of paint and scores of tenants over the years. Now much refurbished, and returned to its original rich brick, it is still stylish. Today there is a fine restaurant on its ground floor. A firm of accountants occupies all the second floor, while the top floor is leased to something called the Achison Consultants Ltd. This firm is reached by the original stairs. There is no lift.

Achison Consultants is quite a legitimate business. In fact, it is a moneymaking enterprise, which deals in commercial development in remote parts of the world. Its real reason for existence, however, is to serve as a cover for a subdepartment of MI6, the branch of the British intelligence apparatus that deals with overseas operations. This subagency, when it is spoken of at all, is referred to as the Special Tasks Branch, or, more commonly, simply "Odd Jobs."

There are very few people on the office staff at Odd Jobs, because most of its personnel work in far places, out of the United Kingdom. But the small home office staff is very bright and generally very experienced, dealing as it does with unusual problems of enormous importance to Great Britain and the West. Sometimes these problems call for violent solutions.

Manton Blake was fifty-seven and balding, slightly rumpled and pudgy, his teeth brownish yellow from the huge briar pipe that perpetually jutted out from his jaw. He sat in his corner of the inner office, which hides behind the agency front. He had his battered brown shoes on his desk, their soles both showing holes, and a cup of tea grew cold on the scratched desktop. All of the desk, save the area occupied by his feet and legs, was covered with files and loose papers. More files were stacked on the ancient bookshelf behind him.

On the wall beside the bookshelf a greengrocer's calendar remained frozen in December 1965. Although it was ten o'clock on a grey gloomy January morning, the shade on the window beside Blake was still pulled all the way down. It was down because Blake seldom looked out the window, which in any case was filthy, and gave a view only of a drab alley and a rank of disheveled garbage cans.

Furthermore, Manton Blake had no interest in much of anything save the files on his desk. He had been a top intelligence analyst for many years, and very little surprised him anymore. But this dreary morning was different. He sat amazed, translating four pages of German typescript before him.

"Jesus Christ," he muttered softly. He rose to his feet and

strode quickly to the rear of the building, passing between two short ranks of desks like his own, each occupied by a civilian man or woman engaged in reading files. As he approached the oak door in the center of the rear wall, a middle-aged secretary seated outside it looked up from her typewriter.

"Manton, good morning. Do you need the skipper?"

Blake nodded. "Badly, Maggie. We've a bitch of a problem. It is quite urgent."

The secretary's eyebrows rose a trifle. "I haven't heard you speak so strongly about anything in years. He's alone, Manton. Go ahead."

Blake rapped softly on the oak door and entered without waiting for an acknowledgment, a privilege earned by many years of sweat and dedication. The small, slim man behind the desk laid his fountain pen on the blotter and regarded Blake calmly over heavy horn-rimmed glasses pushed down on his aquiline nose. He was coatless, a Royal Scots regimental tie hanging unpinned down his stark white shirt. His hair was entirely grey, and a fine David Niven mustache covered his upper lip. His voice was soft, with a broad Highland burr.

"This has got to be interesting, Manton. I know the signs after all these years."

He gestured with his right hand to the battered clubman's wing chair by the side of the desk.

"I can tolerate a little excitement," said the man behind the desk. "Tell me."

Blake seated himself and paused for a moment, collecting his thoughts. Then he spoke. "Okay, skipper. I got a package this morning from our embassy in Bonn, quite tattered, and apparently a long time in transit to them. It came out of Germany in the diplomatic pouch. It purports to be a document signed by Hitler just before the end in Berlin."

He paused, and groped in his pocket for the ancient pipe. "I think it is the real thing. Assuming it is legitimate, it is purest dynamite."

"Tell me about it,"

"There is no return address, for reasons that will presently appear. There is no identification of the sender. There is only a handwritten note inside, written in old-style German script. This is what it says."

He smoothed out a crumpled piece of notepaper on the desktop, and began to read.

> "For many years my husband and I were afraid to tell anyone about this paper. We are not political. We only wanted a little peace in our last days. Now my man is gone and I am dying. I am no longer afraid. I see on the streets today the same ugly faces I saw there in the '20s and '30s. I do not want the Devil loose in Germany again. We were probably cowards not to have sent this to the West long ago. I hope you will understand."

"And that's all there is to the letter, skipper."

He handed the package to his superior. "It's the enclosure

that raised the hair on the back of my neck. I'll let you read it for yourself."

Blake sat quietly, waiting for the diminutive, dapper man to finish reading the contents of the package. Far away outside the paneled room he could hear the boom of traffic in the Haymarket. The only other sound was the dignified ticking of a lovely walnut Georgian desk clock, placidly marking the flow of time from the top of the bookcase behind the desk. At last the Scot raised his head and looked thoughtfully at Blake.

"So, Manton. Now we know why the neo-Nazis are suddenly so interested in Mannheimer, Lammers, Heide, and von Baltheim. And I think it explains what happened to the poor old general. I daresay it also clears up what happened to our mole inside the Fatherland Party."

The small man's pale blue eyes were suddenly hard and piercing, and his voice took on an edge.

"Get on to Berwick. Quickly. Drop everything else until you get to him. If you cannot reach him or the American he works with, Cooper, then call George Martin at the American embassy, or call Mossad and they will connect with their people on the same team. Berwick can get to a safe phone, or Cooper can, and call here. They are to talk *only* to you or to me. No one else is to know. *No one!* I must tell the chief, and he will, of course, see the Minister. But no one else may know, not just yet. No one. Clear, Manton?"

Blake nodded soberly.

"Then get cracking!"

HOF, WEST GERMANY
AFTERNOON, 15 JANUARY 1967

IN THE EARLY AFTERNOON, CLEAR AND BITING COLD, BER-
wick and Moshe found the address Trude had written in her
address book. It was a farmhouse a few kilometers west of the
town of Hof, half-timbered and stuccoed, roofed in reddish-
brown tile, a shadow of prewar Germany. They turned the
Mercedes into a rutted dirt track and into the muddy farmyard,
past a small neat sign labeled simply "Mann."

The two-story house and the barn were a single structure in
the old Bavarian style, separated only by an interior wall. The
building was a uniform shade of faded light brown, broken only
by patches of chalky-white where the old stucco had broken out
and had been mended. The half-timbers were weathered and
splintery, once painted dark brown, now faded to a sort of drift-
wood grey.

In the farmyard steam rose lazily from the inevitable manure
heap in front of the barn. Parked next to it was a shiny new
Deutz tractor and an ancient, battered, honey cart, a wheeled
metal tank from which the farmer sprayed a stinking mixture of

dung and water on his growing crops. Chickens foraged nois-
ily in the barnyard, and pigeons fluttered about the eaves of the
building. A tired brown Opel sedan was parked between the
manure heap and the faded green door of the house. A wisp of
white smoke from the brick chimney announced that someone
was home.

They parked in the farmyard next to the big tractor. As they left
the Mercedes, the farmhouse door opened, and an enormous beefy
man in blue work clothes stood in the doorway, his right hand on
the head of a husky, competent-looking German Shepherd.

Moshe showed his forged census identification, and explained
glibly that they sought Herr Kurt Mann, who gave this address. It
was the matter of a pension from the government. Was he here?

The farmer visibly relaxed. He was Kurt's cousin, and, no,
unfortunately, Kurt was not here. Poor Kurt; the cancer had
him, badly, and he was dying. He could be found at the rest
home just on the edge of Hof, the east side of the town. *Waldesruh*, it was. Did they know it?

No, said Moshe, but they would find it easily. How terrible!
Could Herr Mann be seen? They surely did not want to intrude.

The big man shrugged. Who could tell? Some days he was
awake and alert, sitting up in his wheelchair. On those days he
was able to understand and reply, at least for a little while. Other
days he was not so good. Sometimes you could not reach him at
all. They could only try. But Kurt would be glad of a visit. He
himself could not get over there as often as he would like. The
farm, you know.

Yes, of course, said Moshe. One got so busy; everything

these days took so much time. And with profuse thanks, they got back into the Mercedes and pulled out of the farmyard, shrilly cursed as they left by four terrified hens, fluttering madly out of the car's path.

Waldesruh was a huge, sterile, flat-roofed building, crouched on a modest rise just outside the town. Berwick looked with loathing at the pile of unrelieved concrete, a featureless cube with a few tiny windows in black steel frames. Inside it was all stark surgical-white paint, dull, colorless floor tiles, and unobtrusive fluorescent lighting. *God*, thought Berwick, *how awful for the patients. They have to live in a mausoleum even before they die.*

Moshe smiled broadly at the head nurse behind her counter near the door, and flashed the special census identification that had worked so well in *Berchtesgaden*.

"Herr Mann, *bitte*, Herr Kurt Mann. We are here on a matter of a pension the government wishes to start for him. But there are questions we need to ask him, of course. You know how bureaucracy works."

The nurse nodded, a wrinkled crone with salt-and-pepper hair pulled back into a severe bun beneath her white cap. "We will see how he is, *mein Herr*. I think he may feel well enough today to talk a bit."

She raised a knobby finger in warning, like a schoolteacher admonishing a pupil. "But you must remember, he is very weak. Indeed, he is dying. You must be careful not to overtire him. No more than fifteen or twenty minutes' conversation. You must promise me."

As Moshe smiled and reassured the nurse, Berwick wondered

idly why it was so necessary not to overtire a dying man. But he said nothing. In the end, still repeating her admonitions not to tire Herr Mann, she led them into a huge room filled with modern, ugly, functional furniture of steel and white plastic. It was crowded with patients, many in wheelchairs, most wearing bathrobes, their faces marked by the ravages of long illness. Across the rear of the room, a line of large windows looked out across rolling farmland, now sere and blasted by winter, out toward the East German border only a few kilometers away.

Seppl Heide sat in the far corner of the room, hunched in a wheelchair, his thin shoulders bowed forward under a light green robe that had seen better days. He stared out over the frost-seared fields, and as they approached him, his whole body began to shake with a racking cough, until he buried his face in a handkerchief held in both skeletal hands. They stood quietly beside the nurse until the spasm subsided, and then walked around into the light next to the window so Heide could see them.

"Herr Mann," said the nurse gently. "Herr Mann, here are visitors, some gentlemen from the government, all the way from Nürnberg to see you. Do you feel like talking for a bit?"

The old man slowly turned his head, his rheumy eyes trying to focus on them, his hands still holding the soiled handkerchief near his chin. Berwick saw that it was spotted with yellow phlegm and blood. Heide's hands were claws, all tendons and bone, splotched with the liver spots of age, the skin almost transparent. His face was deeply scored with vertical wrinkles down the cheeks, and he had no teeth. His thin, yellow-grey hair was unkempt, and Berwick detected a distinct bitter, acrid smell about him. He was plainly a dying man.

Berwick pulled up a chair close to the wheelchair, smiled at Heide, and waited until the nurse was out of earshot. He knew the old man's attention span could not be long. If he would talk to them at all, it could only be for a few moments. Berwick would have to be blunt. With luck the old man would not refuse to speak, nor would the shock make him so ill that he could not talk if he wished to.

Berwick waited until the old eyes met his and focused.

"Herr Heide," he said softly. "Herr Heide. You see I use your real name. We are friends. We know who you are, but we mean you no harm. We want only to talk to you awhile, and then we will leave you alone and tell no one. I am from the British government. Do you understand what I have said?"

There was no response. The old man sat frozen in the same position, the dirty handkerchief poised below his mouth. But his eyes were suddenly clear and alert, locked on Berwick's face. And then abruptly the toothless mouth opened and he laughed, a cackling, mechanical sound that rose almost to a shriek, then subsided in another spasm of coughing. Berwick waited.

Finally the awful hacking died away, and there were more blood spots on the filthy handkerchief. Heide's eyes were still clear, however, and now they were also amused.

"So, Englander, it took you this long to find me! My God! I expected you many years ago. But you did not come. You did not come, the years went by, and I decided old Seppl was not of any importance. Everyone else I knew got put in jail, or got de-Nazified in court, or got written about in the papers, or went to

Argentina, or something. But nobody cared about me. I was almost disappointed."

The ancient, runny eyes actually sparkled.

"So, Englander, ask . . . ask whatever you want. Let us be candid, please: I have cancer. It is killing me. You can see that. So it is no longer of much interest to me what I say, or who knows what I was in the old days. We are all equal in the grave, no? And what if anyone did want to send me to court for the things that happened so long ago, eh? What would they do, send a dead man off to Spandau prison?"

Berwick smiled at him. "You are right, of course. And I am not interested in the old days in general, Herr Heide. All I want to know about is the death of Geli Raubal, and why Hitler had her killed on the night of September 18th, 1931. You remember that night, Herr Heide, don't you?"

Heide sat in absolute silence, the eyes intent, wide, and suddenly afraid, no longer sparkling. Then, making an obvious decision, he spoke, nodding as he did so.

"*Ach*, you know already. So why not? What God is doing to me now is far worse than anything any human can do. So what do I care? All right. I don't know why you care, Englander, and I don't give a shit anymore. I will tell you my nasty little story.

"Geli, poor sexy, empty-headed Geli. She was fascinated by Hitler, and repelled by him, too. At first, he was her hero. He was Wotan in a brown uniform and a wrinkled trench coat that was too big for him. He was screwing her, of course, and I don't know what else. The rumor was that he had some very strange ideas, like a fascination with assholes. *Bitte*, a little water? I am

212

not used to talking quite so much."

Berwick poured the old man a glass from the carafe on the table beside his chair. He waited patiently while Heide drank greedily, his trembling hand slopping water down the front of the stained robe.

"*Danke.* Anyway, she began to shy away from him. From fucking him, anyway. I think she cut him off completely by late 1929. Then something really bad happened between them early in 1930, sometime in January, I think. They barely spoke after that.

"And then in the spring, late April or early May of '30, Geli disappeared. Hitler said she had gone to Vienna to study music. The others believed that, or at least they pretended they did.

"But I knew better, oh, yes. I knew better because I saw her often over the next five months."

Heide stopped and clapped the foul handkerchief over his mouth. His thin chest heaved as he fought to hold off the killing cough deep in his wasted lungs. At last the labored breathing eased, and he went on.

"Every couple of weeks I would drive Hitler to the *Berghof*, you know, the house above *Berchtesgaden*. Above the *Obersalzburg*. And she was there, Geli was, living with a housekeeper from the town.

"There were about a dozen beautiful SS men there, too, hand-picked, as a constant security force. Hitler said they were to keep her safe from harm, because people knew she was close to him. But you could see they were also there to restrict her movements. At least, she constantly bitched to the Boss that she wanted to go out. But he wouldn't hear of it, and her mother backed him up.

Old Angela went along on most trips, too, and she always sided with Hitler against her own daughter."

The wrinkled, toothless mouth split in a cavernous grin, and Heide licked his bloodless lips. "And do you know why we went through this stupid charade, Englander?"

He waited expectantly, grinning again as Berwick shook his head.

"Because she was pregnant, man, *pregnant!* And none of the rumors were true, not about the Jew, or Emil Maurice, or any of the rest of that crap. Oh, no, Englander, it was *his* calf she was carrying! His!"

So there it is, thought Berwick. An heir! If she had the child, anyhow. He forced himself to smile at the old man, and waited patiently.

Heide chuckled, a gargling, gasping croak deep in his throat. He paused again, his chest heaving, fighting for air.

"We had always wondered whether he could get it up at all. In the normal way, anyhow. You know the pictures of him in those times? The ones where he stood heroically with his legs apart and his hands clasped over his crotch? Well, those were depression days, and people used to see those pictures and say that Hitler was protecting Germany's last unemployed member!"

Heide began to cackle again, and this time could not hold off a violent paroxysm of coughing. The old man's frail body shook uncontrollably with the effort. There were new and larger blood spots on the handkerchief, this time vivid scarlet. Berwick saw the nurse look across the room at Heide, her face concerned. But she did not approach them, and Heide finally began to control the spasms, sucking in quick, shallow breaths, sweat speckling the pallid skin of his wrinkled face.

"*Ach*, that was bad. I have so very little time." His thin chest heaved with the effort of breathing. "But I will go on while I can. Where was I? Ah.

"So we continued going down to visit Geli, and she got rounder and rounder. Then one night came the call. It was in September, early in the evening. I had to go and get Hitler at the *Buergerbrau Keller*. He was making a big speech that night, and I remember some industrialists came and sat in the back of the hall to listen. They were some of the fat cats who kept the money coming in to the party in those days. And later, too."

Heide wiped the sweat from his forehead with the filthy handkerchief, leaving a streak of blood across the yellow skin.

"So Hitler couldn't cut the speech short. But we got a note in to him. And as soon as the speech was over, and he acknowledged all the *seig heils*, we got on the road to the *Obersalzburg*.

"God, what a ride that was! Hitler kept telling me to go faster, and his sister did a lot of praying. Aloud. I burned up the road, but even so, we got to the *Berghof* after the child was born. Not that Hitler spared any time for Geli, or cared much about how she felt. God, no. To him she was only a brood mare. He only had eyes for the child. 'The heir,' he kept saying, 'the heir!' Very excited. He didn't want to hold the baby, or even touch it, really. To him it was just an object, maybe like a trophy, the cup you get from winning a soccer game.

"That night, Hitler played that damned Victrola of his, on and on and on into the morning. Geli was so tired she slept, but nobody else could get a wink. It was Wagner, of course, 'Siegfried's Rhine Journey,' from *Göterdämmerung*. He played the goddamn thing over and over again, as loud as the Victrola would go."

Berwick interrupted. He had to have one answer before Heide tired, or the coughing overwhelmed him.

"And what happened to the child? Did it live?"

Heide nodded, showing the toothless grin again.

"Oh, yes, indeed. It was a boy, a big baby, and very healthy. It obviously took after Geli, and not our scrawny *Fuehrer*. The baby was called—my God, what else?—Siegfried, and pastured out with a farm couple near the *Berghof*. They were childless, and devoted National Socialists. Everyone was sworn to secrecy, and we all kept our promises, too. You did not talk about things that Hitler did not want you to talk about. It was a quick way to commit suicide."

"And then?"

"Well, the days went by. The baby was obviously going to be a big man, and beautiful and Nordic, like the ideal Aryan. Hitler saw the child once or twice, no more, and he didn't spend much time with the child even when he went to visit. The trouble was, he wouldn't let Geli see the boy at all, and she could not stand it. She got more and more restless. And finally, frightened as she was, she rebelled, and demanded to see the child."

Berwick nodded. "So that was what she meant, that last night of her life, when she argued with Hitler, and shouted that she had to see *him*?"

"Yes, Englander. You begin to see, yes? That was when she

dared to give Hitler her ultimatum, and Hitler called us three together, us the faithful, the trusted ones: Trude, Horst Lammers,
and me. And, well, we did what we did. We fixed it to look like
suicide, but it didn't end there.

"Someone in the ministry of justice arranged things so there
was no investigation worthy of the name. Hitler went about
with a long face, and the child lived on in the farmhouse in the
Obersaltzburg."

He paused, the ravaged face rapt in remembrance.

"But not happily ever after like the fairy stories. Oh, no,
Englander. You see, in the summer five years later, I think in
August, I drove Hitler again to the *Obersalzburg.* And after dark
we drove down to the farmhouse and picked up the boy. Not to
visit this time, as before. This time it was forever, although the
farm couple did not know. They thought the boy was just going
on a little pleasure trip with the savior of their country. They had
taken good care of the heir. And do you know how they were
repaid? Do you?"

Suddenly the old eyes were wet with tears, and a large drop
rolled down his left cheek, running down one of the deep wrinkles
until it dripped off the jawbone, and down the green robe. Another drop followed, and another.

"I did not know I could still cry," said Heide. "It is age, I suppose. Englander, I have been the worst of men in my time; I have
no mercy coming from anybody. But even I could not stomach
what came next. That night the farmhouse burned, very suddenly, with a tremendous heat. Nobody got out. The couple, the
good, simpleminded, loyal people, died in their bed. But the real

horror was this: In what had been the heir's room, they found the charred body of a boy about five years old!"

Heide fell silent, his eyes shut, crying silently. Berwick sat watching him, feeling nauseated. When Heide resumed, his voice was barely audible. "And I did something very stupid. When I first heard about the fire I hid what I felt. But later, almost a year later, I got a little drunk and I let Hitler know how sick it made me. And that was stupid, Englander, *stupid*. For Hitler gave his orders. Two of his beautiful black-uniformed Aryans came for me, and I ran."

Heide's face was chalky-white, and he gasped for every breath.

"But I must finish, Englander. I cannot talk much more. So, after we picked up the boy, I drove Hitler from *Berchtesgaden* to Nürnberg, direct from the *Obersalzburg* without a stop. Just him, and me, and the boy. I remember the boy cried a great deal on the way. He had at least good instincts. He missed the farm couple who had raised him. And he did not like 'Uncle Adolf' very well; he never had. I confess I was a bit amused at the great Leader trying to quiet this small boy, and failing. It was a long drive.

"And then we came to Nürnberg, and Hitler gave me directions, specific ones. I took him to an address on *Streseman-Ring*, in an area reserved for the very rich: nobility, great businesspeople, and industrialists. You had to be filthy with money to live there. We drove up a long drive into one of these huge houses and parked in front. Hitler left the boy with me and went in. He was gone maybe half an hour. Then he came back out with a couple in their forties.

"They were real class; you could tell. Aristocrats to their toes, the kind who are born to it. Hitler always felt inferior around such people. He was *parvenu*, Englander, an upstart peasant. And he both resented and envied these people. He wanted their company. He wanted to travel in their circles. But in his peasant's heart he knew he could never really be like them. It ate at him, like this fucking cancer eats at me.

"Anyhow, this night his attitude was different, as if he had found some reason to lord it over these people. There was nothing said, but you could feel it. The couple looked frightened, although the woman's face lit up when she saw the boy, and she picked him up from the car seat next to me. Even then there were no words between them. Only, when Hitler opened the car door to get in, he looked at the two of them and said, 'Remember.' Only that. He spoke very softly, and his voice was awful.

"They both looked pale and ill at that, and I knew something really terrible had happened in the half hour Hitler was in that house."

THE STRESEMAN-RING, NÜRNBERG, GERMANY
AUGUST 1935

RUDOLF AND ELIZABETE FROMM SAT MOTIONLESS, SIDE BY side on the huge couch covered in rich maroon damask. They were an aristocratic pair in their late forties, slim and impeccably dressed. The woman was lovely, with fair hair piled high above her perfectly shaped oval face and large dark brown eyes. The man was square-jawed, level-eyed, erect, with blond hair cut short in the Prussian manner. Both were clearly terrified, holding their aplomb only with the greatest effort.

They sat in the vast parlor of their home, a gracious chamber of many mirrors, crystal chandeliers, rosewood furniture, and Meissen figurines from the last century. This room had seen balls attended by the cream of Germany's industrialists and merchants, by her soldiers and diplomats, by her aristocracy. There were tall vases of gladiolus on the end tables. Heavy brocade drapes closed the eight-foot french windows opening on the busy Ring.

Across from them sat a nondescript man whom they would never have invited to their home in other days. He was dressed in a wrinkled brown uniform, relieved only by the black-red-white swastika armband on the left sleeve above the elbow. His mouth smiled at them, but his eyes did not. The Fromms, for all their sophistication, sat transfixed by the man, as rodents sit paralyzed by a hunting snake. They could only listen as Hitler spoke and their world crumbled.

"So, you see, I know what you really are. You are Jews! Yes, even though you may deny it, the birth records are quite clear. And you know, I think, what may happen in this country to members of that accursed race. Yes, and to their children, too, and their children's children."

Hitler paused, and smiled his ghastly smile again. "And you have four children, do you not, all married, and young grandchildren, too, *nicht wahr*? Seven, is it? Eight? You are indeed prolific, you sons of Abraham."

In the terrible silence, Fromm finally licked his lips and answered.

"But, *Herr Reichskanzler*, surely, we are Catholic. So were our parents. The records must have also told you that?"

Hitler shrugged and smiled even more broadly. He was enjoying himself.

"*Ach, ja*. I know all that. Your parents converted to Catholicism. But what is that? A thing of words and incense and a little water, nothing more. A piece of paper afterward, and an entry in the church records, a little ink."

His voice rose and even the false smile disappeared. "All that means nothing, I tell you, *nothing at all!* The disease is in your blood, and you cannot cure it by holy water and ceremonies and papers and ink. It is contagious, too, and it passes to your children and grandchildren, as well. There is only one cure for the plague of your race!"

In the dreadful silence a large mantel clock in ormulu and ebony ticked solemnly on. At last Rudolf Fromm spoke, his voice under control, quiet and steady.

"I perceive you wish something of us, *Herr Reichskanzler*; surely you would not come all this distance in person, simply to tell us you know we are of Jewish descent. Please tell us what you want."

The man in the wrinkled brown uniform smiled again.

"Good! That fine intelligence and perception and intellect are what I want. That, and your accumulated culture, and knowledge, and money, and aristocratic bearing and station in life. And your silence."

He hunched forward on his chair, the smile gone, completely serious, and fixed them with his piercing eyes.

"You and your family, all of you, you may continue to live and prosper in the most absolute safety, under my personal protection. The birth records that damn you will conveniently disappear. If there is anything you wish, it shall be yours. No matter what happens to the rest of your stinking race, you shall remain privileged and untouched by any harm. Only I shall know what you really are, only I. To everyone else, you will be what you pretend to be, Catholic and entirely German, more aristocratic than the nobility."

He stared at them, enjoying himself, shifting from one pair of anxious eyes to the other. "But there is a price, and it is this. You shall raise a child in your home, a very special child. He is my heir. His name is Siegfried, and he is the future of this land."

In the crushing silence the Fromms watched the leader of all Germany, both unaware they were holding their breath, waiting for the next words.

"You will raise this child as a relative, perhaps a cousin. We will arrange some distant branch of your family to suit. You will teach him how to behave as an aristocrat, a natural leader of Germany. You will raise him to know music, languages, and history. You will raise him to lead, to be supremely self-confident, to be strong and athletic. I will send you certain directions from time to time."

Hitler leaned closer to the couple, hands on his knees, as if he were about to spring at them. His voice sank to a hissing whisper.

"And this above all! You will raise him to be a dedicated National Socialist, to revere me and my world-solution. You will raise him to detest weakness and Jewishness, to loathe mongrels and defectives and pacifists and other weaklings. *I* shall prescribe what he is to be taught. And in time. . .in time, he will rise to the leadership. When I decide it is time and not before. Until then he will be safe, making ready."

He paused, savoring the drama of the moment. "And if you do this—and I shall be watching—you and your family will prosper and live. And if you do not? Well, remember your children and your grandchildren. You do not want your line to end, root and branch. And do not try to leave Germany! You and your family are watched. You will never all get out; and those who do not succeed in leaving, well . . ."

The handsome clock ticked steadily as the Fromms looked wordlessly at each other. Then, very slowly, Fromm raised his eyes to Hitler. "When do we meet the child?"

Hitler beamed. "Now."

WALDESRUH SANITARIUM, HOF, WEST GERMANY
AFTERNOON, 16 JANUARY 1967

HEIDE WAS STILL, HIS HEAD SUNK ON HIS WASTED CHEST. The breath whistled in his nostrils as he pressed the filthy handkerchief over his mouth again, shuddering when he tried not to cough. Outside, the bitter winter night was coming down over the rolling hills stretching out toward the border. The hills lay barren, cold and dead under the shadows beginning to cover the world, the same shadows that were reaching out for Heide.

Berwick tried to feel pity for this crumbling shell of a man, but he could not. All he could see in his mind's eye were a lonely little boy and a frightened couple, and three charred bodies in the ashes of a Bavarian farmhouse.

But he spoke gently to the dying man.

"Just a little more, Herr Heide. Do you know what happened to the child, Hitler's child, and the family who took him in? Do you remember their names? Please, just this; it is very important."

The watery, sunken old eyes stared back at him from over the bloody handkerchief. Finally Heide nodded.

"They were called Fromm. And I know a little more. Only a little.

"Remember that I ran when the SS came for me. Who would not? And I got clear. It was hard to hide in those days, but I had my half brother's *ausweiss*, his identification card. I kept it when he died of pneumonia the year before; you can never tell when such things may be useful.

"So I changed pictures in the *ausweiss*—it was not hard— and I became Kurt Mann. And I hid where one can be always anonymous. I enlisted in the navy, and asked for submarines. That way, I could be sure of being far from Berlin and Bavaria, and I could wear a beard, too.

"I served in the war, spent a couple of years in the U-boat service. Nine sorties. I served through the great times when the hunting was good, and I served into the dark days when the convoy escorts got more and more numerous and tougher and tougher. And then my boat, U-211, attacked a convoy nearing England, in what you called the Western Approaches. One of your destroyers drove us deep and kept us there, kept us until the air was running out and we had to surface. We had to surface and try to fight.

"I was part of the deck-gun crew, and so I was one of the first on deck. Thank God! For she hit us twice with her forward guns in the first couple of salvos—and she holed the pressure hull and we were sinking. And then she rammed us, Englander! Christ! I can still see that horrible steel knife, that sharp bow coming down on us, with the foam of the bow wave, the bone in her teeth. She ripped through us just behind the conning tower, and

U-211 went down to stay, forever. Only six of us got off."

The old man blinked, and his brow creased and crumpled with the terrible memory.

"The destroyer picked us up, although it was risky for her. She was *H.M.S. Cossack*, a wonderfully handled ship. Remember, Englander? She it was who had put boarders onto our ship *Altmark* in a Norwegian fjord early in the war. *Wunderbar!* Your navy sent men over the side with rifles and bayonets, as they did it in the great old days! Somehow it helped me to know we were sunk by the best."

The rheumy eyes were still clear and alert. Heide looked keenly at Berwick.

"But back to what you want to know, Englander. I know I wander, and I am sorry. It is just that I seldom have anybody to talk to who is still competent. Especially to talk about the old days. Well, I found out a little more about the child later, much later, after I came back from a British PW camp.

"I was in Nürnberg, after the war. I was curious, so I asked about the Fromms. It was easy enough to find out. I said I had worked for them long ago. And it turns out, Englander, that they were dead, dead in Dachau. Not just the people who raised the child, but the whole family, everybody, and all on the same night in 1943."

There were tears in his eyes again.

"And you know who ordered that, Englander, the whole family at once. Surely only Hitler himself."

The old man's voice was barely a whisper, and his thin chest heaved again as another coughing fit began. This time there was no stopping it, and the dirty handkerchief was splashed with more crimson. Berwick rose, and waved for the nurse. There would be no more talking now. Maybe never again.

NÜRNBERG, WEST GERMANY

EVENING, 16 JANUARY 1967

Erich Ritter von und zu Baltheim stood squarely before the full-length mirror in the backstage anteroom. He was pleased with the image that stared back at him. He raised his chin and tilted his head, admiring the effect. His nose was straight and hawkish, his eyes pale blue, his long blond hair almost white, brushed straight back from his high forehead.

It pleased Baltheim when people said he looked like Reinhard Heydrich, the vicious SS Protector of Bohemia and Moravia during the war. He shared with Heydrich a similar tall, commanding figure, and the "ideal" Aryan features so beloved of the National Socialist racial philosophers.

Unfortunately, he also shared with the long-dead Heydrich the too-broad hips and prominent buttocks the Protector had tried so hard to hide under his black uniforms. Baltheim's tailor had worked wonders with the cut of his expensive dark-grey or navy-blue suits. The hips and protruding behind were well-concealed, and his presence was otherwise that of a man born to lead.

He turned to one side and then the other, and struck a

posture, chest thrown out, hands on hips, feet set wide apart. And finally he smiled, at last satisfied, and made a final adjustment, smoothing out a wrinkle in the brilliant armband.

He was proud of the armband; it was his own design. The white circle within the red band was precisely the design of the Nazi insignia. The colors were the same. But the black imperial eagle inside the white circle had been his real inspiration. The Blood Eagle. Who could legally quarrel with that? It was an ancient German symbol. And it was unobjectionable under the German law, even though anyone who saw the armband could easily picture the swastika in place of the eagle.

He glanced at his wristwatch. Almost time. Like distant surf, he could hear the murmur of the great audience in the hall outside. There had been much newspaper comment about the Fatherland Party hiring the hall, but the management could not in the end refuse them, nor could the police prevent the meeting. Baltheim smiled his ferret's smile. How wonderful this democracy, he thought. Just like that rotten Weimar Republic, it protects the very people who will one day bring it down. Even now, there were police in front of the great hall, keeping back the leftists and the stupid oxen of Greens, marching up and down the sidewalk, carrying their silly signs.

He walked to the window of one-way glass, opening onto the auditorium outside. Almost a full house! At last! *That is the sort of public interest I want*, he thought. *Many people revile us. Most newspapers call us neo-Nazis, or dismiss us as crackpots. Or both.*

Baltheim laughed aloud and postured for the mirror.

The left howls for our blood. The fusty socialists dither and say we ought to be banned. But I don't care. I'll welcome public interest any way I can get it. To be known is the thing; what the press and the politicians say means nothing. It never will.

He peered again through the window, and noted the positioning of his security force, the tall, blond young men in black leather jackets and party armbands. There had been rumors that the leftist youth groups had planned disruptions in the hall. Baltheim hoped fervently they would carry them out. The old National Socialists had welcomed combat, and so would he. His men were well-trained and straining at the leash.

He smiled, watching the alert, hawklike stances of his leather-jacketed guards. He could almost picture them in black uniforms. Sooner or later it would come to violence, but the other side would start it. He would see to that. And his men would win; the nation, the world, loved winners. And in time there would be a VAPA martyr, and then more. Again he laughed aloud. His own Horst Wessel, murdered by leftist punks, or maybe by the police.

He turned from the window and paced the room, hands locked behind him. One or two victories in brawls, he thought, and he could attract many of the toughest of the left-wing fighters. He had learned long ago that most extremists had no deep-seated political convictions. They were simply bullies at heart, and all that really mattered to the toughest of them was to be on the winning side. After all, look how neatly many ex-Nazis had adapted to working for the communist East Germans.

He glanced again with pride at his reflection as he passed the long mirror. He struck another pose, legs spread, hands on hips, back arched, and chin up.

"Yes," he said. "It will come little by little, until the masses believe our only god is Germany, free and strong and at peace. And then one day, when we have the strength, we will produce the final surprise. The phoenix will rise, in all its old glory. And after that . . ."

He fell silent, still watching his reflection with satisfaction. Outside he could hear a speaker addressing the audience, and laughter from the full house. Heinrichs, his warm-up speaker, masterfully putting his audience in the mood. He would be talking now about yesterday's conviction of a Green Party leader for sodomy with small boys. A heaven-sent topic. Heinrich's tough and slightly dirty comments would have the audience in the right mood for von Baltheim. And how he would move them, with visions of Germany as she ought to be!

He wheeled as the inner door opened behind him. It was Waldmann, his deputy, slender, erect, fair, and handsome, his eyes frozen blue marbles in a superbly Nordic face. Waldmann was invaluable. Heir to a Rhineland manufacturing empire, he had been one of the earliest followers, and the chief financial support in the formative days.

Waldmann saluted Baltheim with the party greeting, a raising of the right hand to shoulder height, palm open and forward. He also was dressed in a conservative dark suit, the party band brilliant on his left sleeve.

"I'm afraid we will not get our fight tonight, Erich. The damned police are holding the leftist swine back too well. But there is some profit at least. Two of the *Polizei* have been injured so far, and with luck there will be more. The left has no brains at all. They only anger the good law-abiding citizens when they hurt policemen."

He smiled at von Baltheim and stepped close to him. He ran his left hand gently over the taller man's buttocks, caressing and probing. Baltheim stirred, and reached over to smooth Waldmann's long blond hair.

"Enough, my dear," said Baltheim. "Save it for tomorrow, when we celebrate, just the two of us. The escort will be here at any moment."

Waldmann stepped away, still smiling.

"I cannot wait. Have you seen the audience, Erich? This is the biggest crowd ever, I think. I have our applause-leaders carefully distributed in the audience, and the cameras are ready. There is much press coverage. This is our finest moment so far!"

The door to the stage opened abruptly, and the room was flooded with the roar of applause for Heinrich's opening speech and the crash of the band breaking into *"Deutschland, Deutschland ueber Alles."* Baltheim smiled broadly. Every patriotic German loved that anthem; who could object to it?

Before him in the door stood Heinrichs, short, broad, and very tough, once a Tuebingen University professor, now VAPA's finest crowd-warmer. He was flushed and smiling, his face beaded with sweat. He flashed the salute.

"Now, Erich, now! They are ripe, and they are ready. They want fire and blood out there tonight; I can feel it! Do not hold back!"

The two men clasped hands.

"Then I shall give them just that, Otto!" said von Baltheim. "My thanks, my friend. Well done!"

He turned to Waldmann.

"Lead on, Georg. Lead while the applause still goes on and the band still plays."

Baltheim turned to the door to follow Waldmann, seeing before him the runway dimly lit by red floodlights, the huge auditorium otherwise pitch-dark.

The runway was lined with his black-jacketed bodyguards, two by two, standing at rigid attention. As he passed between the first pair, two brilliant spotlights caught him, a single floodlight lit the monstrous party flag hung behind the rostrum, and the applause rose to a thunderous roar. He heard the chant begin, started by his own men, taken up by others, rising to a thunder above the blare of the band. *Balt-heim! Balt-heim! Balt-heim!*

He strode hard up the runway into the blaze of the floodlight, back stiff and head up.

FISCHBACH-AU, BAVARIA

AFTERNOON, 16 JANUARY 1967

IT WAS SNOWING GENTLY OUTSIDE THE *GASTHAUS ZUR Zwiebel,* small wedges of fresh snow already building up in the corners of the diamond-paned windows. Outside in the parking lot, four forlorn cars sat mounded in snow. The inn nestled in a clump of firs, the pale blue of its stucco picked out by the dark brown of its half-timbered framing. Over the arched front door swung the inn's carved sign, a huge blue-and-silver onion reflecting the name of the place. The ground was carpeted with snow, all but the black curve of the road passing in front of the *gasthaus.*

Surrounding the hamlet, looming dimly through the falling snow, bulked the threatening dark mass of the Alps, malevolent giants glowering above the town. A half-dozen neat houses and a closed Esso station beyond the *gasthaus* marked the edge of the postcard village of *Fischbach-Au.* Inside the warmth of the *gasthaus,* Berwick, Cooper, Lore, and Moshe occupied a booth at the far end of the inn's main room. Cooper leaned back wearily.

It had taken a long time to get to the rendezvous. Cooper

and Lore had been on the move since early morning, starting on the early plane from Tempelhof to Frankfurt. He thought they had been followed from the Frankfurt *Flughafen* as they left in the rental car, and they had used almost an hour making certain there was only one car involved in the tail.

Then the followers were cut off in the traffic of downtown Frankfurt. The two young skinheads in it were left swearing futilely at a narrow intersection near the old guard tower called the *Hauptwache*, sitting behind a stalled coal truck provided courtesy of MI6.

After that, it had been a matter of wary, circuitous driving: first down the *autobahn* past Munich, then on south and east toward the valley of the River Inn and the road to Austria, Innsbruck, and the south. As they passed the *autobahn* junction at Rosenheim, the snow stopped and the skies cleared for awhile. For a few hours the crystal-clear weather gave them a colossal view of the Alps, looming abruptly out of the south German plain, snow-draped, eternal, indifferent to the doings of mere humans.

They drove on into Austria at the busy Kufstein crossing, delayed only for the few seconds it took to show Cooper's U.S. Forces ID card, Lore's beautifully forged American passport, and the green card for the automobile. Waved through by an affable Austrian border guard, they drove on into Kufstein and stopped for coffee.

From Kufstein, Cooper took secondary highway 174, winding back west and north from the *autobahn*. They crossed back into Germany over little-used Ursprung Pass, lovely in its solitude, flanked by armies of snow-laden firs, and followed other secondary roads from there, driving north to *Fischbach-Au*. There had been no one behind them on the winding Alpine road.

Berwick leaned forward across the booth table, expression serious, his dark blue eyes intense.

"Okay, everybody, let me sum up where we stand. You all know something about Nazi Germany. You will remember the early days of the Movement, when Hitler finally had enough money to move into decent digs in Munich. It was a big flat in *Prinzregentenplatz*."

The others listened intently.

"Well, Hitler's half sister, Angela Raubal, came to keep house for him, and with her came her daughter, Geli, who would be Hitler's niece. Geli was a tall, lovely woman, very attractive. Also something of an intellectual lightweight. Historians believe she was *der Fuehrer*'s mistress for some two years, maybe more; nobody knows exactly how long.

"Geli Raubal is supposed to have been the great passion of Hitler's life. The party created a mythology about her. Even after the appearance of Eva Braun, the myth went on. Geli became Hitler's inspiration—the spirit of Geli lived on in his heart. And so on and on. The party mythmakers got a lot of mileage out of Hitler's profound sorrow after her death: her spirit inspired him; her picture was his icon, that kind of moonshine."

Berwick picked up his glass of wine and studied it a moment. "In actual fact, she and Hitler quarreled with some frequency. Hitler disapproved of just about everything she wanted to do, other than wait upon his whims. There are also stories about his curious sexual preferences, fascination with the anus and some other rather nasty aberrations. There was even a tale that he like to flog her—and other women—with the whip he was fond of carrying around.

"Anyhow, the whole relationship blew up in 1931, on the evening of the 18th of September. Nobody knows what the two quarreled about, but it was a bloody awful scrap. Finally, Hitler stalked out of the house in a rage, and left on a scheduled motor trip. As he left, she came out on the balcony and shouted something at him. Nobody knows exactly what. His only response was a single sentence: 'No, for the last time, no!'

"But this was no ordinary quarrel. Geli went to bed that night, and that was the last time anybody saw her alive. Next morning, when she did not appear and did not answer knocks on her door, they forced it. The girl was in her bed, shot through the heart with a 6.5 Walther, apparently one of Hitler's own pistols. She was only twenty-three."

Berwick lit a Players Navy-Cut.

"Now this simple case becomes complex. Hitler rushed back to Munich, showing every evidence of a man in deepest grief. Some of the Munich papers made something of the death, and one of them published a story that she had fallen out with Hitler over her plans to move to Vienna and marry a man who lived there.

"The same story asserted the body showed many bruises, and that Geli's nose was broken. There were all manner of other rumors, too, including one that she was pregnant by a Jewish boyfriend and was, therefore, murdered by Himmler. Another was that she was blackmailing Hitler for some reason, and so on.

"There was never any proof of any of these things, and the

whole matter died away soon enough. Hitler played the role of the brokenhearted man for some time. Gregor Strasser—another early party leader—even said that Hitler had to be watched to make certain he did not commit suicide. Now we know that was all party claptrap."

Berwick tapped an ash. "Got to get rid of these things one day," he said with a smile. "But they're so damn good." Abruptly the smile was gone.

"Our story gets curiouser and curiouser. The funeral was held at the Central Cemetery in Vienna, where Geli lived most of her life. She was buried in a Catholic service, and laid in consecrated ground. All this, mind you, in spite of the official verdict of suicide. In those days the Church would not bury suicides in consecrated ground, unless the person was somehow not responsible. Well, there was some gossip about that, but in time interest died away."

Berwick crushed out the cigarette. "Until now, that is. After all these years, suddenly there is intense interest in Geli Raubal again, and in a few people who were close to her. And now we know why. Unquestionably, Geli had a child by Hitler, a boy called Siegfried. You know the rest."

Berwick laid on the table three typed sheets of paper, stapled together at the corner, and set the flat of his hand on them.

"This is a translation of a most curious document, sent me by courier earlier today. Our London people got it out of Berlin, apparently by mail. It was written in April 1945, while the Russians were breaking into Berlin and Hitler was preparing his own death in the bunker. The signature has been identified as his. It is quite straggly and wandering. But that is not surprising. It's the result of the damage done to Hitler's nervous system by the August '44 bomb. Then there was his advanced Parkinson's disease, and the poisonous nostrums his quack doctors were giving him.

"This paper is his philosophical legacy to his child, the next *Fuehrer*. It is, therefore, pure dynamite. I assume it was intended to be flown out of Berlin in the last days. Remember Hitler's pilot, General Bauer, was in the bunker almost to the end. And Berlin could be reached—and left—by aircraft. Hanna Reitsch, the famous test pilot, and the Luftwaffe General von Greim actually landed a light aircraft on *Unter den Linden* in April, and flew out again.

"So why was the legacy not flown out? Who knows? A damaged aircraft, most probably. In the end, I suppose, someone was told off to take it out on foot. It's logical that whoever had the job simply hid it in the utility tunnel. It would have been a death warrant if the Russians had caught him carrying it."

Outside, the short winter day was dying. The *gasthaus* room was suddenly full of old, sad shadows, and a chilly darkness crept steadily from the corners out into the comfortable room. Cooper shivered, and Lore laid a small soft hand on his knee.

"We now have most of the threads in our hands," said Berwick. "Except, of course, the last and critical question: If the child Siegfried is still alive, where is he? The communist hard-liners would want him badly, of course. Think of the propaganda!

"And if he is alive today, and a neo-Nazi himself, so much the better for the Russians. Imagine what a weapon that would be, to raise up all the old ghosts, all that paranoia about a resurgent

Germany. But even if he is not a Nazi, if he is just an ordinary citizen, the Russian propaganda machine will still flog hell out of the German Republic for hiding him all these years. They will imply all manner of dark motives to the Germans and the West generally. The leftwing press in Europe will go absolutely crazy. And millions of people will believe it, including lots of Germans and Americans."

"It would have tremendous impact in Israel," said Lore. "My people have a very long memory. I'm afraid we are not quite rational when it comes to Hitler."

Berwick nodded. "My own country has her own share of nincompoops, too. And they vote. God only knows what the electorates in the West will do with NATO if enough of them think Germany has somehow been hiding Hitler's child all these years."

Berwick took a deep breath, and his expression was closed and hard. "The hard-line Russians would love it. You know the scenario: lots of speeches in the UN, the perfidious West, the specter of another Nazi nightmare, international holocaust, spirit of the Great Patriotic War, all the usual drivel.

"So, I have orders from my superiors to find him, whatever it takes. And I am authorized to say that the American and Israeli leadership concur. There will be other teams assigned, as many as we can muster quickly, but we will stay in the hunt. The orders are simple. We are to find the heir and keep him from the Nazis, or take him away if they have him already."

He paused and met the eyes of each of them in turn. "And we are to do so *at any cost*, at any cost not only to ourselves, but to Siegfried, as well. And we all know what that means. If anyone has trouble with the order to kill Siegfried if we have to, say so now. After all, whatever his parentage, it *is* murder, pure and simple. He may be as innocent as a newborn babe."

They sat for a moment without speaking. Then Lore's soft, cool voice broke the quiet.

"For my part, I have no hesitation. I should not like to do it, especially if Siegfried is today just an ordinary citizen. But I shall. Many, many innocents have already died to hold back the night for another season. Another life is not much more."

She turned to Cooper, her violet eyes level and grave.

"I think of the dead in the camps and the ghettos and the cities. I can still see the little children killed by Syrian tanks. The life of a single person is precious, surely. But it is a small price to pay for what we protect."

Cooper nodded. "That goes for me, too."

"Equally," said Moshe.

The silence returned. Berwick glanced again at each of them. "Right, then, it is clear to us all. If we can find Siegfried and bring him out with us, good. If there is the slightest chance he will fall into the hands of the other side, we will kill him."

The *gasthaus* lights winked on, driving back the ugly shadows crouching in the corners of the dining room. The waiter, a rotund middle-aged Bavarian in knickers, walked back to their table. He smiled broadly and ducked a little brief bow. "So, something to eat? We have today fresh *weisswurst*."

Cooper realized he had not eaten since the morning. "It is made today, yes?"

The waiter looked hurt.

"Naturally, *mein Herr.* It is made fresh always. Everyone knows it must be eaten the same day. Will you have some? I promise it is good."

"With pleasure," said Cooper. "And a *pils, bitte.*"

The others ordered, as well. The ugly thought of what they might have to do was put aside, at least for awhile. As the waiter moved away, Berwick lit another of his Navy-Cuts.

"But now for the last and greatest question. Where is Siegfried? Where do we begin?"

Cooper answered. "Let me speculate out loud, Simon. We can guess that Trude Mannheimer-Baltheim knew about Siegfried. And she knew soon after the child was born. She was a fanatical Nazi, and as far as we know, she never changed. She knew Heide very, very well. Remember that she was so close she knew his new identity. The odds are very high that he would have told her about the child, even if Hitler did not."

The beer arrived, and Cooper waited until the waiter had returned to the kitchen before he went on.

"Remember the snapshots we found in von Baltheim's home. The general did not hide them so carefully because Trude appeared in them, nor because two of them also showed Hitler. The only answer, which seemed nonsense at the time, was that it was the children he wanted to hide. Odd as it seemed to us then, we were right. Except that he was not interested in hiding *all* the children."

Cooper reached in the breast pocket of his jacket and laid three photographs on the table, facedown. Each bore on the back the logo and name of the photographer, Theobald, of Berlin.

Cooper rested his fingertip on the name.

"That's the same man who took the photo of Trude and von Baltheim together, the one we found in his study. These pictures came from the boxful of Trude's keepsakes we found in Dahlem."

He turned the photos over.

"See, they are all family portraits, taken with the two children we know they had. At least, we can safely assume these are their children. Now look closely at the kids. Have you seen these faces before?"

Berwick and Moshe studied the portraits of the smiling family. Berwick nodded.

"I see, of course. They look like two of the three children in the snaps von Baltheim hid so carefully. Moshe?"

"Yes, oh, yes. I think those are their children."

"So do I," said Cooper, and laid two more pictures on the table.

"These are the Minox pictures we took of the photos von Baltheim hid, the ones that include both Trude and Hitler. Compare them with the family portraits, and you will see you're correct. Which leaves one question only. Lore?"

She nodded. "That question is, of course, who is the *third* child in the pictures with Hitler? Look at the background. It is plainly Alpine; it was taken somewhere in the high country, very possibly in the *Obersalzburg*. And see the stone wall. There was the same kind of stone wall around Hitler's residence at the *Berghof*. Last, notice Hitler is wearing *Lederhosen*—shorts—and an open shirt. That was typical for him at the *Berghof*, but after the first years very unusual anyplace else."

A happy, laughing party of six local people entered the *gast-haus*, calling greetings to the host, and went to a table toward the front of the room. They greeted Berwick and his companions, *Gruess Gott*!, in the cheerful Bavarian way, and the Englishman waved in response. Once the laughing newcomers were settled at their table, Lore went on.

"I am inclined to believe the third child in the photo is Sieg-fried. The physical appearance is correct, certainly, and so is the age. And the presence of that child with Hitler, alone apparently, except for Trude's children. Remember the pictures you see of Hitler with children? They were usually taken at large gatherings, carefully orchestrated for publicity purposes. But there is nobody else in these photos. Not in any of them. Nobody but Hitler, Trude, and the children. These were special."

She paused, and reached into her purse.

"And if we need any final confirmation, I think I have it here."

She laid on the table a last picture, a snapshot of a smiling, attractive brunette, dressed prettily in Bavarian *dirndl* and blouse.

"Geli," said Lore simply. "Poor Geli Raubal. Look at that picture, and then at the snapshots from von Baltheim's study, and you will see. The little blond boy is hers, beyond any shadow of a doubt."

There was silence around the well-scrubbed wooden table. Each of them was lost for a moment in thoughts of a time long gone: a lonely child, a frantic mother, a fire raging red in the blackness of the Alpine night.

"So," said Moshe. "We still face the ultimate problem. We know who Siegfried is, but we do not know *where* he is. I take it there was no clue among Trude's souvenirs? Or in your interview with the old woman in Dahlem? Neither Heide nor Lammers could help us with the whereabouts of the child."

Lore shook her head. "No. We do not even know what happened to the heir when the Fromms were murdered in Dachau. We must assume he was moved to a safe place by some henchman of Hitler's. It would have been somebody close to the *Führer*, somebody like Bormann, head of the party chancellery. He had tremendous power in the later days, and he had the confidence of Hitler. And then there is the real possibility the child is dead."

She paused. "But we must assume he is alive, especially since both the Nazis and the KGB are still interested. There is no one left we can go to for more information, no one we know about, at any rate. But there is a possibility, a slim chance, perhaps, but a measurable one."

"Ah," said Cooper, "I begin to see. Erich von Baltheim."

"Exactly. Yes, Trude's son, Erich. We know he is the leading light in the *Vaterlandpartei*. They call him the Chief, and he and his followers are the nearest thing there is to the old Nazis. Who would be more likely to know what Trude knew than her own son?"

She took a sip from her heavy green goblet of wine.

"Who would be most interested in the heir, even more than the Russians? Who would be most anxious to recruit him, to use him, to exploit him? Just think, the actual son of the *Fuehrer*, a link with the great days of the past, the symbol of the future.

Would not Erich von Baltheim give his right arm to have the heir in his camp?

"And who would have a better chance of finding him? This secret has lain dormant, undiscovered, since the '30s. There are no clues for anyone to follow, except maybe somebody who knew Siegfried. Erich was his sometime playmate, and Trude remained a convinced Nazi to the day she died. At the time of her death, Erich was getting into his teens. He was more than old enough to learn devotion to National Socialism from his mother.

"He was also old enough to be told about Siegfried. We don't know what Trude knew, but we do know she worked close to the heart of party affairs. She may well have known where Siegfried was, and what name he had been given. Even the name alone might have been enough to enable von Baltheim to find him when he grew old enough to start his new party."

Lore sighed. "I know this is pretty thin stuff to make decisions on, but I cannot think of any other place to start. Certainly the Fatherlanders know something about the heir. And they know about the handful of people who were involved in the killing of Geli Raubal. They are following the same paths we are. I think they are out to find the heir. Either that, or they have him already, and maybe they want to wipe out the people who know about him, to erase his trail until they're ready to use him."

"What are you suggesting?" said Berwick softly.

Lore glanced to check on the other party. They were engrossed in their own conversation.

"That we kidnap von Baltheim or someone very high in the VAPA leadership, and see what they know. None of us likes

247

Nazis much in any case, so it will not be unpleasant to talk to one of them on our own terms."

Berwick chuckled, his dark blue eyes alight. "Well-reasoned, Lore. I have thought through this thing along with you, and your logic is infallible. And I am not at all sure your theory is 'thin stuff.' In fact, I am so sure your idea *is* the correct approach that I am going to see what homework our leaders have done on Erich and his nasty little party."

He nodded toward the portly waiter, struggling toward them burdened by an enormous tray. "I shall go to the pay phone and call our central. You start on yonder food. And mind you do not eat mine while I am gone."

Berwick made another telephone call during the after-dinner coffee, and returned smiling. "Central is awfully good, indeed. We have more than enough on VAPA to act on. By the way, Erich's boys held rather a large rally in Nürnberg last night. They hold another in Munich tomorrow night. There were leftist riots in Nürnberg, with several policemen hurt. The same thing is almost a certainty in Munich."

Berwick poured himself a second cup of coffee and opened a notebook.

"Central also had some information about the party leadership. It seems von Baltheim has two deputies, both very close to him, both early recruits into the party. They are always near him. They are called Heinrichs and Waldmann. Waldmann is the executive and the personnel man, and, they think, the chief financial supporter. Heinrichs is the orator extraordinaire. He is to VAPA what Goebbels was to the Nazi party.

"I would guess we could take any of the three and get the answers we want, assuming even Baltheim knows where Siegfried is. If we have a choice, I would rather take either Waldmann or Heinrichs. That way there is some chance of avoiding publicity. If we kidnap Baltheim, it is almost sure to make the newspapers. Taking one of the others may not, particularly if VAPA does not report it. In any case, either of the other two will be much easier to take. Baltheim is surrounded by a cadre of guards at all times."

Cooper leaned forward.

"So we have a go at one or the other of the two deputies. I think we must do it in Munich tomorrow night. We can't afford to wait any longer. If Baltheim's goons do not already have the heir, they may be getting close to him."

Berwick nodded. "Right. It's Munich, then, and it's tomorrow night. We have no way of knowing what we'll be getting into, so I have already laid on some extra help from MI6. We will do the actual work, but they will be in close support, to cut off pursuit and otherwise make us hard to catch."

There was silence around the table. Glances were exchanged all around.

"Right," said Berwick. "Doing a snatch at the auditorium is risky. The place will be crawling with VAPA goons, and policemen, too. All the same, I think we ought to try to pick off one of Baltheim's deputies during the party rally there. I have also asked for a plan of the hotel where all the VAPA leadership will stay. We will have people watching both it and the auditorium. I will wake everyone not later than 6:30 tomorrow morning, so settle up tonight."

Berwick finished his coffee. "Tomorrow," he said, "may be a very long day."

MUNICH
8:30 P.M., 17 JANUARY 1967

GEORG WALDMANN PREENED HIMSELF BEFORE THE MIR-
ror in the Blue Room of the auditorium, the small area in which
speakers and actors waited for their cues to walk through the
door to his left, out onto the stage itself. To his right was a similar door, leading off into the backstage areas of the theater, and
to the dressing rooms. He smiled at the mirror. How the rich
dark suit became him! Satisfied, he turned toward the stage door
to listen.

Inside, the audience was in full cry, the cheers and applause
coming in waves, clearly audible through the thick walls. He
could not hear von Baltheim's voice, but Erich was obviously at
the top of his form. It had been a fine night so far. The leftist
radicals and the Greens had been out with their stupid signs, and
there had been considerable violence. Again several of the *Polizei*
had been injured, although they had succeeded in keeping the ri-
oters outside. There had been a wall of black leather jackets just
inside, ready to break heads in the grand old style. Never mind,
he thought, the day would come soon enough. For tonight, that

wonderful reception from the audience was sufficient.

A fresh wave of applause swept over the auditorium, and Waldmann's cruel mouth twisted in a smile. And tomorrow night, after the celebration at a good restaurant, after the well-wishers had gone, he and Erich would be together, naked, on the spacious hotel bed. He licked his lips in anticipation.

Waldmann turned, startled, when the door to the dressing rooms swung open behind him. He frowned as he saw the two green-coated Bavarian police officers enter the room, the first officer a slim man with very dark hair and striking dark blue eyes.

"Well?" demanded Waldmann coldly. It amused him to strut before these peasant policemen, so courteous and restrained. So stupid.

"We do not require police. You have no business here. Unless there something wrong, please leave. The Chief will be coming here in only a quarter of an hour or so."

Waldmann's scowl deepened as the leading policeman, without answering, marched up to him. Waldman's lip curled, and he started to speak again.

Waldmann's thin mouth opened into a startled, soundless "O" as the blue-eyed policeman hit him hard in the solar plexus, a short, straight right-hand punch that drove the wind from Waldmann's lungs. He dropped to his knees, hands clutched across his midsection. His mouth worked furiously, but nothing came out. He could only see, as if he were a spectator, the two policemen approach him, grab him under the armpits, lift him, and drop him in a chair. The second officer, a husky, green-eyed man, pushed a thin wooden wedge under the lockless door.

The man who hit Waldmann removed from his pocket a black plastic case. Waldmann, gagging for breath, could only watch as the policeman removed a hypodermic syringe, fitted with a needle, and about half-full of a greenish fluid. Waldmann wanted to cry out, to run, to resist, but the second man held a crushing grip on both his biceps, and Waldmann's airless lungs could not force out any noise but a sort of soft mewing sound.

The slender man deftly pushed up Waldmann's sleeve, and he felt the prick of the needle. Before the needle was out of his arm, the drug hit him, and his head dropped forward on his chest.

The man moved to the window and raised the sash, admitting a rush of cold, fresh air. He leaned out to look down into the alley twenty feet below. Except for a wan bulb over a back door, away to his left, the alley was dark. At either end were police barricades and solid phalanxes of police officers, all facing away from the alley, intent on keeping the leftist mob away from the rear of the theater. The buildings across the from him were dark.

Below him was a parked Mercedes truck. He reached into the pocket of his immaculate green jacket, and produced a large bolt, which he dropped onto the canvas top of the truck. Instantly another man in police uniform rolled back the canvas top from behind the truck cab, and removed two of the bows that supported the top.

With another glance at each end of the alley, the man turned to the second police officer, and the two lifted Waldmann by the back of the collar and the waistband of his tailored trousers. They dragged the Nazi to the window, looked quickly left and right, heaved the unconscious man through the window, and dropped him through the opening in the canvas top of the Mercedes onto a stack of mattresses piled in the bed of the truck. The two bows were quickly replaced, and the canvas refastened over them.

The Munich policeman below them, a small man with a neat black beard, jumped out of the back of the truck, raised his head and nodded at the window, and then mounted the running board on the driver's side of the truck. The engine coughed and came to life, the lights came on, and the truck moved slowly down the alley.

Cooper chuckled at the showgirl with the vacant smile and the incredibly large bosom painted on the canvas side of the truck. *Blum's Spedition*, trumpeted a bright yellow sign, *schnell und gut*! the best in all of Munich! He watched as the police cordon, in response to the waves and calls of the officer on the running board, parted the barricade and the crowd to let the truck pass through.

Cooper turned from the window, smiling.

Berwick smiled in return. "Well done, Thomas. A lovely throw that was. And Moshe has another triumph with that nude on his truck—right up there with the big plastic cockroach. Right, then, unbar yon door and let's be off. I want to be out of here by the time that rabble-rouser finishes."

Cooper deftly removed the wedge from the door, and the two men fell into step and marched briskly down the corridor toward the dressing rooms. Behind them another wave of fervent applause shook the auditorium. Von Baltheim was outdoing himself.

Berwick and Cooper marched briskly down the long corridor from the Blue Room, staying in step and moving like men with a purpose. Cooper noticed with amusement that Berwick ostentatiously carried a clipboard bearing their floor plan of the building, obviously marked with red and blue arrows and lines. He was the very picture of the efficient policeman, concerned only with the security of the building.

Cooper remembered advice he'd gotten from an old colonel many years before, when he wore the gold bar of a brand-new second lieutenant. "Son," said the veteran, "son, if you ever need to go someplace and you don't want to be delayed or questioned, walk quickly and carry a clipboard." And there was Berwick, walking quickly and carrying a clipboard, and no one backstage in the theater looked at them twice.

They clattered down long steel stairs to the ground floor, then marched along a side corridor, their shoes making little sound on the deep carpet. The noise of the crowd inside was louder, a steady rise and fall of heavy applause, and behind it the strong tenor of Baltheim's voice. They could not distinguish his words, but the variation in pitch and tone, the emphasis and pace, were plainly those of a polished orator.

Halfway down the corridor they halted next to a door marked *Putzfrauen*, the daytime lair of the cleaning ladies. As Berwick watched the corridor in both directions, Cooper knelt, small steel picklock in his right hand. The simple lock opened easily, and the two men entered, closing the door behind them.

They emerged cautiously four or five minutes later, dressed in dark business suits, the police uniforms dropped down the trash chute leading to the incinerator in the basement. They walked casually down the long corridor toward the front of the building, and Berwick had time for a cigarette before von Baltheim's speech ended. As the band blared against the solid wall of applause, the chanting began again: *Balt-heim! Balt-heim! Balt-heim*! louder and louder, rising to a thunder that entirely drowned out the band. The crowd was stamping to the rhythm of the chant, and Cooper could feel a light tremor in the floor of the huge auditorium. *Balt-heim!*

Cooper and Berwick looked at one another. Down a long, shadowy corridor from another time rang a similar chant, *Sieg-heil!* Berwick shook his head, and his eyes were grim.

At last the chant subsided, and the first of the crowd began to push out through the exit doors into the lobby, still excited, talking animatedly. Behind them the band was finally audible again, playing *"Alte Kameraden,"* the old German army marching song.

Cooper had to concede Baltheim's cleverness. There were no speeches, no slogans, no music specifically connected with the old Nazi Party. Everything was properly patriotic. *"Alte Kameraden,"* for example, was the favorite marching song of the German army, and was associated only with honorable service over several generations of ordinary Germans. Like *"Deutschland Ueber Alles,"* it struck a chord in every loyal German's heart, and no politician or government functionary could object.

As the crowd poured out across the lobby into the street, the two men joined the throng, passing unnoticed out into the noise and bustle of the broad *Theresien-Hoehe*, the wide boulevard still crowded with cars.

Out of the curtain of gently falling snow loomed the enormous, heroic female figure of Germania, standing stolidly under a blanket of white. Beyond her, hidden in the gloom, lay the broad expanse of *Theresien-Weise* park. They walked rapidly down the *Hoehe* toward their car, the snowflakes big and wet on their faces.

MUNICH-SCHWABING
10:00 P.M., 17 JANUARY 1967

THEIR SAFE HOUSE WAS UP IN THE SUBURB OF *SCHWABING*, northeast across the Isar River, which rolled through the city to join the Danube far to the north. Cooper drove, easing the Mercedes out of the thick traffic on the *Theresien-Hoehe*, swinging around the park on the *Bavaria-Ring*. Berwick reached under the dashboard below the radio, and pulled out a car-telephone handset, hidden in its retaining clips out of sight. He punched in a number.

"Bravo, Alfa here. Success. Situation, please. Over."

The response was instant, a flat, clear, expressionless English voice.

"Alfa, this is Bravo. I understand success. Your second team has reported clear. But be advised that we have visitors here. Come quickly. Over."

Berwick frowned, and keyed the mike again. "Alpha. Wilco. About ten minutes. Out."

Berwick turned to Cooper. "They have trouble at Baltheim's hotel. It may be the Russians are there. Tom, it's out in *Bogen-*

hausen, so stay on the *Ring* and go clear around the park, then right to *Bayerstrasse*. And push it as hard as you can."

Cooper nodded. "I know the way."

He stepped down on the accelerator, and the Mercedes surged smoothly in response. He swung the car through the traffic, still fairly heavy in spite of the steady snowfall. He left the great dark bulk of St. Paul's Cathedral behind on his right, then swung into a second broad street, heading east for the river and the suburb called *Bogenhausen*.

He spoke to Berwick without taking his eyes off the road. "I assume Moshe and Lore got clear all right?"

"Yes. Sorry I didn't tell you. Our people at the hotel said they've rogered. They're out."

The traffic was beginning to thin out, and Cooper drove faster on the broad thoroughfare, well-lit by the streetlights' glare, glowing a strange bone-white through the falling snow. He turned first north, then gently northeast and east through the broad *Maximilianplatz*.

As the traffic lightened still further, the snow increased, swirling in thick clouds through the headlight beams, and piling up in windrows against the wiper blades. Cooper could hear the click, snap, and dull ring of metal on metal in the backseat as Berwick loaded weapons.

Now they were headed east, directly for the Isar bridge. Cooper could not help remembering that only a few blocks to the right lay the *Odeonsplatz*. There, on a dismal November day, a handful of police riflemen had stopped Hitler's 1923 beer-hall *putsch*. The man beside Hitler had been killed, Cooper remembered. He shook his head. God, what a blessing had that bullet found the *Fuehrer* instead.

The car rolled on through the thick snow, nearing the bridge, and Cooper was touched again by the dead and clammy hand of history.

"Simon. Just glance up a moment. On the right. This is *Prinzregentenplatz*, where Hitler had his big, gaudy apartment, where Geli Raubal died. This is where it all began."

"Spooky," said Berwick softly, "especially considering our mission this night. It's a night for ghosts and devils anyway. Can you make out the house itself?"

"No," said Cooper. "It's close by here somewhere, or it was. Everything looks the same in this snow, and the area has changed. But I can feel it. I sound like an old woman, I know; I guess I've been on this case too long. But the taste of evil is almost palpable to me. The smell of murder is still here."

Berwick spoke in a hushed tone, staring out into the gloom and the swirling snow.

"My grandmother was Irish, and a little fey. She said that evil stays on in a place long after the people leave it. It will lurk there, and fester, maybe forever. And I believe that. Tom, you're no old woman. You just feel the evil of those days. That's all. So do I."

They drove across the bridge, the lovely Isar dull as concrete below them through the curtain of snow. They were in *Bogenhausen*, and the hotel was close. Berwick peered into the gloom ahead.

"Tom, first we see the chaps in the surveillance car. They're in a side street near the hotel; I'll show you. If the hostiles are still in the hotel, we may have to take some action. We can't have the Russians—or whoever they are—snatching von Baltheim or Heinrichs. If they make a move before the VAPA realizes Waldmann is missing, the Fatherlanders will not have tightened up their own security.

"If the Russians know we're in the hunt, it's open warfare. Tonight is not the time to be retiring and subtle. We do anything we have to, and no *glasnost*. The KGB station-chief here is called Balcheff. He's a Bulgarian, 100-percent bastard. You'll know him if you see him, which I hope you don't. He's short and dumpy, with a really ugly scar across the center of his forehead. Anything this important, Balcheff will be in on personally, so we want to be very careful. He's smart, and he's absolutely ruthless. Tom, you're the one least likely to be recognized. You take the floor Baltheim's suite is on. I'll go in on the floor above. You can take the lift up, but walk the last couple of floors. This is a posh hotel. The carpet will be too thick for anyone to hear you coming. I'll use the back stairs.

"And be careful, Tom. Balcheff looks like a fat slob, but he's not. He's very quick, and if he's there, he will not be alone. Whoever else the Russians use on this one will surely be good. So watch your arse. You'll have the radio; yell for help if you even suspect you need it."

Cooper grinned. "I'm very fond of my fanny, Simon. I'll be careful."

Berwick chuckled and again peered into the snow ahead.

"That's the hotel, Thomas. See, there on the right, with all the lights. Drive on past it, then turn into the alley on the other side of the building and find a place to park. We need to pass out the tools."

HOTEL AUGSBURGER HOF, BOGENHAUSEN, MUNICH
10:30 P.M., 17 JANUARY 1967

COOPER HOBBLED DOWN THE FOURTH-FLOOR HALL FROM the broad stairway. He wore his suit coat draped over his shoulders like a cape. His left forearm was encased in a plaster cast, supported by a white linen neck sling. He limped heavily, supporting himself with a plain wooden cane in his right hand. His progress was slow and laborious.

The corridor was deeply carpeted; deserted. He had seen nothing on his way up the stairs, only a few hotel guests and a bellboy hurrying down the third-floor corridor with a vast tray of beer and cold meat. The hotel could not be more quiet and peaceful.

He passed Baltheim's suite without glancing at it and plodded on down the hall. He was walking close to the right-hand wall, and so he came upon the alcove suddenly, not guessing it was there. It was small, large enough only for a pair of soft chairs and a little table in between. There were two men sitting in it, two men in rumpled dark suits sharing a half-bottle of wine.

Cooper's heart jumped. They could be anyone, but they were

263

sitting close enough to Baltheim's door to see it. Cooper nodded at the two, and spoke in German.

"*Gruess Gott.* It is horrible weather, is it not?"

The nearer man, a tall, cadaverous forty-something-year-old with oddly blank pale eyes, looked at him steadily without expression, only nodding slightly in acknowledgment of the greeting. The other man, short, dark, and powerful-looking, glanced at Cooper briefly, from eyes so hooded Cooper could not see their color.

It was the first man's eyes that warned him he had been recognized. Cooper saw the sudden widening of the cold, pale irises even before the tall man jerked upright in his chair and reached under the lapel of his coat.

Cooper pointed the wooden cane at the tall man and pressed the stud under the curve of the handle. The twanging sound as the spring released was soft, but the needle-thin six-inch dart was driven up to the feathers in the tall man's neck. He stiffened and started to rise, his eyes glaring, his left hand reaching up to claw wildly at the plastic feathers of the dart. Before he got completely to his feet, both hands flew up to his throat, and his face convulsed into a ghastly rictus, a snarling, hideous mask. He dropped forward onto the thick rose carpet, flopping, convulsing, gargling and gagging deep in his throat.

The second man was fast. He had his right hand on the Makarov automatic in his hip-holster before Cooper even turned to him. But as the man half-rose, and the Makarov's muzzle cleared the holster, Cooper shot him four times with the silenced PPK inside the false cast.

For a moment the Russian stood frozen, his hand still on the Makarov at his hip. His mouth hung open, his eyes widened in amazement, and he stared down at the four red holes bunched in the center of his white shirt, in a group no larger than a saucer. Then he sat slowly back down on his chair, and his head and chest dropped forward on his knees. He made no sound and sat absolutely still, his chin on his knees, both arms hanging down to the carpet as if he were reaching for something on the floor.

The tall man was also still, his convulsions finished. Cooper glanced down the long hall. It was empty and silent still. He looked back to his left—there was no one on the stair landing. He turned back down the hall toward von Baltheim's suite, pulling the false cast from his arm, and the sling from around his neck. He dropped both into a steel waste container, and pulled his suit coat back on. He changed magazines in the PPK, shoved the automatic into the waistband of his trousers, and buttoned the coat.

Cooper pulled the transmitter from his coat pocket and keyed it twice, signaling success. There was no answer. *Hell,* he thought, *the steel in the damned building has cut off my signal. I'll have to move down toward the stairwell—maybe it'll go better there.* He turned to walk back down the hall.

And stopped dead. Balcheff was walking straight down the long hall toward him. Cooper saw the dumpy figure, the bad suit, and the scar, and knew it couldn't be anyone else. Behind Balcheff were two more men. One was short, almost a dwarf; the other was a gangling youth with black, stringy hair hanging lankly over his shoulders. He carried a leather attaché case.

There was no place to take cover. Balcheff had seen him, and the Bulgarian had also seen the two dead men in the alcove. With a single grunted word to his companions, Balcheff drove his right hand under his coat, reaching for a weapon. The dwarf reached behind him, under the tail of his suit coat, and the young man popped open the attaché case with one hand and reached inside with the other.

Cooper did the only thing he could. Digging for the PPK in his waistband, he drove hard with his shoulder at the nearest room door. Pain lanced down the shoulder; the door sagged and the frame cracked, but it did not open. The PPK snagged on his waistband, and he wrenched at it to get it clear. Down the hall Balcheff and the dwarf had both drawn silenced automatic pistols; the youth was pulling a folding-stock AK-47 from the open attaché case.

Cooper hurled himself desperately at the door again, and this time the frame gave with a sharp cracking and splintering, and he plunged headlong into the room. Behind him he heard two sharp pops from the silenced weapons, and the crunch as one slug buried itself in the door frame.

The room was brightly lit, its centerpiece a king-sized bed with an enormous white canopy. In the very center of the bed, a lovely African woman and a husky blond European man were entwined in the act of love. The woman, on her back, had her long, slender legs locked around the man's hips as he drove into her. Frozen, they stared at Cooper as he ran past them.

"Hit the floor!" gasped Cooper. *"Volle deckung!"* and he launched himself in a karate kick at what he hoped was the door to an adjoining room and not a closet. The lock and molding gave with a splintering crash, and he stumbled into the room next door. It was empty. He swung the shattered connecting door shut behind him.

Panting, Cooper dropped flat on the rose-colored carpet of the empty room, breathing deeply to slow his hammering heart, hearing running footsteps enter the room he had just left. He waited until the charging footsteps were close to the connecting door, then drove three rounds from the PPK through the door at belt-level. There was a gurgling cry from beyond the door, and the sound of something heavy falling.

Then someone swore in Russian, and the door panel began to splinter, small chunks of wood flying into the room. Cooper could hear the baritone coughing of the silenced AK beyond the door.

He rolled to his right, getting the bed between his body and the splintered door. Then he rose to one knee, his elbows on the bed, and put two more rounds through the door next to the door jamb. The AK stopped.

Suddenly there was no sound at all. Cooper's panting sounded thunderous in his ears, like a rasp on hard wood. He scrambled across the bed and moved swiftly up beside the door, keeping his body behind the wall next to it, then eased the door open, pushing it wide with the tip of the cane. There was no shooting from the other side, no noise of any kind.

Cooper thought frantically. He could not stay where he was, to be boxed in by the police, or by VAPA goons. Or the Russians, if they were still around. He had to move. Better the way he came than straight into the hall. He took a deep breath and jumped sideways into the doorway, dropping into a fighting crouch, the PPK pointed, two-handed, into the next room.

Balcheff and the youth were gone. Only the dwarf, remained, lying on the brocade carpet on his back, quite dead, with a hole in his forehead and another in his chest. His pistol was gone.

Cooper walked cautiously into the next room, still ready to shoot. The couple remained on the bed, the woman's long, graceful legs locked around the man's hips. They were motionless, the man's eyes wide with surprise and fear.

"*Bitte weiterfuehren,*" said Cooper. "Please carry on."

The man remained frozen in shock, but the black woman smiled broadly, her voice low and melodious in purest university German. bow. *That*, he thought, *is real class.*

"*Kein problem,*" she said. "*Es macht nichts.*" No problem. It is not a big thing.

Cooper returned the smile and gave the naked woman a courtly bow. He peered cautiously around the shattered doorjamb into the long hall. It was empty.

Cooper trotted down the corridor past the alcove with its two bodies. He was driven now with the need for haste. He did not know which way Balcheff and the skinny man had gone, but he reasoned they would have run to the nearest stairwell. They would not have taken the time to call the elevator.

At the corner he halted, and peered around the edge of the wall with one eye. But the stairway down to the next landing was empty. He reached for the transmitter, and this time pressed it three times, signaling danger to anyone who could hear him.

He keyed again, and this time a beep in his earphone told him someone had heard.

He keyed the mike again and spoke softly into it. "Tom. Three down on the fifth floor. Balcheff is gone, with one other. Don't know which way. Over."

He knew the tinny voice replying was Berwick. "Understood. Get out. Quickly. Exit rear. I'll catch up. Over."

"Wilco, out," Cooper acknowledged and trotted on down the stairs, the PPK back in its shoulder holster. He remained wary, but was beginning to think the worst of the danger had probably passed. The couple in the room would be calling the *Polizei* by now, and the hotel would be crawling with them in minutes. At least VAPA, returning to the hotel, would be alerted, and Baltheim and Heinrichs should be safe. He turned into a cross-corridor leading toward the rear of the building. He was preternaturally wary, breathing rapidly, and moving as soundlessly as he could. Balcheff and the other man could also have chosen to leave through the rear of the building. They could even be waiting for him to take the back way out.

But they were not. He trotted down four flights without seeing anyone, and found the back door easily. Two laughing, slightly tipsy couples passed him in the door, and did not glance at him twice. He took a deep breath, and walked through swiftly. He moved to the far side of the walk outside, to minimize the time he would be silhouetted against the light of the broad arched doorway.

The snow was falling heavily, thick and wet. It felt clean and soothing on his face. He shook his head. He felt dirty and hot, in spite of the cold of the night.

Berwick was waiting for him next to the Mercedes. He could see the concern and sudden relief on the Englishman's face. They climbed into the dark car and sat in silence for a few seconds. Then Berwick grunted, "Go. *Schwabing*," and Tom slipped the car into gear. The Mercedes purred smoothly from the hotel lot into the shelter of the falling snow.

Berwick turned to Cooper, his expression grim. "Tell me, Tom."

"I got two on Baltheim's floor," said Cooper. "I'm not sure who they were, but they were pros. Almost surely Russians. And then I ran head-on into Balcheff and two others I didn't recognize. One was tall, long stringy hair; the other was small, almost a dwarf."

Berwick nodded. "I don't think I know the tall one. The short one, the dwarf, is called Kolitsky, I think. He's also a Bulgarian."

"Was," said Cooper. "I got him, too. But Balcheff and the other man had too much firepower, an AK. Silenced. They didn't miss me by much. I couldn't tell which way they went."

"Well done, Tom. It's my fault. I didn't think they'd have so many people close to Baltheim's suite. I killed another one on the floor above. In any case, Baltheim and his people will be careful now. Balcheff has probably run. A hotel full of corpses is no place for a Russian hatchetman in this time of peace and openness."

He dug in his coat pocket for his crumpled pack of Players.

"God! What the German press won't say about this one! In the States it might pass as a gang war. But over here they conclude automatically that foreign powers are using Germany as a battle-ground. Unfortunately, it will be food for the Greens and the other nitwits who think all you need for peace is good intentions."

Berwick lit the cigarette and pulled hungrily at it.

Cooper reached over to lay his hand on the Englishman's shoulder.

"It couldn't be helped, Simon. We had no choice but to go in there and interrupt whatever Balcheff had in mind. And we did. No, it was a good call. I'd have done it the same way, if that's any comfort."

Berwick smiled a thin sardonic smile, without humor. "Thank you, Tom. That helps. Even though you're sure a decision is professionally correct, you can't help second-guessing when something goes bad."

There was little traffic now, and Cooper pushed the car expertly north through *Bogenhausen*, then swung gradually west on the broad Isar Ring, crossing the river again on the John F. Kennedy Bridge. A police van rushed past them out of the swirling snow, driving hard back toward *Bogenhausen*, its blue light turning the sheets of snow a strange shimmering aquamarine. Cooper watched the street behind them for a trailing car. He could not be certain in the darkness and snow, but he did not think they had been followed.

They left the broad expanse of the English Gardens behind them, sere and barren in the heart of winter, then turned south into the rabbit warren of *Schwabing*'s small streets and squares. Tom began a complex series of turns, punctuated by halts to watch the street behind. Once they were certain there was no tail, they drove deeper into *Schwabing*, and finally onto a one-block street close to the university. The few streetlights silhouetted a row of leafless, naked trees, grotesque skeletons against the pale yellow light and the curtain of snow. Out of the swirling snow Cooper could see a faded, listing blue sign identifying this drab, tired street as *Lübecker Strasse.*

Midway down the block Berwick pointed left, and Tom turned into a narrow, cobblestoned alley, and again left into a still smaller alley running behind the old, sedate stucco houses fronting on *Lübecker Strasse.* They stopped briefly while Berwick got out and opened the door of one of the sagging wooden garages lining the alley. Then they pulled inside, locked the garage door into the alley, and walked through a garden, now dreary, dark, and heaped with snow.

Lore opened the door to Berwick's coded knock, and Cooper warmed to the look of relief on her face when she saw him. The house was full of the aroma of coffee, and of food—something warm and delicious. Cooper was suddenly very hungry as the adrenaline ebbed away. His mouth began to water, and the warmth of the house felt wonderful.

They walked on past the peeling, faded paint of the dark entry hall, into a living room lit by a single lamp, hanging from a ceiling cord. The battered furniture was all in startling prints, mostly enormous roses, threadbare and faded from long years and hard use. On the worn, dirty mock-Oriental carpet lay Waldmann, his natty black suit rumpled, his right wrist handcuffed to the hot-water pipe feeding the radiator. He was semiconscious, beginning to stir, and mumbling to himself.

Moshe sat near Waldmann on a wildly flowered overstuffed chair. He smiled up at Cooper. "*Shalom*, Tom; I'm glad to see you." And then the smile faded. "Bad?"

Cooper nodded. "Bad, Moshe. We had a hell of a fight. I'll tell you about it."

Lore stepped up beside him and squeezed his hand. "Tom, you should eat. I have an *eintopf* out there, mostly pea soup with some *wurst* and onions. It's good. May I bring you some? And coffee?"

Cooper looked down into the huge violet eyes and smiled, the ugliness of the last hour beginning to fade. "Both, please, Lore. And a bottle of beer, if you have some."

She nodded and left the room.

Berwick dropped his heavy duffel coat on the couch.

"Sit down and eat, Tom. You've done more than your share tonight."

He turned to Moshe. "Is he ready?"

Moshe nodded. "I think so. It took longer than we planned. He reacted to the first drug more strongly than most people do. I had to use the antidote. But now he's coming out of it. Another couple of minutes, Simon."

Cooper sank wearily on another overstuffed chair and pulled a side table in front of him. He sighed, reached behind him, pulled the PPK from the waistband of his trousers, and laid it on the floor beside the chair. Lore set an enormous bowl of steaming stew in front of him, along with an open bottle of *Hackerbrau* and a fragrant cup of coffee.

He smiled up at her, and she laid her hand on the nape of

273

his neck. He took a long drink of the cool beer and dug into the stew, thick, hot, and delicious. He watched Waldmann, trying to sit up, and looking around him at the strange, dreary room and the silent, grim people, obviously terrified and trying not to show it.

Berwick walked over to Waldmann, grabbed him by the hair, and dragged him up into a sitting position against the wall. The young man cowered and shrank from Berwick, trying to shield his face with his free left hand. Berwick knocked the hand down and knelt next to Waldmann. His voice was soft and gentle, and there was no light in the cobalt eyes. He spoke in German, slowly and clearly.

"Listen to me, you Nazi son of a bitch. Pay *very* close attention to every word I say. Your worthless life depends on it."

Waldmann kept his eyes fixed on the shabby carpet. He would not meet Berwick's glare. Berwick grabbed him by his long blond hair and jerked his head up.

"*Look* at me, asshole! To me, you are just a piece of Nazi shit. A dog turd in the gutter has more value. I would enjoy killing you. You have only one chance to save your dirty little life, and that is to tell us the answers to our questions. I will know if you try to lie to me."

Waldmann tried to bluster. "I will not! I demand to see a magistrate! You cannot keep me without charges like this. And I can pay, if that is what you want. I have money . . ."

Berwick laughed, and slammed the man's head back against the radiator. "Magistrate? You're stupider than you look, Nazi. We are not the police, and we have no scruples at all. We don't want money, but we will do whatever we must to get answers from you."

His voice dropped again to that soft, lethal whisper.

"One thing we can do is give you certain drugs. If the first dose does not make you talk, we will give you more and more, and finally you will tell us what we want to know. And those drugs, Nazi hero, if we give you enough, will scramble your brains. Permanently."

He paused, seeing the terror in Waldmann's eyes.

"You will be a screaming vegetable for the rest of your days, Waldmann. You will cower slobbering in the corner of some dirty asylum, your life one long nightmare. You will wet your pants and foul your trousers, and every moment of the day and night you will see hideous visions. Would you like that, Nazi?"

Waldmann could only stare at Berwick, mute with fear. He wet his lips, but he could not speak. Berwick stood up, and Waldmann's horrified eyes followed him.

"Well?" asked Berwick gently. "Now it is time to choose. Which will it be? Moshe?"

Moshe held up a hypodermic syringe, filled with a clear liquid. Berwick reached for it. Waldmann followed the syringe with his eyes, licking his lips again. Once more he tried to speak and could not make a sound. Berwick took the syringe from Moshe, raised it slowly up against the light from the floor lamp, and carefully depressed the plunger until a single drop of liquid oozed from the tip of the needle and dropped to the carpet.

Waldmann watched it fall. "Wait," he cried, almost inaudibly, his eyes still on the tiny wet spot on the carpet. "What do you want to know?"

Cooper swallowed another spoonful of the wonderful stew, and washed it down with a sip of beer. So the punk had broken. Good. They were in a hurry, and the drugs were bad to watch. He did not care much about trash like Waldmann, but the drugs produced ugly delusions, and later convulsions. Cooper had had enough horror for this day.

Berwick pulled a straight wooden chair up in front of Waldmann and sat down. He kept the syringe in his right hand, close to Waldmann's face, where the man had to see it. He went right to the point, seizing the moment of abject surrender.

"Hitler's child, Waldmann, the heir. Where is he? Exactly, and in detail, where is he?"

Waldmann's eyes widened. "My God, not that, I cannot! Erich would have me killed! Tortured to death! You do not know what he is capable of. My God! Please, please, ask me anything at all but that. In the name of God!"

Berwick's voice dripped with contempt. "What does a prick like you know of God? Don't talk about something you don't understand, trash! Understand that Baltheim cannot reach you now. *But I can*, and that is what you must worry about, for I am a much worse enemy than he could ever be. If you talk to me, you may live. If you don't, then you will die in great agony, or live the rest of your life an idiot."

He held the syringe no more than an inch from Waldmann's right eye, and his voice dropped almost to a whisper.

"Where is the heir?"

Cooper watched the Nazi deflate, as if something inside him

had sprung a leak. His shoulders sagged, and he made a sobbing noise.

"All right. Please take that thing away from my eyes. He is at the *Berghof*, above *Berchtesgaden*. He has been there for many years. How long exactly, I do not know. Since before I became a party leader anyhow, and that is four years ago."

"The *Berghof*!" exclaimed Berwick. "Tell me the truth, Nazi. The *Berghof* was destroyed in the 1950s, what was left of it after the war. It has not been rebuilt."

Waldmann nodded, eager to talk now that his will to resist had broken.

"That is so, yes, but the tunnels remain, the old tunnels that run forever under the mountain. Yes, they were sealed when the *Berghof* was blown up. But they have been cleared again, or some of them have, and the system has been expanded. Downhill from where the old house was there are two vacation homes, you see, all very innocent. We built them both, and that is where the system comes out. That is where the generators are, for power, and the blowers for ventilation. And there is another exit, back up in the hills. The whole complex is quite something. Who would suspect? And that is where the heir is kept."

Berwick sat intently watching Waldmann's pale, frightened face.

"I will take the handcuff from your right wrist, and you will draw me a detailed diagram of all this. *Very* detailed, including the guard posts, the ventilators, the living quarters, everything. Including the precise location of the son."

Berwick paused menacingly. "And if you send us into a trap,

remember that I will leave a man with you here. If anything happens to us, you will die, Waldmann. You will die hard, and it will take a long time, for I will have the man begin by removing your testicles. How many guards are there?"

Waldmann rubbed his right wrist when Berwick slipped off the cuff. "Only four or five, normally. They live in the two vacation houses I mentioned. I will show you. But the Chief will go back there from Munich; he is on the way now, probably, especially if he has realized I am missing. And when he is there, there will be at least a dozen men with him, maybe more. And they are well-armed, man. You will not have an easy time."

Berwick nodded. "My worry. Yours is staying alive and in one piece. Here is a pad of paper and a pencil. Be thorough. Be as quick as you can, but thorough. Remember, your future depends on our success. One last thing, Nazi: Were you supposed to join Baltheim tonight? Do not try to lie to me."

Waldmann shook his head. "No, not until tomorrow."

"And did he expect to meet you at the auditorium?"

"Yes."

"Well, then, you are going to make a telephone call to someone who can pass a message to Baltheim. You will explain that you have been in an automobile accident. It is minor, but it prevented you from reaching the auditorium in time. You are so sorry to have missed his triumph, but you will congratulate him tomorrow night."

Without warning Berwick knelt and struck Waldmann in the testicles. The Nazi gagged and doubled up, clutching his crotch. The Englishman stood again, and watched Waldmann without expression for a moment.

"Just a reminder, Nazi. Don't try to alert anyone during that call. No code words. If we fail in the *Obersalzburg*, you will die the hard way. That little caress was just a hint of what you will face."

He rose and turned away.

Cooper finished with relish the last spoonful of stew. Berwick stopped beside his chair. "Feel better, Thomas?"

Cooper smiled and nodded. "Lord, yes. I've got some more mileage left in me tonight. I take it we drive to the *Obersalzburg* now, before von Baltheim decides to move and take the heir with him. He's got to know about the Russians by now, and all the bodies strewn around the hotel in *Bogenhausen*."

"Absolutely," said Berwick. "We can't wait. There will be the four of us and the four men from the surveillance teams. I'd like to have a few SAS lads, but they can't get here in time. This weather blocks all flying, and they're all the way up north in Minden. Your people are too far away, too. The German border police are tough and efficient, but getting help from the Germans takes clearances, and we can't afford the time."

Berwick paused and looked at each of them in turn.

"We will go with what we've got. Fifteen minutes."

THE BERCHTESGADEN ROAD
MIDNIGHT, 17 JANUARY 1967

THE SNOW POURED DOWN, SWIRLING ACROSS THE WAN yellow tunnels of the headlamps, starting to pile up against the windshield wipers. Lore swung the car off the empty *autobahn*, then south into the raging night, toward the Alps, brooding invisibly in the gloom. The road was narrow, curving and beginning to rise through stands of evergreen, grey-black in the darkness, torn by a shrieking east wind.

Buildings loomed suddenly out of the night. Drab houses, deserted streets, the pleasant spa town of *Bad Reichenhall* slumbering in the icy darkness, looking like a city of ornate tombs. The bitter wind howled through the empty streets, skeletal trees bending wearily before it. There was no light but the spaced pools of dirty yellow cast by the streetlights. Down narrow side streets lines of eyes stared unwinkingly at them, the parking lamps of snow-heaped cars.

And then the town was gone, vanished in the darkness like a phantom, a city of nightmares. They climbed more steeply, the road a twisting tunnel through the darkness of the trees, crowding in close to the road's edge.

Ahead a light gleamed suddenly through the snow, a farm-house window probably, bright and warm against the gloom. Then it was gone as suddenly, and the night rushed back, darker than before. The snow was wet and sticky on the windshield, thick clots of it clinging to the swinging wipers.

"It's getting thicker," said Lore, her eyes on the twisting blacktop ahead. "The road's all right for now, but visibility will be zero by the time we reach the high country."

Berwick glanced at the luminous dial of his watch. "Zero three hundred. The road doesn't get any better, Lore. I'd guess we still have an hour to the *Berghof*."

She nodded. "At least in this muck. And if it gets worse, then longer. We ought to be all right. The road is fine blacktop all the way, and the snow is no problem yet."

Berwick watched the car's headlights probing at the black-ness and the swirling snow. Only days since he and Moshe had found the old Nazi in *Berchtesgaden* . . . and watched him die there. Only days since the lush waitress at the *Hof.* It seemed ages ago. He shook himself back to the present, and turned to Cooper in the backseat.

"Weapons, Thomas. Let's check the gear now, while there's leisure."

Cooper undid the straps securing the rucksack on the seat between him and Moshe. Metal clinked as he removed the con-tents and handed them, item by item, to the Israeli.

"Three Uzis, Simon, and a twelve-gauge riot gun. I've checked the actions, and everything works smoothly. Thirty-round magazines for the Uzis. Lots of ammo. The nine millimeter is wad-cutter; no jacketed bullets. The shotgun loads are magnum buckshot."

He dug further into the rucksack.

"We've also got half a dozen fragmentation grenades and two white phosphorus. Best of all, there are eight stun grenades. I can't imagine much use for the frags or the willy-peter in those tunnels, but the flash-bangs will be handy."

He emptied the rest of the contents on the seat.

"There are also four sets of web harness and four knives, two Kabars, a Fairbairn, and an enormous damn Gurkha *kukri*. I take it the *kukri* is yours. And last but not least, some *plastique* and a pair of LAW anti-armor rockets. If we have to blow away a door, they'll do the job."

Cooper looked up at Berwick.

"That's it. There's a similar lot with the backup team in the other car. What's your preference?"

"Take your pick, you three. Lore?"

"An Uzi, please. It's my national weapon."

"Me, too," said Moshe. "I am an artist with that gun."

"The shotgun for me," said Cooper.

Berwick nodded. "All right, then. Let's talk about the operation. According to the miserable Waldmann, the main entrance is the cellar of the larger of those two guesthouses."

He snapped on a penlight and unfolded the sketch Waldmann had drawn in the Munich safe house.

"Once in the tunnel, we have about two hundred meters to the suite where the heir lives. There are other rooms along the way—see, here, here, and here. Most of them are empty, but the guard room is here"—he pointed on the sketch—"just as you come to the heir's quarters."

Out of the blackness ahead an Alpine railway engine shrieked like a banshee, once, twice, and again. For a moment the brilliant shaft of its headlight stabbed through the night, a long bright blade cutting through the darkness.

"Goods train," said Berwick. "On its way over the summit to the Austrian frontier and Salzburg. As long as the *Bundesbahn* runs, our road is probably still passable high up. We're not far from *Berchtesgaden*, Lore. We won't go through the town; I don't know what eyes VAPA may have there. I'll show you where to turn off."

Lore nodded, all her concentration on the road ahead.

"Now, back to the problem. I assume we'll have to shoot our way in. And there's another way out of those tunnels. As Waldmann drew it, it leads out through one of the old ventilators built in Hitler's day. They are farther uphill, in the thick woods toward the General Patton Hotel. That exit has got to be stopped up, or we may lose Baltheim and the heir. Lore, you and Moshe will cover that exit."

There was an edge to Lore's voice, although she kept her eyes on the road.

"Damn it, Simon, that's a sideshow! Can't you use two of your own four men? Moshe and I ought to be in at the kill."

"Lore, it's no sideshow. If I were Baltheim, I'd sacrifice my guard force; I'd buy a few minutes to get out, me and my most precious asset. And the only way he can do that is by the ventilator exit."

Berwick's voice was low.

"I know you want to be in at the death, both of you. You deserve it. And you may be. They may well try to come out through you. If we don't achieve surprise, they certainly *will* come out through you. I must be absolutely sure that bolt-hole is closed."

Lore sighed, holding the car into another tight turn, the tires skipping and slithering across the snowy road.

"All right, Simon, you're in command. We'll be the stopper in the bathtub."

She swung into another curve, and this time the car broke loose and slid sickeningly toward the bank before the tires caught and it pulled on through the turn. She shook her head.

"Road's getting worse. I think we'll make it, but I'll have to slow down a little."

Simon peered through the side window, into the driving snow.

"Just keep it on the road, Lore. We're not far out."

He flicked on the penlight again, and spread out a map of the *Obersalzburg* on the seat next to him.

"We'll come to a *gasthaus* on the right. It's called *Waldhaus*, and it's about two hundred meters below the house, but it's separated from it by two curves. We'll park there and go through the woods on foot. It'll be slow going, but the sight of a car near the house at this hour will alert any sentry. I wish we had some protective clothing."

Cooper chuckled. "We do. I stole all the sheets off the beds before we left the safe house. I'll cut slits in them, and we can wear them like ponchos. Not stylish, but they'll do."

"Well done," said Berwick. He stretched out his arm and touched each of them on the shoulder. "Good hunting, children. We have got to make this work, whatever it costs. I am happy to say I could not go into this in better company."

THE OBERSALZBURG
2:00 A.M., 18 JANUARY 1967

THE *OBERSALZBURG* IS A LOVELY LAND, A FINGER OF ALPINE beauty pointing southeast from southern Bavaria, surrounded on three sides by Austria. At its southern tip, in Austrian territory, lies Mozart's city, the ancient jewel called Salzburg. The *Obersalzburg* is a paradise of high peaks of incredible beauty, endless evergreen forests, and ice-cold crystal streams.

Hitler began coming to this unspoiled country in the 1920s. After his release from Landsberg Prison, where he served his sentence for the failed 1923 *putsch*, he finished *Mein Kampf* in a house high above *Berchtesgaden*. Soon after, he bought a typical, modest, five-room home there, in those peaceful days called *Haus Wachenfeld*.

This house he later expanded into his personal retreat. He named it the *Berghof,* which literally means "mountain farmhouse." It came to be much more luxurious than any other farmhouse in those lovely hills, although the rustic name remained. Gradually, massive infusions of party money turned it into a cold, forbidding congeries of huge rooms, filled with too much overstuffed furniture and cluttered with a bewildering array of sculpture and paintings of every school, hung everywhere without system or order.

In time, the *Berghof* was surrounded by garages and guard barracks and other crude concrete structures, scabbing over the lovely Alpine hillside like foul boils on a fair skin. The whole area was taken over by Hitler's guards and support services, and by his cronies. The other private owners in the area had sold out, some under Nazi Party pressure. Goering built an elaborate home nearby; so did Martin Bormann, the powerful grey eminence of the party chancellery. The area became honeycombed with a long and complex system of tunnels. Lying an average of one hundred feet underground, extending for thousands of meters, they once held shelters, command centers, switchboards, kitchens, even kennels for the guard dogs.

Not far away, uphill, stood the *Platterhof,* Hitler's favorite hotel. It was soon taken over by the party and turned into a "national hotel." At the first, any ordinary German wishing to visit Hitler's hideaway could stay at the *Platterhof* for only a single *Reichsmark*. By late in the '30s, though, luxuriously rebuilt, it was affordable only by the upper classes of the Nazi society.

High above to the east stood *Kehlsteinhaus*, the famous Eagle's Nest. Perched high on towering *Kehlstein* rock, it was reached by a 150-foot tunnel deep into the granite, from the end of which a 350-foot elevator shaft moved visitors to the summit. Built at vast expense, it was used by Hitler only five times. Today, it is a restaurant. The food is not memorable, but the view is inspiring.

After the war, most of the structures that made it through British and American bombing were razed. The tunnels were sealed. Of the *Berghof,* no trace remained except its garage. The *Platterhof* survived, once more bright and new, reborn as the General Walker Hotel, a resort for American service personnel and their families.

The Nazi leaders are dead. Most of their works are gone. But on the right sort of gloomy night, surrounded by the endless black forests and the Wagnerian bulk of the Alps, sheets of swirling snow and a howling, freezing wind, there are still malignant ghosts wandering in the *Obersalzburg.* The weed of evil has very deep roots.

Cooper and Berwick lay side by side, belly-down in the snow, deep under a stand of thick firs, black against the night sky. Berwick's four MI6 agents lay in the snow behind them, almost invisible in their makeshift snow parkas. It was still snowing, but more lightly, wet flakes dancing out of the night to slap against their faces.

Both men intently watched the two houses below them. There were dim lights in both, but no sign of movement. Far to their front, and uphill from the valley in which the houses lay, a single bright light gleamed in the night. That would be the General Walker Hotel, full of soundly sleeping American service personnel and their families, up to the *Obersalzburg* to ski and rest.

To their right, invisible in the murk, lay Skytop and Evergreen Lodge, also part of the American recreation area complex. Across the road from the houses, far below the Walker, buried deep beneath the rock and sod, ran the tunnel complex built for Hitler and his staff so long ago. Just across the road in front of them lay the stone-and-concrete remains of the *Berghof*'s garage.

Cooper cuddled the shotgun lying across his arms beneath the improvised parka, and reflected on the job before them. They would have to go in before daylight, and God only knew what they would find. Waldmann had assured them they would face only conventional weapons. He was positive there were no mines, no gas, no exotic defense devices, but Cooper wondered. Waldmann had told the truth. Cooper was sure of that. The man was too terrified of Berwick to do anything else. Still, it was entirely possible that von Baltheim did not tell his deputy everything.

"Well," said Berwick, looking at his watch, "Moshe and Lore will be in position by now. It seems quiet enough down there. By now, Baltheim and the heir should be here. In any case, we cannot afford to wait longer. There will be daylight of a sort in a few more hours, and I want to clear out of this area before daylight if we can."

Cooper nodded, but his thoughts were of Lore and Moshe, hidden near the old ventilator, uphill in the howling darkness. Waldmann had told them it was a last-resort escape route. Surely two people could hold it against any number of escapers; and yet, and yet. The gnawing worm of worry would not go away.

Lore, thought Cooper, *little Lore. I've done it, I've let her inside me, when I swore I would never do it again.* "God," he murmured, *"I've done a lot of things I shouldn't, and I haven't paid the attention to you as I should. But please, please take care of Lore. If one of us has to get hurt tonight, let it be me."*

Berwick raised his radio to his lips and spoke softly.

"We are going in now. Be careful." And a tiny voice, far out in the snow and the black night, acknowledged.

Cooper and Berwick chose the bigger house, the building that contained the tunnel entrance. They took one agent with them, a skinny cockney youngster with a wispy red mustache and a fighter's flattened nose. They left the other three agents to take out the guards in the second house. They crossed the snow-covered porch without sound, and paused. Berwick softly tried the door, and found it locked. He turned to Cooper, nodding. Cooper shut his eyes to preserve his night vision and blew the lock clear through the polished pine door with the shotgun.

Cooper kicked open the splintered door, and moved into the room, Berwick and the skinny agent close behind him. The living room, lit by a single dim table lamp, was furnished in plain, polished, Alpine-style pine furniture. It was empty except for a single guard. He had been dozing, sitting on the couch, and was only halfway to his feet, reaching for his AK-47, when Cooper blew a fist-sized hole in his chest with the riot gun.

Berwick did not break stride as the guard flopped back onto the couch. He pointed to the kitchen entrance to their right, and the other agent turned in that direction without a word.

There were two other exits from the pine-paneled room: to the left, a closed door; dead ahead, across the living room, a dark hallway. Berwick pointed left, and Cooper turned sharply for the closed door. Berwick ran on down the hall, flicking a light switch to his left as he entered the corridor, filling the passage with light.

Cooper pressed down on the brass door handle; the door was unlocked. He shoved it hard, so that it swung back against the wall with a crash, and took one step inside, the twelve-gauge at his shoulder, ready to fire.

The room was small, also pine-paneled, furnished chiefly with an enormous Bavarian wooden bed, hand-painted with floral designs in crimson and bright green. It was occupied by two blond young men. They sat up in surprise as light flooded the room, fuddled with sleep, both quite naked.

"*Hände hoch*! Hands up!" shouted Cooper. "Where is Baltheim? Answer quickly!"

Behind him, down the hall, Cooper heard the hammer of an Uzi, and the cutoff scream of a human in agony. The man to Cooper's left threw his hands over his head, his eyes wide with terror. "*Unten! Unten!*" he blurted in a high, shaky voice. "Below! Below in the tunnel!"

As he cried out the last word, the other man reached for the automatic pistol beside him on the nightstand. He was not nearly fast enough. Cooper blew the side of his head away before the man's hand even touched the weapon.

Cooper swung the weapon on to the second man: his arms were stretched above his head as far as he could reach, his mouth working but making no sound. Cooper gritted his teeth and shot the terrified man full in the face and watched what was left of him flop forward onto the bedcovers away from the hideous splash of blood and brains across the wall behind the bed. The first man still sat up in bed, his head tilted back against the headboard, his eyes open, seeing nothing.

Cooper turned back into the living room, thumbing shells into the shotgun as he went, sick at what he had had to do. But there could be no prisoners. Berwick's men were too few.

Berwick and the young agent returned from the hall. "Four more down there," said Berwick. "Got them all."

Cooper nodded. "Two in the bedroom, both dead. Baltheim's in the tunnel."

"All right," said Berwick. "I'll call the other team, and we'll have a go." He spoke into the radio.

All three men started at the ripping hammer of automatic-weapons fire below them, down the hill at the second guesthouse: two long bursts, then silence.

Berwick turned to Cooper. "That tears it, Tom. The people in the tunnel may have heard that even if they didn't hear us."

He nodded to the skinny kid with the straggly mustache. "Now, Bert, hurry, we can't wait. Noise doesn't matter anymore."

They trotted down the cellar stairs, turning on the lights as they went. The cellar was huge, its walls lined with shelves piled with boxed supplies: canned and dried food, clothing, ammunition. In an adjoining room, Cooper could make out the bulk of a big diesel generator, silent now, topped with an elaborate exhaust system. Behind it a bank of storage batteries stood on a rack against the wall.

The tunnel entrance was directly in front of them, a heavy steel door, closed but unlocked. Behind it, the passage led straight back into the mountain, dimly lit by widely spaced low-wattage bulbs strung along the rock ceiling. They plunged into it, moving swiftly along clean, dry duckboard flooring.

There was no sound but their soft-soled boots on the wooden floor. They were perhaps fifty feet inside when a leather-jacketed man stepped out of a side room, an AK-47 cradled in his arms. His eyes widened at the sight of them. A burst from Berwick's Uzi hurled him back against the edge of the doorjamb, and he slid bonelessly to the floor, leaving an ugly crimson smear on the whitewashed stone.

There were shouts inside the room from which the man had come, and an alarm bell began to ring stridently, shattering the silence of the tunnel.

"Cover me," hissed Berwick, and ran crouching down the wall toward the room door. Cooper and the young agent knelt, firing at the angle of the doorjamb, keeping the occupants of the room penned inside. Berwick halted next to the door and pulled the pin on a concussion grenade. Cooper saw him let the spoon fly loose and hold the grenade for a count of three. Then Berwick tossed the grenade sidearm into the room, and Cooper opened his mouth against the concussion to come.

The bright yellow flash and the explosion were almost instantaneous, a roar that shook the tunnel and knocked bits of dirt and mortar from the ceiling. The lights flickered, but stayed on. Berwick was into the doorway right behind the blast, and fired an entire magazine from the Uzi into the room.

It was over by the time Cooper got to the door: six black-jacketed young men sprawled across the floor in a clutter of overturned chairs, broken coffee cups, paperback books, and AK-47s. There were beds against the wall, and a table in the center of the room, knocked on its side. This had been the guard room.

They returned to the corridor and ran on. Suddenly the tunnel sides were damp, and there was a slight odor of rot and mildew in the air. This was part of the old tunnel system. They ran on past dark passages opening on both sides, smelling more and more of age and decay.

Two more figures appeared farther down the dim corridor, and from one of them came the yellow-white wink of muzzle flashes and the roar of a submachine gun. Behind Cooper a bullet struck with the ugly sound of a cleaver chopping meat, and the skinny cockney kid grunted and went down on the duckboard. Their answering fire swept both figures away, and there was silence. They pushed on toward the two bodies.

"Christ," said Berwick. "This one's a woman!"

She lay on her back, eyes open, a matronly woman in late middle-age, her greying blond hair cut short, dressed in the same dark clothing Baltheim's bodyguards wore. She and the other figure, a male guard, had been moving toward a closed door just to Cooper's right, a door marked *PRIVAT! EINTRITT NUR MIT ERLAUPNIS!*

"Here," said Cooper. "This has got to be it."

The door was locked, and Cooper blew the lock away with the shotgun. As the door swung back, bright light streamed into the corridor. Berwick edged through the door, his lithe body tense, the submachinegun raised to his shoulder, Cooper right behind him, jacking another round into the chamber of the shotgun.

The room was enormous, warm and carpeted, painted a bright yellow. One whole wall was covered with a wallpaper mural of a magnificent Alpine scene. To their left was a large closet, its doors open, filled with lines of ceremonial black uniforms and a rank of shiny boots. The far wall was covered with shelves, lined with hundreds of toy soldiers and model cars and trucks. On a large table below the shelves stood the biggest electric train layout Cooper had ever seen.

There were two men in the room. Von Baltheim stood backed up against the train table, wearing a short maroon robe bearing the party emblem on the right side of the chest. He was barefoot. A pistol was clutched in his right hand, but the hand hung limply from his shoulder, the muzzle of the weapon pointed at the floor. Baltheim's mouth worked silently, and he held his left arm straight out toward them, the palm open as if to stop them, as if to ward off violence. His eyes were terrified.

Cooper smiled. "Mine," he said quietly, and shot the man precisely through the raised palm, the buckshot tearing most of his hand off and smashing through to strike Baltheim in the center of the chest. The VAPA leader, his eyes still open and horrified, dropped to his knees, then tipped slowly forward on his face in the position a Muslim assumes to pray. The short robe had opened and slid forward, and Baltheim's buttocks protruded obscenely.

The other man was sitting up in the big bed in the corner of the room. He was huge, broad-shouldered, fair-skinned, with long blond hair. He was wonderfully muscled, and handsome. But he was dressed incongrously in white pajamas, with tiny figures of Mickey Mouse printed on them, and there was something wrong with one corner of his mouth. As they watched, he began to slobber a little. He was crying silently, huge tears running down to mix with the saliva from his slobbering mouth. As they moved closer to him, he shrank against the head of the bed. His left hand groped for something among the bedcovers.

As both Cooper and Berwick raised their weapons, the big blond man pulled from the quilts a large brown teddy bear in red velvet trousers, and hugged it to himself. He was racked with sobs.

"No hurt Sigi," he said in high-pitched, singsong German. "No hurt Sigi; Sigi good."

Berwick lowered the Uzi. "My God," he said softly. "Merciful God. Thomas, I give you Siegfried, Hitler's heir. I think his brain's about four years old."

THE BERGHOF TUNNEL
3:30 A.M.

THEY THREW A BLANKET AROUND THE HUGE, BLUBBERING man and led him gently to the door, still clutching the teddy bear. Berwick spoke quietly to him, as one would to a child, patted him on the shoulder, and turned him over to the three other agents as they came up outside the room door.

"Be gentle with him, will you? He's retarded. He's only a little child in a man's body. Just take him out of here."

The others left the bright room leading the big, blubbering man, turning left down the dim tunnel toward the basement entrance. It was silent in the corridor.

On impulse, Cooper picked up two more of Siegfried's stuffed toys. He shook his head. The poor creature was frightened enough without at least a few familiar things around him. He left the room, carrying an enormous stuffed elephant and a koala bear with a shiny black nose, the butt of his shotgun tucked under his right arm.

As he turned to follow Berwick, he glanced casually to his right, and looked straight into the eyes of the second of the skinny men he had seen in the surveillance photo of Baltheim's Munich hotel. Behind the skinny man, some twenty feet back in the shadowy tunnel, were four or five other men in ski parkas. They did not look like VAPA goons.

The skinny man had his AK-47 raised, aiming at the backs of Cooper's companions. Now, startled, his eyes jerked to Cooper; he swung the muzzle of the AK and fired. Cooper was smashed back against the door frame, the stuffed animals torn from his grasp. A hammer blow struck his left shoulder and a splinter from the door frame tore into his left cheek. Off balance, Cooper squeezed off a round one-handed, and cut the skinny man's legs from under him.

A thunder of firing erupted in the corridor. Somebody screamed. Cooper huddled just inside the door frame. He did not dare lean out to shoot. But leaning far to his left inside the doorway, he could just see the skinny man, slowly twisting on the floor, trying to pull himself back down the corridor, dragging his shattered legs. Cooper's left arm hung uselessly at his side, but he pointed the riot gun one-handed again, and hit the skinny man in the center of the back. There was no more movement.

The orange-yellow flame of muzzle flashes flickered in the corridor outside, and ricochets howled and screeched off the stone and concrete of the old walls. Then two stun grenades went off almost simultaneously to his right, and the firing abruptly slackened. Two more grenades followed, and there was no more shooting from his right.

Berwick, a smear of blood on his cheek, sprinted past the door, firing. Cooper stepped into the corridor in time to see Berwick fire a long burst down the corridor and another into five dark forms on the tunnel floor. Berwick ran back toward him, changing magazines on the Uzi, concern stamped on his lean face.

"Tom! Tom! Are you all right?"

"Yes. Hurt but mobile. Simon, those people had to be Russians!"

"I know. And they came from the ventilator end of the tunnel."

They turned down the corridor. One of Berwick's men lay still on the floor in a widening pool of blood. Farther down the corridor, the other two men were still on their feet, holding Sigi by the elbows. The man was sobbing uncontrollably, covering his face with both hands.

"Let's go back through the cellar," said Berwick. "Maybe we can beat them to the surface."

He turned to his two agents.

"Get him out. Take a car and get him to the safe house. If you can't get clear, shoot him. On your way out, bleed the fuel oil tanks in the house basements and set fire to them."

He gestured toward the agent on the floor of the tunnel. "Tommy's finished. We'll have to leave him. See to Bert on your way out."

The agents nodded, and led Sigi off down the corridor.

Cooper and Berwick ran back toward the cellar entrance. The Russians had farther to go than they did, but Cooper and Berwick would have to find the ventilator in the howling storm. Cooper clamped his teeth tightly together. Pain lanced up the left arm with every step, but he ran hard.

Lore, he thought, Jesus! Lore! The Russians must have surprised them at the ventilator. God, he prayed, gritting his teeth against the fire in his arm, *God, please save her for me. Don't let it happen twice.*

They ran on through the door into the cellar, and took the stairs two at a time.

ABOVE THE BERGHOF TUNNEL
3:40 A.M.

THE SNOW STILL FELL IN GREAT SWEEPING SHEETS, WHIRL-ing out of the blackness of the trees, until each man was alone in the darkness, by himself, cut off from everything beyond arm's reach and from all the world of men. The wind moaned and shrieked in the pines overhead.

Cooper ran desperately, slipping in the snow, frantic with fear for the woman somewhere up in front of him in the storm. His mind raced. The KGB had guessed about the *Obersalzburg*, or maybe they had caught Heinrichs, or another VAPA man who knew the secret. And they had hit the party at the ventilator tunnel from behind, out of this wild night. He tried to will his legs to go faster through the deep snow.

He sank into the drifted snow below the ridge at every step, panting, dodging trees, trying to keep sight of the white smock ahead of him, Berwick, running tirelessly up toward the ventilator. Cooper could hear nothing over the howl of the wind.

The ridge got steeper and steeper, tapering up almost to a knife-edge, and Cooper knew they had to be close to the ventilator. He pushed harder. He had closed a step on Berwick when he lost his footing and fell, his momentum carrying him violently downhill, slipping, sliding, trying desperately to keep from falling on his injured left shoulder. He bounced off a small fir, felt the pain shoot through his shoulder, and then rolled on down the slope, a parachute landing-fall roll that brought him up in the deep snow at the base of the ridge, utterly alone.

He pushed to his feet, still clutching the shotgun, and climbed diagonally back up the slope, sliding down a foot for every two feet he gained, trying to estimate the angle that would bring him to the ridge close to the ventilator. He could hear nothing but the howl of the wind, see nothing but the cloud of falling snow against the deeper black of the trees.

And then above and to his left, the blue-white glare of a powerful light split the night, and he pushed on, close to the crest of the ridge, until he could see the top at last.

Berwick crouched, holding a brilliant flashlight leveled along the barrel of his Uzi, snow thick in his dark hair, his chest heaving with the effort of his run. The beam of the light was centered on two men wearing dark ski clothing, crouched over their own weapons some twenty feet away.

Bald and dumpy, Balcheff stood next to a very tall, thin, black-haired man holding an AK-47. Lore stood in front of Balcheff, between him and Berwick. Balcheff held her by the ponytail into which she had pulled her long hair. Her head was pulled back at an agonizing angle, and her wrists were wired together behind her back.

Balcheff held a Makarov automatic pressed against the nape

of her neck and kept her body pulled tightly against his. The left shoulder, side, and back of her white snow parka were soaked in blood. Around her in the snow lay four other still bodies. Cooper knew one of them had to be Moshe.

They can't see past the light. They don't know Berwick is alone. And they don't know I'm here. He bit his lip against his own pain, and sank down behind a downed log, trying to stabilize his breathing. *Goddamn it!* He couldn't use the shotgun; he'd hit her, too.

Cooper fumbled under the makeshift parka and drew his PPK. Awkwardly, he thumbed back the hammer and laid his right arm across the top of the log. He aligned the rudimentary sights as best he could on the heavy man's head, holding just below the temple.

He dared not shoot, not as long as that pistol muzzle rested against his woman's neck. He could not be sure Balcheff's pistol would not go off, even if he killed cleanly. The Bulgarian's weapon would surely have a very light trigger pull; a professional like Balcheff would make certain of that.

The squat Bulgarian called to Berwick, shouting against the storm.

"So, Englishman, I thought it might be you. We have what the Yankees call a Mexican standoff. I have this so-lovely agent of yours. You shoot, she dies. I will trade her for the heir, and we will go. There will be no more killing. This lady should live long, and bear children; there is no point in her dying in this miserable place. There is no point in any of us dying here. Decide, Englishman; decide quickly!" His voice was hard and penetrating, even over the screech of the wind.

Berwick's voice was like the ring of steel on steel.

"No deal, Balcheff. You know that. I will do one thing, however: I will trade your lives for hers. Period. You leave in safety, she stays with us. But nothing more. I have more men close by. You do not." His Uzi did not waver.

And then the skinny gunman made his move. He stepped behind Balcheff and Lore, and with his left hand tossed an oval black object underhand at Berwick. At that instant, as the skinny man turned and ran into the darkness, Berwick dropped flat to avoid his grenade. As Berwick's light dropped into the snow and the primordial darkness rushed in, the muzzle of Balcheff's Makarov wavered. And in that fraction of an instant, Cooper fired.

The night flashed into brilliant yellow and crimson as the grenade went off. The roar of it racketed up the Alpine valleys in all directions, its echoes calling each to the other again and again through the howling night. And then the blackness surged back, deeper than ever.

Cooper dropped the PPK in his pocket and scrambled up the steep slope in the dark, pulling himself with saplings and leafless brush, his shoulder afire. Just before he reached the crest, Berwick pulled the light from the snow, and its brilliance flooded the ridge.

Balcheff lay on his back, mouth and eyes open, the top of his skull gone. Lore lay facedown, bleeding heavily, the snow reddening under her left shoulder. But her face was turned toward Cooper, and the big violet eyes were open. He dropped on his knees beside her as Berwick scrambled past him, the light probing the stygian blackness into which the skinny man had gone. There was nothing in the beam of light except the gloom of the pines, and a torrent of huge snowflakes.

Cooper quickly unwound the wire that bit into Lore's wrists. He turned her over gently in the snow, and she managed a wan smile. He was appalled by the amount of bright blood soaked into her parka.

Then Berwick was kneeling beside him. "Let me take her, Tom; I've got two good arms. You take the light and lead. We've got to get her off this bloody mountain."

Cooper looked back at Moshe, his black eyes closed, his face calm, the heavy snow already powdering the neat black beard.

Berwick touched Cooper gently on the good shoulder. "Leave him, Tom. We can't help him now."

Berwick slung the Uzi and picked Lore up. He looked back only once, to the darkness into which the Russian had run.

"*Dosvedanya*," Berwick muttered. "*Dosvedanya*, you bastard. Farewell. There'll be another day."

Cooper turned the light and started downhill. Ahead, through the falling snow, he could see the flicker of flames from the nearest house. The tunnel entrances would be clogged and covered for a long time to come.

They fought their way back downhill through the snow, Cooper trying to shut out the fire in his left shoulder, Berwick staggering in the drifts under Lore's weight. But they made the car at last, and the road was still empty. The other car was gone, so Berwick's men had gotten Sigi away. The snow danced around them, scarlet and yellow with the glare of the fires.

Cooper pulled himself into the rear seat of the Mercedes, black spots of exhaustion dancing in front of his eyes. Berwick, panting, handing Lore in to him, wrenched open the driver's door, and fumbled the key into the ignition. The car started on the first try, and Berwick pulled onto the blacktop in a shower of snow.

Cooper huddled in the backseat of the Mercedes, cradling Lore as Berwick pushed the car hard through the night, taking chances through the curves, down the snow-covered road toward *Bad Reichenhall.* In the sleepy town Berwick found a pay phone and called his Munich contact, and then they raced on through the blackness, up on to the *autobahn*, and west into the teeth of the storm.

"How is she, Tom?"

"Unconscious, Simon, and her breathing is ragged. She's gasping. I think the bleeding has stopped, but I don't know what's happening internally. I know we can't use a civilian doctor, but for Christ's sake, how long does she have to do without?"

"The ambulance will meet us on the way, Tom. There's a doctor onboard. He's one of our people; the whole ambulance crew is. Hang on; it won't be long. Just a short run the other side of Rosenheim."

The Mercedes roared on into the howling night.

ROTHENBURG-OP-DER-TAUBER
FEBRURARY 1967

THE ANCIENT STONE OF THE CITY WALL STRETCHED AWAY into the darkness, its lichen-crusted top covered with a thin layer of snow. Far below, the walls fell away to a snow-covered slope, a dozen shades of white and light grey, dropping into the valley of the little river Tauber far below. The night was clear, lit by a pale half-moon riding high in an obsidian sky dusted with a scattering of brilliant stars. Down the wall loomed a massive stone watchtower, square and black against the night sky, still standing guard against nameless evils outside the old walls.

Rothenburg was one with the centuries this cold, clear night, its narrow cobbled streets empty of traffic, but filled with ghosts of years long passed away. Across the red-tiled roofs a single bell began to strike, a clear, sweet, soprano chime telling the passing of the night.

Cooper stood at the open hotel window overlooking the fifteenth-century wall, sucking in the chill, rich, clean air. The ancient city had never lost its charm for him, the keen sense that time had no real meaning here. Within these walls, in the watches of the night, the filth, and ugliness, and uncertainty of the world were shut out. Evil was impotent to touch those inside this magic city. Cooper smiled at his own fantasy.

An enormous owl sailed past Cooper's window, a great grey wraith in the gloom, bound on some mysterious errand of his own.

Cooper absently rubbed the dull ache in his left shoulder, remembering. Big, pitiful Siegfried was gone, living happily in a quiet, expensive Catholic nursing home on Lake Constance. He would be content there, watched over by kindly nursing sisters, surrounded by his new toys and his old stuffed animals, paid for, like the home, by Her Britannic Majesty's government.

And Berwick, the man who had come to be his friend. Cooper shook his head. It was not good to have friends in this lousy business, but occasionally you could not help it. The Englishman was gone back into the twilight, to fight the battles of the West without medals or trumpets. Cooper had an address in a tiny village on Dart Moor. It was only a mail drop, but any letter he sent would be forwarded. Somewhere. And someday, if their luck held, they would meet again.

Now across the roofs and chimney pots a deep, deliberate, baritone bell answered the sweet chime. Then it, too, fell silent, and the deep quiet of the ages settled again over the sleeping city. Cooper smiled, at peace, shivered, and closed the window.

As he turned from the window, the bathroom door opened, and Lore stepped into the room in a faint cloud of steam. Her hair was down over the shoulders of her white robe and she smelled wonderfully of soap and cologne. The wide mouth and huge violet eyes smiled at Cooper.

"I heard the bells, Thomas, those beautiful bells. I realized I feel safe. My God, how long it has been since I really felt safe. I can sleep soundly tonight and look forward to a big breakfast and a walk in this lovely town. I can walk with my man and never have to look over my shoulder. It has been so long since I've been sure there would even *be* a tomorrow."

The gentle smile returned. "And we have two whole weeks, my love. I don't intend to waste it. Are you prepared for a needy, demanding, lascivious woman?"

Cooper smiled back into those wonderful eyes. "As long as it's you, my sexy wench, always. But with a useless, strapped-up arm apiece, how are we going to manage this?"

Lore's impish smile broadened. "We each have one arm that works; we'll just have to cooperate. And anyhow, the parts of us that we're going to use work just fine."

She shrugged the robe from her shoulders, and stood before Cooper, slim and bare and lovely. She held out her good arm to him.

"Come, my dearest. We'll think of something."

Robert Barr Smith

photo by Olan Mills

Robert Barr Smith entered the United States Army as a private in 1958, and was commissioned in the following year. He served in Vietnam with 4th Infantry Division, two tours in Germany — a total of more than seven years — and with troop units and on posts throughout the United States, retiring as a Colonel. He is a Senior Parachutist, and holds the Legion of Merit (two awards), the Bronze Star, and other decorations.

He has served as the Staff Judge Advocate — senior lawyer and legal advisor to the commanding general — for the 82nd Airborne Division, 1st Armored Division, 7th Infantry Division and Fort Ord, California, Fort Benning, Georgia, and V U.S. Army Corps. He also served as a trial judge and as Executive Officer of two judge advocate offices.

He grew up in Palo Alto, California, then earned a BA in History and a Doctor of Laws at Stanford University. He is a professor of law at the University of Oklahoma, where he served six years as Associate Dean for Academics and Associate Director of the Law Center.

He lectures extensively on military and western history, and is the author or co-author of nine books and more than a hundred magazine articles in military and western history.

FINAL STROKE

MICHAEL BERES

Retired government agents in Florida cling to a decades-old secret that threatens to wreak havoc on the American political system.

A right-brain stroke victim related to a high profile mobster dies mysteriously at a Chicago rehabilitation facility.

A fellow rehab patient with a left-brain stroke who was a detective in his former life launches his own investigation.

The detective's wife, desperate to help her husband connect to his past, joins the investigation, makes very large waves, and is kidnapped. An environmental activist is murdered while driving his hybrid vehicle to a clandestine meeting. An aide at the rehab facility, who stumbles into the plot while ripping off the health care system, becomes yet another victim. Saint Mel in the Woods Rehabilitation Facility, aptly nicknamed Hell in the Woods by residents and employees, is the last place you'd expect violence on this scale.

The mob, family legacy, health care scams, a troubled environment, crooked politics, and federal agents authorized to commit murder . . . Why is it all zeroing in on a rehabilitation facility?

Final Stroke. The ultimate in stroke rehab . . . Figure it out, or die trying.

ISBN#9781932815955
Platinum Imprint / Thriller
US $24.95 / CDN $33.95
Available Now

For more information

about other great titles from

MEDALLION PRESS, visit

www.medallionpress.com

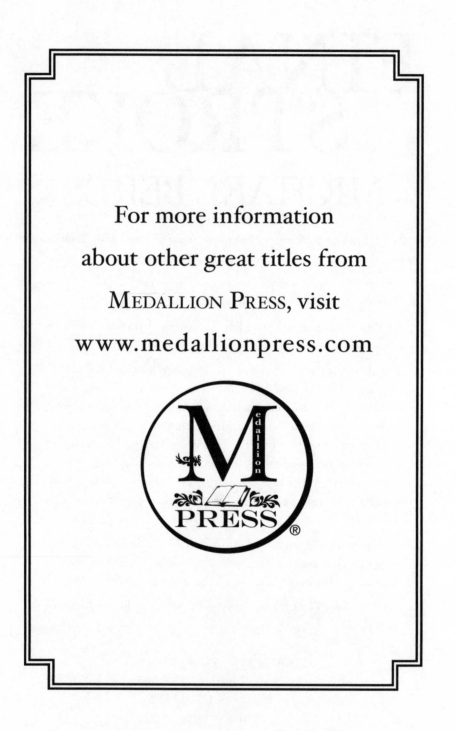